The End of Us

The End of Us

SANDRA PROUDMAN

joy revolution

Joy Revolution
An imprint of Random House Children's Books
A division of Penguin Random House LLC
1745 Broadway, New York, NY 10019
penguinrandomhouse.com
getunderlined.com

Editor: Bria Ragin
Cover Designer: Tatiana Guel
Interior Designer: Megan Shortt
Production Editor: Jamie Johnson
Managing Editor: Tamar Schwartz
Production Manager: Shameiza Ally

Library of Congress Cataloging-in-Publication Data

Names: Proudman, Sandra author
Title: The end of us / Sandra Proudman.
Description: New York, NY : Joy Revolution, [2026] | Audience term: Teenagers | Audience: Ages 12 and up | Audience: Grades 7–9 | Summary: Jules and Rico have always had each other in the post-apocalyptic world they live in, but when Rico wins a lottery to live in the last safe haven, he sacrifices his place for Jules, and the two fight their way back to each other as a rigged system and a rebellion threaten both their survival and their love. Provided by publisher.
Identifiers: LCCN 2025049424 (print) | LCCN 2025049425 (ebook) |
ISBN 979-8-217-11819-9 hardcover | ISBN 979-8-217-11822-9 paperback |
ISBN 979-8-217-11821-2 library binding | ISBN 979-8-217-11820-5 ebook
Subjects: CYAC: Dystopias | Government, Resistance to | Romance stories |
LCGFT: Dystopian fiction | Novels
Classification: LCC PZ7.1.P7835 En 2026 (print) | LCC PZ7.1.P7835 (ebook)

The text of this book is set in 10-point Tiempos Text.

Manufactured in the United States of America
1st Printing

TO THE READERS WHO BELIEVE IN
FIGHTING FOR A BETTER WORLD.
THIS ONE IS FOR YOU.

PART I

THE LOTTERY & MICTLĀN

CHAPTER 1
Jules

It's lottery day.

I hate lottery days in the fall, when cooler times remain out of reach and random heat waves make even the night miserable.

It's nearing sunrise in the burnt and ravaged part of San Francisco that was once downtown. The temperature in the Scar—this canyon of scorched buildings—is already rising, and it'll be hot as hellfire in a few hours when daylight breaks. Rico sings to himself like we have no problems whatsoever. My lungs, meanwhile, squeeze with every breath, the thin air painful despite our mostly full oxygen tanks and protective suits. The air is the least of our concerns today, though. Even after hours, we haven't scavenged anything worthwhile. The area's been picked clean, but Rico wants to salvage the night, so here we are still at work.

I turn back to the car in front of me. I use a pipe to break the last of the glass in the window. The noise ricochets in the emptiness of the Scar. I clean the jagged shards away from the edges, then reach inside and unlock the door. It's a miracle we found a vehicle that hasn't been searched.

Then again, there're skeletons in the front seats, arms wrapped around each other, that weren't visible through the tinted windows. I've seen dead bodies before, especially in this area where the annual fires trapped so many, but my heartbeat quickens as a too-familiar emotion roars within. This type of mental ache transcends death and is ruefully shared by those who witness it. Even scavengers like me.

Will Rico and I end up like this one day? In love, but ultimately unable to protect each other from the world around us. I should search their pockets and the car, but I can't bring myself to tear them apart. I understand why no one has moved them. It's a sign we haven't all fully lost our humanity yet. I close the door. Squeeze my eyes shut and tell myself not to cry. Doing so in my protective suit always fogs the visor of my helmet.

I turn to Rico and try not to think about how much I need him. In a time of hurt, he's my comfort.

Static bursts to life in the ear of my helmet from the small radios that Rico linked in our suits. It's how we communicate while we scavenge. "¡Jules, ven aqui! Come and look at this. Finally found something good," Rico calls from where he digs underneath a half-charred car a block away.

I approach him and pretend I'm not out of breath from the short walk over.

He stands. Between his forefinger and thumb, he holds

up a diamond ring. It shimmers against the light of my headlamp.

I smile and press the button on the side of my visor to turn on my own radio. "That can't be real."

He lowers to one knee. His protective suit stretches and rubs against debris on the ground. I make a mental note that I'll need to replace the fabric soon. He grins through his helmet, the way only he can because life sucks. I recognize the gesture. I saw it in fifty-year-old magazines right before I traded them.

"Juliana, will you marry me?" he asks.

I smack his arm and tell him, "Knock it off." His expression softens into a thoughtful gaze. *He's serious*. He wants me to *marry* him. We're literally in a hellhole and *that's* where his head's at?

I *should* say yes. What is there to lose? What is there to wait for? Instead, I shake my head and laugh it off. "Don't you think we have more important things to worry about?"

"I know. I'm joking, anyway." It's not true. His smile fades as he stands, and I regret letting the moment pass as soon as it's gone. But we still have time. If we're lucky, and if we do good work for the Sheriff, we'll have a whole lifetime together ahead of us.

I ask, "What do you think the Sheriff's Station will give us for the ring?"

He winks, and the twinkle returns to his eyes. "Let's go find out."

We pocket what little we have, eager to beat the sunrise to

the Wharf, where the Sheriff's Station is located in an underground bunker. We've been scavengers for the Sheriff for a few months now. Working the Scar for the man who oversees San Francisco is the best way to get a survivable amount of food and correctly processed desalinated water rations—without having to steal or murder for them. That's not to say the job is without its dangers. It may kill you if your protective suit rips and you suffer ash inhalation, or you can get attacked by someone trying to rob you. Out here, even the natural world is dangerous. We're mindful of the ravens that'll eat you while you're still alive. And the killer bees that've evolved to not die after they've stung you with venom that'll leave you numb for days. Many scavengers come back empty-handed or simply disappear. It's worth the risk. To us, anyway. Because it's allowed us to believe that we can make it.

Working the Scar is also the best way to earn extra tickets for the lottery to get into the Oasis, a lavish mountainous haven protected by an impenetrable dome that people would kill to live in if they could. As the leader of our isolation city, appointed by the last President Burberry, the Sheriff helps run the lottery in San Francisco, while two other sheriffs run those in San Jose and Sacramento. Between our three cities, we make up 90 percent of survivors in California. But only those who win a spot in the Oasis truly live. Maybe Rico and I will both be chosen one day. I try my best to buy into it, but every time we don't get picked, it's like a match has been lit to our paper dreams.

Still, Rico gets lost in the reverie.

We jog, which I hate almost as much as lottery days.

It's the only way to get anywhere quickly without a vehicle, though. As we go, others emerge from the several thousand connected underground bunkers below the high-rises that once dominated the sky. We're like ants coming out of a colony, using the cool earth to hide from the scorching heat of the day and any possible fires topside. The bunkers are discolored, unkempt, and dirty, overcrowded with families and also kids who'll grow up without families, like we did—but livable unless the air-conditioning stops. Fortunately, ours is close to the Sheriff's Station.

To our knowledge, the Oasis is the only place in what was the United States where people still live aboveground. Not that anyone truly knows what exists beyond the Oasis. Radios are localized. There are no supplies left to create ships or planes. And even when there were, people left and never returned.

People theorize that outside California's four isolation cities—the Oasis, San Francisco, San Jose, and Sacramento—Sibervirus never stopped spreading. By the time widespread communications were disrupted, 40 percent of the population had already succumbed to the severe flu-like illness that came from deep drilling in the Arctic. But there have to be others like us. I'm sure of it. And one day, we'll find them. Or they'll find us. And maybe life will be better.

For now, the surface is unrecognizable from what it used to be when my mami was my age. After over a decade without maintenance, the buildings around us show their signs of wear—sun-spotted walls that are falling apart, shattered windows, and graffiti galore. What were malls, bookstores, and schools have long ago been foraged and repurposed—turned into underground homes.

The crowd at the Wharf seems to be winding down when we arrive, as most people are headed to Union Square, where there will be free fresh food and water at today's lottery. Mami told me the area used to be called Fisherman's Wharf back in the Old Epoch. A fun area families went to shop and to enjoy the ocean, where people made lasting memories. Now the territory is all part of the Sheriff's Station. In it, his deputies govern the fifteen thousand people who live in San Francisco. Whatever we find in the Scar, we bring to the station. And in return, we get food, shelter, and extra lottery tickets. With all the competition, we have to watch our backs.

Not that I'm a fighter. I have Rico for that, who is strong and has a reputation for being as fast as a cat. No one's ever been able to hit him. In our darkest days, we used to count on it during the street fights Rico competed in to feed us. He's as vigilant as ever. As we weave our way to the Sheriff's Station, Rico shoves a few suspicious people out of the way.

We pass other scavengers as we head underground. Out in the Scar, we see them but can hardly ever recognize anyone with our suits on. With our helmets off, everyone we walk by has this same worn expression. Their eyes twitch or are bloodshot, and their noses are scrunched up, giving the impression of perpetual rage. Others have scratches or burn scars. We live among those already gone.

We enter the overcrowded man-made grotto, where people have congregated into the two-hundred-foot rectangle. The bunker walls were created with a gray cement that makes everything extra dark. The lights in the Sheriff's Station bunker are interspersed along the ceiling. The dusky smell gets worse the farther we go into the crowd.

We head right, to the three ticket booths meant to process small items, which the Sheriff's deputies run. They've been set up against the far wall, shielded by impenetrable plexiglass.

We choose the shortest line and wait our turn as other people who work for the Sheriff try to make a stop for extra lottery tickets. I don't recognize the deputy at our ticket window. He's too tall and big, made more intimidating by his sharp and serious glower. Even his top-grade navy-blue protective suit can't hide how his nostrils flare at every interaction. He's a killer; all of the Sheriff's deputies are. My hands sweat from the nervousness. If the station worker is having a bad day, we have one, too. And bad days are unpredictable.

When our turn comes, Rico and I walk up to the booth together. At the window, we get our retinas scanned by a machine. When it's confirmed that we're in good standing with the Sheriff and our IDs have been verified, the deputy signals to the slot where we can pass through any pocket-sized items. Rico glances both ways before he puts the ring and the few other items we found through the small slot in the ticket counter. Sometimes people will step in and rob you before you can set your items down, and whoever sets them down owns the payment, so you have to act fast. The deputy scrapes everything else aside and picks up the ring. He examines it closely in a machine by his side, which gives a positive beep, and without a single word to us sends through only one lottery ticket.

Far too exhausted to hold it together, I shout, "Are you kidding me?"

"Jules—" Rico starts, caution in his tone.

This deputy must be having a seriously horrible day. I want to rip off the stupid star-shaped pin centered above his heart on his protective suit and throw it in his face.

"No," I snap back, then I whirl on the deputy and hit the plastic booth once with the palm of my right hand. It stings and everyone around us freezes like this ends one way: Rico dragging my dead body out of this place. But I can't stay quiet. "We just found a *diamond ring*," I say and add, "and you're trying to pull one over on us." The deputy hits Rico with a *you-should-keep-your-girl-in-check* look that angers me more. Rico pulls my arm. I tug away out of his grip, nervousness be damned. "This is worth at least six lottery tickets. *You know it*."

The man pushes the plexiglass up, the material squeaking as it moves. I've never seen that happen. And maybe the heaviness of what I'm doing should stop me. I've made a mistake and should apologize, but I am *so* angry. *All the time.* Like rage boils inside me and I can't ever fully get my frustration out. So I blow up. Rico alone helps me stay levelheaded.

"I know it?" the deputy says. His voice booms. I take a couple steps back on impulse. He snickers at this, so I freeze and stand my ground. "Look around you, girl. This is one of few jobs left in the Wasteland, and you should be thankful to have it. Normally, I'd have made the call to end your life, right here and now, and not even given it a second thought. But I was there when the Sheriff hired you. Boss has a weak spot for the two of you. So I'll let the attitude pass. This. One. Time. Take the extra lottery ticket and get out of here before I change my mind." There are too many deputies to remember him from the day the Sheriff offered us our jobs. Then again, all I ever strive to do is forget my past. I only have the future. Unless my temper gets me killed.

"Juliana, please," Rico repeats, with more force this time. Saying my whole name means he's being extra serious. "It's not worth our lives. Vámonos. Let's go to the lottery."

The *our* out of his lips douses my burning cheeks. Tears sit, ready to expel themselves from my eyes. I hate how weak crying would make me appear. They're both right. Part of me understands that diamond rings don't matter anymore when they've all been traded in for food and water. One that size might have been worth tens of thousands of dollars sixty years ago in the Old Epoch. In the New Epoch, it's worth *one* lottery ticket. Mami used to say anger is pain incarnate. Perhaps it isn't that I'm angry all the time. What I really hate is how raw life has become.

I should have said yes when Rico asked me to marry him and kept the ring. I want to imagine that reality. But I can only guess at what that kind of happiness is like.

I picture the people who came here for fun during the Old Epoch and laughed down these streets. I reach out to take the lottery ticket—a gold chip that has a mountain valley, an etching of the Oasis, on one side and a star symbol on the other to match the Sheriff's golden badge. I run my finger over the unique serial number on the coin, then take the hand Rico offers me.

"Let it go," he says as he cups my face with one hand. I can't help but melt into his touch. He kisses me once, lips not smooth but still soft, a reminder that we're okay.

Then Rico and I head to the lottery, straight toward more disappointment but at least we're together. And perhaps that's all that matters. That's love in the Wasteland.

CHAPTER 2
Jules

At Union Square, I tilt my head sideways to read the melted and bent-over digital gauge set up in the middle of the open area. I grumble a wild array of colorful words under my breath as I replay what happened earlier at the Sheriff's Station. The solar-powered thermostat on the gauge reads 115 degrees in digital red letters as we near five-thirty a.m.

Despite it being ten degrees less than usual, our protective suits only cool us down so much. I should be happy that we have suits, another perk of scavenging for the Sheriff—we found enough good material that I could sew them together. An ability I'm thankful to Mami for. Especially since, before them, we were only able to be aboveground for a couple of hours a day safely. Sweat rolls down my forehead, neck, back—*everywhere*. The suit clings tight to my skin, and the salt stings my eyes and lips. But we don't have a choice except to wait through the heat. If you don't get to the lottery early enough, they run out of food and water. The generosity of the Oasis goes only so far, enough to keep us from storming the haven with hard, stale bread and a lot of false hope. You stay long after you've eaten since you *must* be present to win.

I stare at the empty building Mami once sold protective suits out of. I recall the way I used to beg her to take me with her. I liked to run through the lines of women sewing, learning and having fun with them. I watched them all die. Until just Mami was left. Maybe I should have taken up her work. Given more people a chance to walk in the sun. But any fabric I find now, I trade it in to the Sheriff to eat.

After waiting in line for forty minutes, Rico and I insert half our extra lottery tickets into one of the several machines that count them, each ticket making a clink, until the meter on the screen reads sixteen total tickets. Fifteen extra, hard-earned tickets and the free one that comes included with each buzzer. The machine spits out a buzzer, which contains a digital version of my lottery tickets, and Rico hands it to me. The buzzer itself is a palm-sized, heavy gray disk. It has an image of the Oasis etched on one side, same as the coin, and a barcode on the other. We repeat the process for Rico. We always split our extra tickets evenly. If one of the numbers from our coins matches that of the number pulled, the buzzer will flash and vibrate, and someone will come and whisk the winner off to the Oasis.

I saw it happen to someone I knew once, to my tía on my mami's side, when I was twelve years old.

"I'll find us a seat," I tell Rico. It's risky to split up, but it's the way to both get food and water and not have to stand for the entire lottery.

"I have a good feeling about this drawing," he tells me through our radios.

My belly complains. But at least Rico believes. In goodness. In a future. In us.

"Oh yeah? So, tell me, what exactly are we going to do when we both win?" It's a great question. One I almost never think about. Otherwise, my thoughts run away with dreams that'll never happen. But I need a serotonin boost after that encounter with the deputy.

"We're going to be even happier."

I don't know if I'm happy now. Or if I'm not happy. I worry so much about losing what I've been able to hold on to, and that's mostly him, anything more seems like such a stretch—a fantasy, really. But I don't tell Rico that. Instead, I say, "That's a big promise. What if you find a fancy Oasis girl who says yes to your proposal and you forget about me?"

He chuckles. "I would never fall for anyone else, but you wouldn't have to worry about me following you around everywhere like a puppy anymore."

I laugh. We need each other, but I need him more. I'd follow him into any hellfire or oasis.

"I'd say yes in the Oasis," I whisper, so low I kind of hope he doesn't notice.

"I have a good feeling about this lottery," he repeats, and I can hear his smile in every word.

Can something so liberating ever happen to us? Or is it only reserved for . . . what? Other people?

When I'm quiet, he says, "You okay?"

I nod, though he can't see me. There's a knot in my throat I have to push back. "Yeah," I answer. "I'm just thinking."

"I love you, Jules," he says, his voice so gentle. "And that giant overthinking brain of yours."

"I love you, too," I reply without hesitation.

Rico walks back from the food line. Despite the protection the mask offers, and how it allows me to breathe clean instead of ash-filled air, I remove it from my face and my protective suit so he can find me in the crowd. I wave. His face lights up when our eyes meet. Rico weaves through hundreds of people to get to me. I've snagged seats for us on the top step of the plaza. My shoulders drop when he finally reaches our spot, and my body relaxes.

I take the meal he hands me with restrained eagerness. My portion is a thin plastic bowl filled to the brim with cold noodles and an eight-ounce plastic cup with fresh water instead of the desalinated yet still contaminated ocean water available to us every other day. The latter has the worst aftertaste. Not ready to sip the Oasis water, I rest the cup at my feet.

Rico also passes me my buzzer, which he had to scan to get my portion, then sits and waits until I take my first bite. The noodles are salty yet embarrassingly delicious. He grins at the pleasure painted plainly on my face before he devours his own bowl in ravenous gulps.

"Riquísimo," I mumble, noodles slipping from my mouth. "So good."

"You're so good," Rico says. He moves closer so our legs touch. The warmth of his thigh against mine through our suits is welcome. His eyes wander behind me. Vigilant as always. Meanwhile, I concentrate on his lips, which I can never get enough of. I note that they're cracked and bleeding as he refocuses on me. He then adds, "Best part's coming." I follow his gaze to the water and to the two buzzers at our feet. It isn't every day the Oasis has room for new residents. It happens like three times a month tops as folks in said paradise pass away.

Rico eyes our buzzers with confidence, as if he's prophesized that we'll be lucky enough to enter the haven today. *Yeah, right.* Crowded into the city blocks around Union Square are thousands of other people, forced to sit in the sweltering heat, waiting for their own numbers to be drawn. And this is just San Francisco. There are another thirty thousand people split between San Jose and Sacramento. The odds both of us will be picked are dismal.

Rico waves his hand right in front of my face. "Earth to Juliana." I was frozen mid-bite, distracted by the thought of how pointless this feels. Don't get me wrong, I'll take the food and drink, but waiting for my life to change by magic doesn't sit well with me.

I try to finish the noodles, but my stomach has shrunk since the last time I ate this much.

"Here, comete esto. Eat up." I give Rico a soft nudge with my shoulder as I shove my leftovers at him. After all, he needs the food more than I do. He's too scrawny for his height. Flaco. Tall and hollowed out, and he won't stay fast as a cat if he doesn't have the energy to move.

To my joy, he relishes the extra bites.

The lights around the plaza flash on, a signal the lottery drawing is about to start. The sharp beams paint flames along the glass windows of the old department store buildings around us. The blazes didn't reach this part of San Francisco. Not like they ravaged the Scar, southwest of Union Square. There, the area is uninhabitable. The buildings aboveground tumbled over by earthquakes or burned in the aftermath by uncontrollable fires. The plaza at Union Square is the epicenter of the relatively small safe zone.

Once Rico slurps the remainder of my noodles, I hand him one of the plastic cups and take the other in my hand. I set my optimistic expression in place and snap myself out of gloomy thoughts of the past. "¡Salud! Here's to making it to another week," I say.

"¡Salud! Here's to making it into the Oasis next." Rico clinks his cup with mine. The plastic edges crinkle and bend together. We're careful not to spill a precious drop.

I elbow him lightly. "You really think today's our lucky day? I've lost track of how many lotteries we've been to."

He brings forth one of his warm grins. "The fifty hundredth time's the charm. We got this." We both chuckle. He wipes away some of the sweat trickling down my forehead, some of the blood off my own lips. He pauses for a moment, and everything around us disappears as he cups my face with his hand, then kisses me gently on the mouth and once on my forehead. It's this feeling of being cared about that keeps me going.

"We're going to be okay," he promises, even as his eyes

trail behind me again. For a moment, with his hand still against my cheek, he goes stiff. He puts on the same stone-like expression he has when he's about to get into a fight. His hand goes to his neck on instinct, to the beginnings of a burn scar that covers most of his back. A morbid memento of his time with the San Francisco organization his tía started, Mictlān. And what it cost him as her protégé, and next in line to lead, to get out after she died.

I didn't know about his involvement when we first met. If I had, I wouldn't have trusted him. But he was another hungry kid like me, and we saved each other. I give his arm a quick squeeze now and hold our little bubble together. "Hey, focus on me. The past is the past," I say.

"Yeah—sorry. I thought I saw Jesus," he says before he turns his attention back to his water. "The strange things you imagine when you're dehydrated, right?"

I don't laugh. Jesus is Rico's cousin, and the current leader of Mictlān. From what Rico's told me, Jesus blames him for his mami's death. "Jesus wouldn't be planning another move on the Oasis, would he?"

Rico thinks for a moment before he replies, "Nah. We should drink up. Water is probably getting warm."

My lips hover near the rim of the cup for a full minute before I take my first sip. The water is *actually* still cold—crystal clear and uncontaminated. I drink until the liquid is gone. I lick every inch of the cup, my thirst barely mollified. In my periphery, Rico continues to look around. The hairs on the back of my neck tingle. What would happen if Jesus ever tried to come back into Rico's life? Rico wouldn't return to Mictlān, right?

The loudspeakers on either side of the building awaken with a piercing screech. The rest of the speakers, set up erratically around the area, follow suit. Lofty banners have been raised next to the main screen. They show the glorious valley that the Masterdome is built over, reinforcing why we're here: the picture-perfect home that awaits us if we win.

I glimpse the Sheriff on his usual chair, to the right of one of the banners, sitting where everyone can see him. It's his presence alone that keeps the crowd in check during lottery days. No one, and I mean absolutely no one, wants to be on the Sheriff's wrong side.

He's the age I think my parents would have been, his hair starting to whiten, his face a smooth tan, his eyes lined with deep-set wrinkles. There's a sharp edge to him. The way his face is like steel, the way he hardly ever blinks.

I once saw him give the order to quell fifty people when a fight broke out at a lottery event. His deputies hadn't hesitated or questioned him. Since then, I do my best to get us a seat we can easily run from. And am grateful that he does—for some strange reason—look out for Rico and me.

He's an enigma to everyone, a god to those in San Francisco. He's not the type of god you expect miracles from, though—he's the type that you're expected to pray to if you don't want to be sacrificed. The deputy from the ticket booth approaches the Sheriff and whispers something in his ear. I glare in the man's direction. He is so huge and muscular . . . *What was I thinking?*

Maddison Burberry, the third Burberry to become California's president, appears in a broadcast that's being live streamed from the mountain. She's probably in her early fifties, her white-blond hair held in a high, tight bun today. As she speaks, her face softens. Her voice loosens. For good reason.

The people out here are hungry, thirsty, and hopeless. The last thing they need is a giant, haughty face reminding them that some people are not, in fact, miserable. The Sheriff always stares at her like he hates her with the fire of a thousand suns. I find it amusing. I'm also trying to figure out why. I suppose the reason is obvious enough—he's jealous. She's the leader of a paradise and he of a crumbling San Francisco.

Rico sets his hand on my knee. He sees a light at the end of the tunnel, and I've long felt that if I hold on to him tight enough, he'll pull me through along with him, no matter how jaded I am. I want to believe like he does, and I do on some level, but it's buried under so much that if there *is* a flame of optimism burning deep inside me, I can't see it in the dark.

Rico winks at me. I do a drumroll with my pointer fingers playfully on his hand, adding to his enthusiasm.

Burberry clears her throat, lifts her chin to someone outside the camera's view, surely to signal them to commence the lottery-drawing countdown, and gives us her speech.

"Citizens of California, it is with a heavy heart that I must announce the passing of three of our beloved constituents in the Oasis. Although these deaths pain me, it is my great pleasure to announce we can welcome three new residents into our isolation city. Our inhabitants are chosen by a lottery and can only be replaced after they have died. This has been our way since my father began the lottery system after the Great Earthquake of 2065 ravaged the Wasteland. But like our Masterdome, we stand tall. And I am proud to continue his legacy.

"Soon, our computer system will select three barcodes at random. If yours is one of them, your buzzer will light up and vibrate, and you will be taken by one of our representatives and delivered to us, where you will be given the chance to live a new life in a world void of hardship. You will not need any of your former belongings. Though, I pray you have all brought your most prized possessions—you will not be given the chance to go home and grab them.

"We ask everyone to please respect the winners. Do not touch, attack, or jeer your fellow citizens. If you are *not* chosen, we ask you to remember that even if you were not picked *this time*, to not lose faith. It is with great difficulty we cannot accept everyone within our walls, but we will continue to offer fresh water collected from our precious reservoir and a free meal at lottery events. We'll continue to search for a way to allow more of you into the Oasis or at least bring pieces of it to you.

"Now, out of respect for the dead, we will count down the last minute in silence."

The crowd seems to find it within themselves to stay silent for the *whole* minute. This moment always surprises me. Maybe they're thinking about the deceased, but more likely they're all dreaming about what their first day in paradise will be like. About all the food they'll eat. About all the uncontaminated water they'll drink. The clothes they'll get to wear. How they'll pass out at night, full and merry and clean and unable to believe how lucky they are. How they'll get to see actual sunlight without worrying about their skin burning.

I calculate how much metal and wiring we'll need to strip from the few remaining light posts within the Scar so we can eat this week. It's only Wednesday, so we might still be able to gather enough for a good amount of water that'll last us into next week, too.

I keep my eyes open and lean against Rico's bony shoulder. Rico keeps his hand on my leg, caressing me with his thumb. He grabs his buzzer in the other for good luck.

When the minute is over, everything remains silent, soundless. It's the usual prolonged stillness amid massive anticipation. While everyone else has their eyes shut, I scan the filled-up area. My gaze lands on the Sheriff, who hasn't closed his eyes either. And I swear, he's watching me. Suddenly, a buzz arises and echoes against the buildings surrounding the square, like there's a bee right beside my ear. As soon as the sound rings again, Rico's eyes burst open, and he squeezes my leg. I'm not imagining the noise or how close it is.

I glance from Rico's lit buzzer to his face in utter disbelief. He's as surprised as I am, but there's also an *I-knew-it* look in his sparkling eyes. I am terrified at once. Rico has won a spot in the Oasis and is going to leave me. *This very minute.* I will never see him again. I want to grab the thing out of his hand and throw it into the crowd. I want to be completely selfish.

That dreaded pain that he makes better hits me all at once and across my entire body. The fear of being alone consumes me. But I need to stifle everything and be happy for Rico. He will be safe, and I am absolutely in love with that thought. And isn't that enough for me?

In an odd way, the thought lessens the tension in my muscles so much I'm weightless. I love Rico with all my heart, and he's guaranteed to live a beautiful life from now on.

I'm about to say goodbye when Rico grabs my buzzer and stuffs it into his pocket. Then he wraps my trembling hands around the winning one before anyone notices.

My voice squeaks as I manage to say, "What are you doing? Take it back!"

I follow him as he moves away. I ignore the wave of whispers in the air as people turn their attention toward us.

Rico still smiles his toothy grin. "Jules, this was the plan; they won't let—"

"We talked about this. You said you'd just lie."

He grabs my shoulders for a moment and shakes his head. "They'd see through the lie. My tía began Mictlān. I didn't have a choice to be involved or not, but the role I played in it was too large—they won't let me in. My win has *always* had your name on it. If there's any way for us to be together again, I promise, I'll find it. But for now, you're going."

"I didn't bring any of my belongings with me." If I leave, I'm giving up the last photograph of my family I have. Bile rises up my throat as a sudden dizzy spell wafts over me. I wait for Rico to say he loves me; that will settle my stomach. If this is the last time we'll be together, I *need* him to say it to be okay.

Rico kisses my lips, hugs me tight. "I'll keep everything safe."

This feels like the end of us. Tremors take me over. I'm about to kiss him again when the representative assigned to our location seizes Rico's arm, as if fully aware Rico's the true winner. Rico yanks free before nudging me forward to take his place. For one moment, I lock eyes with the representative.

"She's the winner," Rico says firmly.

Hesitating, the representative looks from Rico to me, then from me to Rico, who retreats out of immediate reach. Without any other choice, the representative relents and pulls out a plastic water bottle from a backpack he's carrying, what seems to be his proof that he's from the Oasis. He throws the water bottle into the crowd, a way to distract the thirsty people around us, before firmly grasping my wrist and dragging me with him.

I turn back. Take Rico in before he fully disappears and sear into memory what he looks, sounds, *feels* like. His beautiful brown face; his dark, messily chopped hair that falls down past his ears now; his full lips and always-alert eyes. His husky voice. The way he makes me laugh. The way he never lets me down. How safe we've been together.

The day we met, both of us were dehydrated and starved. I was in the food line at a lottery, right behind him. He got the last bowl of food and I ended up with half a cup of water. He sat next to me, and for the first of many times, we shared our meal with each other. We didn't say a word until the event was over, but we never left each other's sides after that day. How cruel it is that the lottery that gave him to me is now taking him away?

Any one of the people around would trade places with me in an instant. I consider it. All I need to do is give the Oasis's representative another arm to drag so I'm not separated from Rico. But someone reaches out to shake my hand. More reach out to pat my back or to try to touch my face. The crowd surrounds us. People block our path to the north, south, east, west. A circle forms around our two bodies until we can't move freely anymore.

Suddenly, a few people make it through the rest to shove me or throw weak punches at me. They yell at me to let them take my place. Some tell me they're sick. Others that they have no one left. Many verbally attack me. I've seen the horde before with tía Ines and the others who have won in San Francisco, but to experience it firsthand is something else. My immediate train of thought veers from what *has* happened to what *might* occur in the aftermath of the lottery drawing. I was mostly safe amid the crowd sixty seconds ago. *One* minute ago, I was still one of them. Not anymore. Not when I'm a winner. Now, those outside the haven see me as one of the people who will thrive while they slowly starve.

I fight back and send my fist against the lips, eyes, noses, throats of strangers. It doesn't make a difference. For every person I shove back, there're a hundred more coming at me.

A push from behind throws me forward, and I fall to

the ground, scraping the mask of my protective suit against the pavement. I roll onto my back but take on the crushing weight of someone who lands on top of me. I try to move them off but can't. For a moment, everyone else fades. I squeeze my eyes shut in anticipation. Then they're pulled back by another person, who's probably eager to take their place at the front of the *steal-Jules's-spot* line. The Oasis's representative reappears and manages to haul me to my feet.

As soon as I'm up, a rock hits my shoulder. Hot air burns through the hole in my protective suit. A reminder that I'll never get to patch up Rico's suit. I squeal, the new cut bleeding. After a woman spits on my visor, the representative thrusts her back hard enough that she falls to the ground. Bones crunch as she's trampled by the incoming wave of others.

The representative calls my attention to him. He's wearing a protective suit, too, but through his face mask and visor, he has skin darker than mine and chrome-colored eyes. In one quick motion, he cleans my mask and keeps us moving through the pandemonium.

I'm cornered. I either go to the Oasis and leave Rico behind or die in the middle of Union Square. I'm not ready to leave this world when a beautiful life awaits me. The snake of bodies constricts us until we're unable to move an inch farther. The end of the crowd is a mere hundred feet away, but there's no real way to reach it. The bodies squeeze tighter around me. My bones hurt; I'm worried they're going to crack. And I don't spot Rico anywhere.

The people who press against me scream as those behind

us suffocate them as well, until three shots ring out. The representative points a gun at the nearest person, who cowers away. He moves the weapon at different targets. I gasp in air as an empty circle appears around us.

The focus of the crowd shifts away from me. Guns are rare as most have been traded for tickets to the Sheriff "to help maintain order in the City" or taken by his deputies by force. The gun is a prize in itself—another trophy people are willing to fight and kill for. The representative must sense the shift and pitches the weapon into the swarm, as far away from us as possible. He uses the diversion to push us forward the rest of the way.

As we're about to get to the street, a hand squeezes my shoulder, and nails dig into my skin where my suit was ripped. A shot reverberates from behind me. I freeze, body giving in to the shakes. I relax once the hand slips away. I'm unhurt. Another shot sounds farther behind us as people continue to fight to take control of the weapon, even when half of them don't have any protective suits. I don't dare glimpse back. Neither does the representative. With any luck, Rico has fled Union Square already and the Sheriff's deputies are regaining control.

The Oasis's representative leads me to a black sedan parked on an eerily still side street. He opens the rear door of the car and stuffs me into the back seat. Plexiglass separates the two sections of the car. He gets into the driver's seat, starts the vehicle, and speeds away—dodging the relentless people in the street. Some throw debris at the windshield of the car but don't manage to break the glass. As soon as we drive out of the city limits and onto the empty highway, my adrenaline wanes. I burrow into the cushion, exhausted.

And then there's radio static in my ear, and the best voice in this whole entire world cuts through to say, "Jules, can you hear me?"

CHAPTER 3
Rico

I don't waste time after the representative and Jules drive away, not even when my eyebrow starts bleeding all over the place. I'm usually faster, but I wasn't able to evade a good elbow to the face as I yanked people away from her. The deputies clear the area and collect the buzzers everyone has left on the ground. I need to get to the highest vantage point of Coit Tower, one of the few tall buildings that haven't fallen apart, before Jules gets too far away.

I dash past a kid around my age who plays a drum set made of green glass bottles and upside-down white plastic buckets. They're good, their dreadlocks swaying to the rhythm of the beat they create. But their neon-green shirt has swallowed their body. Like there's a skeleton underneath the fabric. Yet they still perform with so much energy, and it courses through me. We might be dying, but the people of the Wasteland are so full of soul, nobody can diminish us. Not even the deputies who harass the kid to stop the music and give up their buzzer.

It didn't take the deputies long to regain control of the crowd. A few heads bashed in with metal batons later, and it's mostly cleanup time.

I hand the buzzer I took from Jules to the nearest deputy. The Sheriff executes a kill-on-first-refusal order against anyone who neglects to return their buzzer, a rule enacted a few years ago after folks tried to cheat the system by hoarding them. If I tried to hide the buzzer, they'd track it down.

After, I run at full speed from the area. Everyone I pass ignores me, including those who would normally try to rob someone injured like I am. There will be riots soon. Like there are after every lottery. People are too angry and upset that they're not the ones heading to the Oasis.

But I couldn't be happier about today's outcome.

Coit Tower is several blocks away. I press on my wound and hurry into the stairwell once I get to the building. I apologize to the people I knock into in my rush up, those who head down before the day gets too hot to be in the tower.

When I reach the roof, I'm out of breath. My face is drenched in sweat, my eye gluing itself shut. I go to the observation deck where the tourist telescopes are dirty and cracked but still clear enough to see through. I point one toward the bridge straight ahead. It's hard to be certain, but with my good eye, I think I spot a car moving.

I snap on the radio in my protective suit. Blink away the fogginess of my vision as I try to get a clear picture through the viewfinder. "Jules, can you hear me?"

There's the crackle of static on the other end, then a

whisper: "Rico?" Her voice breaks as she says my name. Jules's voice is eternal bliss, but the danger is far from over until she reaches the Oasis. I have to believe I made the right choice, though, even when the weight of my pain drops me to my knees.

"There you are. Are you okay? Are you injured?"

She quietly gives an "I'm okay."

"When you get further, you won't be able to talk to me anymore. You'll need to find a radio booster for the suit when you get to the haven. Don't say anything else so the representative doesn't take the radio away. If you find the booster, we'll be able to talk, and I'll know you made it there safely."

She speaks, but another voice that must be the representative's makes her stop.

"Listen, Jules," I add. "You're still going to have to go through No Man's Land. It'll be really dangerous, and you have to promise to listen to the representative. He'll get you through the area alive. Even if it's something that you wouldn't normally do, or that I wouldn't even ask you to do, you *have* to listen to him."

There's a small noise that I take as a yes on the other end. "I love you, so much," I manage to say before the radio goes dark. As they drive out of range, my throat squeezes. "Good luck, Jules," I whisper to the impending dawn, unsure what to do next.

Not that I'm given the space to ponder. The moment I stand, there's a shuffling behind me. Someone drapes a bag over my head, and my world goes black.

I wake with a jolt in an oversized brown leather chair. I bolt to my feet, glad I'm at least able to do that. The room I'm in has gray walls and dim lights. I'm in a bunker. There's a glass wall on one side with a murky underwater view. I'm at the Wharf. When I turn, my good eye takes in the Sheriff. He stops what he's doing and sets his rimless glasses down onto the wild array of papers spread across his vintage mahogany desk.

"Thought you'd never wake up, mi hijo," he says.

I exhale a semblance of relief. "Sheriff Ramos . . . why?" I shake my head as I try to make sense of what's happening. Could it be connected to the incident earlier with the deputy?

"Sometimes I give instructions that aren't very clear. I told my men to bring you to me. They thought you'd fight back. So they kind of knocked you out. But don't worry, you're safe. I promise, I didn't bring you here to harm you."

He stands, approaches, then embraces me. It's odd and comforting at the same time. No one's hugged me except for Jules since tía Linda, Jesus's mom, died. Not even my cousin or anyone else at Mictlān. Still, the hug is laced with darkness. The Sheriff does not look like an evil man. No, he has the appearance of someone's abuelito—a grandfather with whitening hair, a wrinkled face, worn and calloused hands, and a bright smile he likely mastered during the Old Epoch when he was part of the San Francisco Police Department. But appearances can deceive. He's not someone to anger, no matter how much he seems to have a soft spot for me.

“We need to talk,” he says as he lets go. “Sit.”

I listen, and he returns to the chair behind his desk. He scratches at his ear.

“Did I do something wrong?”

I’m surprised when he says, “Yes, actually, you did. You weren’t supposed to give the winning buzzer to Juliana.”

I try to process his words but ultimately come up short. “I’m confused.”

“I rigged the lottery.” He says it like he hasn’t just revealed something shocking. He connects his hands, sets them atop his desk, and waits for my reaction.

I rub at my face, wince at the pulse of pain when I press too close to my injured eyebrow, then try to piece things together. But I can’t. Why would he have rigged it so that I, of all people, won? And *how* could he have rigged it? So many questions zip through my brain all at once.

When I don’t reply and just sit there with my mouth hanging in a large O, he continues. “I was going to give you a mission that I wanted you to complete inside the Oasis.”

“A mission? What kind of mission?” I ask when I’m able to talk again.

He opens one of his desk drawers, pulls out a small piece of paper, and slides it over to me.

I flip it over. It’s an old and worn picture of an adorable toddler with pigtails and tan skin, wearing a red-and-black plaid Christmas dress, white stockings, and shiny white shoes. The picturesque background gives me the impression it was taken inside the haven. My confusion hits an all-time high. When I don’t say anything, he adds, “I’ll just come out and say it. I hired you and Juliana because your cousin told me that we *needed* you for our plan . . ."

My throat tightens at the mention of Jesus, and all the joy I felt at seeing Jules being driven away vanishes into thin air. "Don't turn pale," the Sheriff continues. It's an order I literally have zero ability to obey. "Your tía caused her own downfall. In being greedy, she refused my help when she tried to break into the Oasis. And failed because of it. But I see something in you. You're a good kid, Rico. Trust me when I tell you that today marks a day that'll change your life forever, so don't make the same mistake your aunt did, and don't refuse me before I tell you what I need your help for."

Tía Linda is gone because of me. She took me in when I was orphaned, gave me a home, and I failed to crack the code that would get us through the hangar door of the train depot and into the Oasis, and she was shot by their sheriff. I'm not the right person for his plan, whatever it is. But I'm rendered speechless again, as prickles of fear now run through my body.

He keeps going. "Now, don't give me that look. Linda was an incredible woman who many admired and loved. I had nothing but respect for your tía. I wish I could say the same about her toward me. At any rate, here's the deal: I need you to go into the haven and do me a few favors. If you do them for me, Juliana will stay safe, and I'll promise you and her a place in the new Oasis we're planning. If you don't, well, your girlfriend's trip to paradise will be short-lived."

I'm unable to make eye contact, suddenly drained of what little energy I had left. My working eye is as heavy as the injured one. Just when I thought Jesus couldn't go any lower, he's working with the Sheriff to blackmail me.

"But why me? If you could rig the lottery, can't you get what you need done with the help of someone already inside?"

"Unfortunately, it's not that easy. You're smart like your aunt and more levelheaded than your cousin. We need someone like you to be a ghost in the Masterdome."

"What do you want with the girl in the photo? Are you going to hurt her?" I ask next, my voice cracking.

He cocks his head backward and chortles before his face turns to stone again. "She's my granddaughter." The Sheriff may be ruthless, but he's not a liar. Someone who has this much power doesn't have to be.

He gives me the information freely. "When Hunter Burberry hired me to be the sheriff of San Francisco, part of the deal was that I was allowed to send one person into the haven at any point. Ultimately, I chose to send my granddaughter. There, she would be safe in a way my own daughter hadn't been."

"What happened to your daughter?" I ask, unable to keep back my curiosity.

"My brother wanted to take my place as sheriff, so he took my daughter as leverage. By the time my deputies found her, it was too late. Luckily, we were able to save the baby in her belly. My granddaughter, Sidra. Three years ago, I asked for Sidra to be returned to San Francisco, to me. Our current president refused, stopped communications with me except to tell me that my granddaughter would die if I ceased cooperating. She holds me and my granddaughter hostage.

Enough is enough. If Burberry won't send Sidra back, I've decided I'll go to her and take the rest of that city while I'm at it. But I need Sidra out of harm's way before I act. As long as Burberry has Sidra, she has control over me. Sidra is my last tie to my daughter. We had elections once. Soon enough, we'll have them again, but I need my granddaughter safe before I can snuff out the Burberry lineage."

I try to figure a way out of this, but even if I said no, I am in *his* domain. I am literally in his office. Plus, there's a look of pain in his eyes that sticks with me. He's no longer one of the most powerful men in the Wasteland, but an old man defeated and asking me to help him get his granddaughter back. And there's Jules. I can't take the risk he'll hurt her. The irony is not lost on me that he's holding my family hostage to save his own.

"Okay," I reply, my mouth so dry even water couldn't quench my thirst.

Sheriff Ramos claps once and says, "That's my boy."

I play along the best I can. "So . . . we wait for the next lottery? And what about my ties to Mictlān? I figured they wouldn't let me in if they knew I was tía Linda's nephew." If I wait, it will give me time to see if Jules can find a signal booster for her radio. If she finds one and I can talk to her, we can figure out how to get out of this mess.

The Sheriff shakes his head. "I don't have that sort of time. We've created the necessary crack in the Masterdome as a fail-safe plan. A digital camouflage, if you will, that is temporary to get you in and keep you hidden once inside. But you need to enter the Masterdome in the next three days.

In terms of how you'll get to the Oasis, Jesus told me about the train. I want you to fix it." The Sheriff puts on that self-assured smile of his. The one so at ease I don't think anything could ever burden the man. He is the calm river that flows into the ocean. That's why he's the one in charge.

I reply honestly. "I don't know if I can fix it that fast. I haven't even seen the train in years."

His smile isn't cruel, but it is condescending.

"You'll find a way to make it happen," he replies before he moves on. "Some logistics: I have a disciple on the inside. A close friend who will govern the haven with me. She used to be a representative until we got too close. Now, Burberry doesn't let her leave the South Shore. So she's been secretly building up our rebellion from within. Her name is Viola Hershall. You track her down, and she will help you get my granddaughter. Sidra will be fine with Viola. Listen to her. I'll need you to send an unmanned train down to me. It'll be as hard as work in the Scar. Nothing more. And I guarantee your cousin and your girlfriend will both stay safe."

He grabs something else from the same drawer he got the picture from. They're bracelets, made of slate-blue fabric, each holding a small rectangular silver device.

"These are special key fobs that give the wearer access to everything inside the Oasis. As long as you wear these key fobs, no one will question you, not Burberry or her soldiers. You can use them to purchase what you need and to travel the area. They are one of a kind, so do not lose them. Viola sent me three: one for you, and two for your cousin if he needs another pair of hands. Whatever happened between the two of you, I want you to put it aside. You'll need to work together to see this through for me."

I try to give back the photo, but the Sheriff puts up his hand.

"Take the picture, take the key fobs, fix the train with Jesus, ride the train into the city, find Viola Hershall, get my granddaughter safely into Viola's hands, and follow her next steps. If you can handle all that, you and Juliana will live out your happily ever after. Do we have a deal?"

He stretches out his hand like I have a choice. I take it.

"And I have another surprise, but your cousin is the one who wants to break the news to you," Sheriff Ramos says.

Oh, great. "Just who I want to see," I reply as I stand.

I make my way out of the Sheriff's office on wobbly legs, missing Jules now more than ever.

CHAPTER 4

Jules

The moment Rico's line goes static, I miss his voice. I squeeze my eyes. I can do this. I'm not fully alone like I thought I was. I have my radio and all I need to do is find a radio booster in the Oasis. Then I can talk to Rico again. God, I would talk to him every day. It might not be enough, but it *will* do until I figure out what comes next.

"Did you hear me? We're almost to No Man's Land," the representative repeats from the front seat. I don't reply, unsure of what exactly he wants from me.

Growing up, I heard so many stories of people dying in No Man's Land. Anarchy spread as government officials fled to safer places, leaving the general populace as the world fell apart. At that point, the last of humanity fought for what limited supplies were left, from water bottles to canned food. At first, it was violent groups that emerged to take control of any place governing forces abandoned.

The crimes drove people into the three lower isolation cities in California, all of which combined became known as the Wasteland, where sheriffs govern with iron fists. Led by the state's president, the sheriffs have their own ways of keeping peace and stopping the violence from becoming too extreme.

From that moment on, we entered the New Epoch. One where people no longer had the ability to move wherever they wanted without risk of dying. One where people started to feel truly trapped. I don't want to talk about No Man's Land. And I definitely don't want to cross it.

Staying silent on the matter must not be an option, though. The representative stops and turns the car off. As soon as he does, sweat re-forms on my brow, lip, chin, armpits, and back. My eyes are swollen from crying. My hands, bloated like I've got balloons for fingers. My head pulses painfully, right in the middle of my forehead, as if someone took a hammer to it. The representative's footsteps crunch on uneven gravel as he gets out and walks back to the trunk to grab something. He comes around, opens my door, and hands me a stainless steel canteen.

I relax a bit and remove the helmet of my protective suit. I take the bottle and drink from the water container as soon as I've got the cap off. The liquid bottlenecks in my throat. It tastes so fresh—and ice frickin' cold.

"I'm Rodrick Green, by the way. It's my job to get you to the haven alive," the representative says, reaching out his hand to me. I don't take it—my manners faded along with my mami. When he gets the hint, he reaches for my arm instead, to study the cut from the rock thrown at me. It still bleeds, but I'm more worried about my protective suit. Will I be able to find the fabric I need to repair it in the Oasis? "You know what is waiting for us the further we go down this route, right?" Rodrick's voice is muffled underneath his own suit.

I nod with caution.

"Good," he answers. "We're about a mile out from the border into No Man's Land. I have to cover a few things before we keep going. If you thought things got bad in Union Square, they're about to get a hundred times worse. The people we'll run into are not just going to want to kill us; they're going to want to have fun while doing it. If they catch us, they'll torture us, might even eat us. As you likely already know, what keeps them out of the isolation cities are the sheriffs and their deputies. Out here, they're not afraid of anyone, so our one goal over the next two hours is to make sure we make it to the train we need to catch before the sunrise that's set to crest at about seven-thirty today."

"Can't we"—I clear my throat—"go around them?"

"There's no way around. And drink it all," he says, pointing to the canteen. I gulp the rest of the clean water but still crave more, a river's worth. I huff and hand the container back to Rodrick. Through the visor of his protective suit, his chrome eyes are concerned as he takes in my worn-out face. He pulls a peach out of thin air and hands it to me.

A magic trick. He's just done a magic trick.

I'm giddy with innocent excitement—a kid for the first time in years.

I haven't eaten a decent piece of fruit in so long. I blink a few times in disbelief and snatch the peach away from him like an animal. I dig my teeth into its skin, which is sweet, cool, refreshing. I sigh as its nectar soothes my cracked lips and sore throat, its liquid trickling down my neck. I wipe it off with the back of my arm and wish Rico were here for me to share this with.

Rodrick takes off his helmet. I hadn't noticed while he dragged me through San Francisco that he can't be much older than me, if at all. He's tall and lean, with a square chin, dark brown skin, and focused eyes. What would compel someone our age to come out of the Oasis? Is it punishment? Or something else—a savior complex?

Whatever the reason, the boy is brave. Most people wouldn't have done what he did. Most people would have left me in Union Square after the mob attacked.

"Once we cross the border, you must listen to every single thing I say. If I say jump, you jump. If I say duck, you duck. If I tell you that you need to get out of the car and it's moving, you—"

"—jump out," I finish. Rico told me to follow orders, too. I may not be prepared for whatever is out there, but I am fully committed to surviving.

Rodrick shoots me a quick side grin. "You have to use the restroom or anything?" He looks around for a moment. I shake my head. I don't want to leave this car.

"What about the other winners?" I ask.

"There's a rendezvous point near the train depot. The distance there is about the same from all three cities, so we'll arrive at approximately the same time."

When I think he's about to go back to the driver's seat, Rodrick reaches behind his back and pulls out another gun.

He double-checks it to make sure the safety is on and tries to hand it to me, but I refuse it.

"I'm not a great shot, so I'd rather not."

Rodrick sighs as I take another bite of the peach. He leans in closer. "Pacifism isn't a choice for us out here. I can't defend us alone. We need to haul ass and get to the train that'll take us to the Masterdome before the sun comes up. Take the gun. For protection. Once we're safe, you can give it back."

I have no other choice but to grab it. Instantly, I feel the weight of every bullet inside. I know the burden each one carries. Has every lottery winner done something like this? Did Rico suspect this would be necessary for me to stay alive? Does he know that I could die out here? By what he said on the radio, the answer is yes.

"What's your name?" he asks.

"Juliana, or Jules," I reply.

"What do you say we get you home, Jules?"

"Okay." I linger on the word *home*, and I truly can't believe that Rico won the lottery. How is this even my life right now?

Rodrick sets his helmet back in place, returns to the driver's seat, and asks me to buckle my seat belt and hang on. My parents owned a car for a couple of years until it seemed like the whole world ran out of gas, but they never went this fast. I grasp the handlebar of the door so tight my knuckles hurt.

"Here we go," he mumbles.

It's quiet outside for a long while. Who would be out there? There's no one coming to hunt us down.

I've just let go of the door handle when the car is sent in

a 360-degree tailspin. My heart clenches; my stomach flips. I shut my eyes and grit my teeth, the seat belt holding me tight, thank God.

"Stay with me, Juliana!" Rodrick says from the front. He straightens out the car and accelerates again. There's a massive dent in the door on the side of the car that was hit. If I had been on that side instead of this one, I would've been injured. Or worse—

I examine the gun, find the safety, and keep it ready. My hand quivers as I search all around us for our attackers. At first, there's no one. Then one, three, five, ten vehicles appear. But they're not like this one. They're bulkier and covered with armor. There're massive spikes coming out of the cars, so they seem more like giant steroid-enraged porcupines.

"Go faster!" I yell as one of the spikes is catapulted into the back window with a violent crash. The edge of the spike nicks my hair. It cuts a piece clean off so it flies all over my lap, but the spike leaves my skull intact as it enters the front passenger headrest.

"Stay down!" Rodrick screams at me like I don't already know I should.

But I don't listen. I need to prove to him that I'm a fighter, worthy of making it into the Oasis. Otherwise, I left Rico for nothing.

I grasp the spike lodged into the passenger seat and, with all my might, pull it free and chuck it out the back window. The car lightens and picks up speed. The spike rolls behind us. *Most* of the cars pursuing us dodge it, but one of them doesn't move in time. It goes flying sideways as the spike tangles with its wheels, rolling twice before it stops with a screech.

"Woo-hoo!" Rodrick laughs. I turn to him. We lock eyes through the rearview mirror for a second. "Hold on tight, Jules!"

I take hold of my gun once more and focus on our tail. I aim through the opening at the back. I get my first decent look at the drivers of the armored cars. They have shaved heads painted dark with ash, so they blend in with the darkness of their vehicles in the night. *Who are these people?*

"They're getting closer!" I shout.

Rodrick doesn't answer me for a minute. Just when I think he isn't going to, he says, "So fire at them!"

I aim the weapon, take a deep breath, and squeeze. The kickback jolts me uncomfortably.

I miss the first car entirely. Once. Twice. Three times.

I told Rodrick I'm a terrible shot. I yell out my frustration. The moment I go to squeeze a fourth shot out, another car like ours comes out of nowhere and rams the porcupine vehicle closest to us. It ricochets against the others.

"There she is!" Rodrick says. He hits the wheel with excitement and glances back.

"Who?" I can't make anyone out in the vehicle behind the darkened windshield.

Shots fire and tires burst open on our attackers' cars. They all stop, unable to follow us any longer. A third black car appears in front of us, this one an SUV. Three cars. Three winners and their representatives. Six people against madmen cannibals sounds more like the kind of odds I can get behind.

We drive, all in a row, our car in the middle.

"That'll be the worst of it, if we're lucky not to go into another group's territory," Rodrick says.

I nod at his back, relax into the seat once more.

A good ten minutes later, Rodrick whispers, "We're almost at the train depot. Once we get there, we'll need to make it onto the actual train." He pauses to check his wristwatch. "Which will be at the station in exactly thirty minutes. It's operated by a timer, so it won't wait for us—be ready to run as fast as you can. If we miss our window, there won't be another train until the next drawing. It'd be a miracle to make it out in No Man's Land for that long. We'd have to backtrack to San Francisco, which doesn't seem like a good option either."

I don't know what to say, so I don't speak. I wait and stay vigilant. It remains peaceful for all of five minutes.

I'm reminded that we're still in No Man's Land and thus in danger by an explosion in front of us. The force of it sends the representative's SUV that's in front careening over our vehicle. I wrap my arms around my head to shield me from the weight of the car that never comes.

"What? No. No. No!" Rodrick yells.

The SUV crashes behind us, causing the other representative's car to swerve. We might have been able to turn back and help them, but another porcupine throws some kind of explosive at the fallen vehicle.

"No. No," Rodrick repeats from the front. He sounds like

he's going to cry. Still, he drives with unwavering focus, and at least the other car remains all right. "We're five minutes away. Say a prayer, Jules."

A prayer . . . How do I tell Rodrick that I don't have anything close to that left in me?

Papá used to talk about God a lot, especially once the water wars began, after the Great Earthquake of 2065, after the fires, after the new wave of Sibervirus spread so ruthlessly that nothing helped the sick breathe and it always led to seizures. He was obsessed with prayer. When my middle brother died, he prayed. When my younger brother was on his deathbed, half burned, flesh rotted, feverish and seizing from Sibervirus, he prayed. But prayer never saved him. And it didn't save Mami or anyone else in our family.

Praying is useless when humans are heartless. I don't pray. Instead, fiery tears escape from my eyes.

"We're five minutes away," Rodrick says again, almost more to himself than to me this time.

I nod and grip my weapon so tight it's hard to move my fingers. I force them to loosen, even as my body screams *Get out of this car and find your way back to San Francisco.* Although Rico is the optimist, I did have a sliver of hope that leaving the area would be my salvation. What's happened in the last few minutes has taught me otherwise. Is there even a safe place left in this terrible world? Perhaps the answer is no, and all I can really hope for is another day. There's only survival. But I don't need to go to the haven for that. Rico made living worthwhile at least.

The tires screech as the car comes to a halt. "Get out and

follow me," Rodrick says. A young woman with another winner jumps out of the car behind us. Rodrick quickens his pace, and I make sure to keep up.

The area we've stopped at is empty of buildings. It's a strange open field with what looks like a fish-shaped bunker door protruding from the ground.

We don't get far. There must be twenty people waiting in front of the entryway. By the tattered clothing they're wearing and the expressions of hate on their ashen faces, I don't think they're part of the Oasis welcoming committee.

We stand side by side. Me, Rodrick, the other girl, and the boy next to her. There should have been six of us. But the other winner and their representative are gone. Are we next?

We all must seem so silly to these people in our protective suits. Something tells me that they are way more used to fighting in daylight than any of us. Our luck will only get worse as the first rays of the day creep across the horizon and we're forced to move in temperatures we're not used to.

"Willa," Rodrick whispers.

"I know. I can see them," Willa replies through gritted teeth.

She sounds my age. Are we all teens out here bracing ourselves against adults wielding all types of weapons? And there are *all* types of weapons in their hands, from spiked bats to chains to swords to guns. *Yeah.*

This is how I'm going to die.

I wish I had gotten to say goodbye to Rico properly.

But as soon as I have the thought, Rodrick and Willa move away from us and toward our attackers. Before I can even process what's happening, Rodrick takes out what looks like an oversized gun, but when he pulls the trigger, a large swell of light shoots out. I thought laser weapons were only part of comic books and movies. The person he hits drops to the ground, immobile. It's unlike anything I've ever seen.

Weapons clatter and clash. Rodrick and Willa fight on their own. A beeping sound rings. I don't know where it's coming from.

"Run inside! The train is coming," Willa shouts at the boy and me.

At first, I don't react.

Then the other winner takes my hand. He pulls me straight toward the mouth of the giant stone fish.

We don't make it far before someone grasps my injured shoulder and pulls me to the ground. I yelp as a long serrated knife appears in front of my face. I barely register it in time to roll out of the way. The knife digs into the dirt next to my head. It's stuck, but my attacker takes my throat and squeezes. I gasp for breath, but it's impossible. I kick my legs, trying to move in any direction that might help me. The world turns white too fast.

Freeing myself is *not* impossible, though.

Rico taught me how to get out of this kind of situation. All I need to do is calm down. I refocus and wrap my legs tight around my attacker's neck and lift my back up, removing their hands from my throat. I shift their body with my legs to the right. They fight against me, but I have them in my grip. Problem is, I don't know how to get up from here. The moment I move my legs they'll be free to kill me. They squirm and push away. My thighs begin to slip from their shoulders, and there's a paralyzing fear that comes with it.

Rico would be proud even though I failed.

But then Rodrick reaches me and kicks my attacker's head. There's a loud crunch, and the man becomes unconscious or perhaps is already gone from this world. I take Rodrick's hand when he offers it and get to my feet. He pulls me into the mouth of the fish, which seems to lead down into a tunnel.

I slip close to the bottom and take Rodrick with me so we fall along the final five steps. Something's wrong; my ankle throbs as if I've twisted it. But I stand, and this time, I'm the one who helps Rodrick up.

Rodrick glances at his watch as he rights himself and finally stops the beeping.

There's a padlocked gate between the train platform and us. Rodrick punches in a code that is too long for me to memorize, but he obviously knows it by heart.

"Thank the Lord," he says when the door opens, though his relief wanes as he turns back toward the staircase. Willa and the other winner haven't appeared yet.

"We should go back," I say and refuse to step through the threshold. Rico would tell me to keep going. But that isn't me. Still, I can't move since Rodrick holds me in place.

"No," he says. But he cares about Willa, doesn't he? He adds in, "My job is to get you onto the train. If they don't show up in one minute, you're going to get on and *I'll* go up."

The bright headlights of a train appear in the darkness. I don't think we have a minute.

"What a morning," he says. He turns to me and adds, "When it stops, you'll have exactly fifteen seconds to make it through the doors before the train pulls off. You need to move fast, you got it?"

"Affirmative," I say. Sweat drips in my mask and clouds my visor so my vision is blurred.

I turn to the stairs again when there's the familiar scream of someone getting injured.

Rodrick's expression falters. The train is almost to us, and if we miss it, that's it. But I don't know—something comes over me. I've lived through so many terrible deaths. I won't let Willa or the other winner die, too. Not without trying to save them.

I wriggle out of Rodrick's grasp and ascend the stairs, skipping up them two at a time. My ankle burns at the acceleration. The sun creeps up the horizon. The light blinds me for a moment, but I spot them.

The boy drags Willa, whose leg is bleeding. She cries out in pain. I run to them and help the boy hold her weight.

Rodrick appears. "I got her," he says to us. He takes Willa in his arms and cradles her like a baby. "Go! Run!"

We move fast, Rodrick with Willa on our heels. I'm amazed he doesn't fall or trip down the stairs after us.

The moment we set foot back on the platform, the doors to the train open.

"Get in, get in!" Rodrick yells as he turns around to shut the padlocked gate.

In front of me, the boy doesn't hesitate and crashes into the wall on the other side of the door. I jump in too fast, ram into him, then roll out of the way to give Rodrick and Willa space.

The doors begin to close before they've made it through, so I leap back up. I take one side of the door with both hands, while the boy grabs the other. My hands, my arms, my legs all shake. And my ankle still screams at me to settle down. Tears brim in my eyes as I struggle to hold my side open. Thankfully, the pair enter in a matter of seconds. Once they're both in, the boy and I let go at the same time and the doors slam shut.

I had thought Union Square would be the worst of it, but as Rodrick promised, this was so much crueler.

The other winner gives me a slight nod.

"Thank you," Willa says. She shudders as she handles the gash going across her lower leg.

I nod and lean back against the doors, the weight of events too much to bear as we speed off toward the Oasis.

CHAPTER 5
Jules

The boy and I don't say a word as we take seats across from each other and stare at the metallic table between us.

In another train booth, Rodrick mends Willa's leg with a first aid kit. Her gash is gnarly, bone visible through open skin, so there's blood everywhere. Yet Willa barely screams as Rodrick stitches her up. The sheen of sweat on her freckled face, which makes locks of her bright red hair stick to her forehead, is the only evidence of her discomfort.

The last hour of the train ride goes by too slow. The tunnel is pitch-dark, especially when the lights on the train have dimmed. It's a struggle to stay awake and alert. But I can't close my eyes again, terrified we'll be attacked once more.

Rodrick and Willa exchange a glance, in a way I often do with Rico. They're in love. I can tell from being around them for a few minutes. They risked their lives, their life together, for us. It doesn't make sense to me, but I'm grateful, nonetheless.

Across from me, the boy lets out a long exhale as if the fact that we made it onto the train alive has just hit him. He takes off his mask. He's a big sweaty mess, too. We all are. His long hair is pulled back into a ponytail, and his dark and alert eyes are a moss green.

I need to make conversation to avoid crashing, so I ask, "What's your name?"

"Samuel," he whispers. "Sam."

"Sam," I repeat. "I'm Juliana. Or Jules. Whichever you prefer. Where did you come from?"

"Sacramento lottery."

"Did you know the other winner?"

Sam shakes his head. "No, I was the only one who won in Sacramento."

That means the other winner came from San Jose.

"It was bad luck, what happened," Rodrick says as he sniffles. "Gregory was our senior representative for this trip. He was a great mentor. It's a big loss, but we're all familiar with the dangers."

"Then why do it?" I ask.

Willa grimaces before she gazes at Rodrick as if the loss of their mentor hurts her more than her wound.

Before either of them can respond, a stream of sunlight catches our attention as we come out of the tunnel. The Oasis comes into view to our right. I move to the other side of the train and stare out the window, mouth agape. The golden protective dome that surrounds the haven isn't exactly transparent the way I imagined it'd be. Rather, it has honeycomb-shaped metallic sections. The spaces within these sections are translucent, with a slight shimmer and yellow tint. Past the dome, there is a multitude of colors inside emanating from tall buildings and so many trees.

I smile to myself as I take it in. I'm one of the lucky few who get to live here. My heart breaks for the winner who lost their life.

"I've never seen anything more beautiful," Rodrick says. Willa clears her throat, so he adds, "Except for you, of course."

The view of the Masterdome ends as we enter another tunnel. At least it's a short one. The train rolls into a large hangar and stops where the tracks end.

A large group of people become visible in the darkness of the hangar, armed and dressed in metallic green suits and caps. Their stern faces don't instill confidence, and when the door to the train doesn't open, my heartbeat quickens.

To my relief, it isn't a deputy who walks in when they finally get the doors ajar—it's a woman in a long-sleeve black dress, cut with a diagonal slit at her knees and adorned with shimmering silver beads. She wears elaborate pearlescent-pink platform high heels. I'm still staring at her shoes when she says the last thing I would ever expect.

"Juliana?"

My eyes meet hers, and it's like I've seen a ghost with pink eye shadow. I might be dead. My mom is right in front of me. It all connects. It's not Mami. She's gone. This is someone exactly like her, except younger. It's my tía, the one who won the lottery years ago.

My voice teems with excitement as I ask, "Tía?" When I

stand and rush to her, she hugs me so tight that it's hard to breathe, but I don't even care.

"Mi querida," she says. It's been seven years since tía Ines won a spot in the Oasis. I never thought I'd see her again. Hadn't even remembered her on the train ride. Now she's right in front of me, and my fear evaporates.

"Mom?" Willa says. *Mom?* I turn to Willa, confused. Did I hear wrong?

"Dios santo, what happened?" tía Ines says as she turns her attention to Willa. Still, my aunt doesn't let my hand go as she approaches Willa. She pulls me with her.

Willa gives tía Ines a large fake grin coated in pain. "A sword."

"She's okay, though," Rodrick quickly adds.

Tía Ines nods, exhales, and for a moment, we're all silent, waiting for a million explanations.

"Willa," she finally says, "this is your cousin. My sister's daughter, Juliana." When she turns to me, she adds, "Willa is the daughter of my late husband. God rest his soul."

Tears form in my eyes at the memory of everyone we've lost. There's no one, not even Rico, who would understand my pain except for my tía. I had another cousin once. Tía Ines's biological daughter died before my aunt won the lottery. The knowledge that my aunt has been happy here, has a new family, one that perhaps can be my family, too, is everything.

Willa smiles. "I've always wanted a cousin." She sniffles as tears brim in her eyes now as well. Before I know it, the three of us are laughing. "Especially one as badass as you are. Thank you again for holding the door open."

I try to hold it together so I don't ugly cry.

Tía Ines hugs me again, tight, and kisses me on the forehead.

"I think we should get you all to the infirmary," she says to us, then asks, "Are you ready?"

Tía Ines still holds my hand as we walk out of the train. Cheers and claps erupt around us. There must be a hundred people here—the actual Oasis welcoming committee. Some hold signs that say things like *Welcome Home!* or *Your New Life Awaits!* They're all a sea of metallic clothing, bright makeup, and cheery faces. Sam and I exchange a knowing glance, aware of how new we must seem to these people. The awkwardness makes my belly squirm.

We walk by a wall with three giant picture frames that hold portrait paintings of California's last three presidents: Ronald Burberry, the billionaire who created this upper isolation city; his son, Hunter Burberry, the man who launched the lottery; and the current president, Hunter Burberry's daughter, Maddison Burberry, the woman who continues their legacy.

"We owe them so much," tía Ines tells me as I gawk, my ankle throbbing with every step. "The Burberrys really stepped up when the United States government collapsed during the first wave of the Sibervirus. No one could have predicted that it would get so bad, so fast. Did you know that within weeks, the president and half of the Congress of the United States died? States were forced to govern themselves. Ronald Burberry saved us all during those first dark days."

"By bringing everyone together?" Sam asks.

"By using the billions of dollars he had to keep a semblance of order. He became the president of California—governing the lower cities and the Oasis—as all states became autonomous," tía Ines replies with a smile. "Now, c'mon, let's get you all to the medical bay."

I nod and swallow hard as I wonder: Will I live up to their standards?

"The first place every lottery winner is taken is the infirmary for a checkup," tía Ines says from a motorized walkway that takes us up three floors. "We're currently located in one of several bunkers that exist at the entrance of the haven, embedded into the mountain range and connected to the train depot for arrivals."

We step off the walkway and head past several people who give tía Ines slight bows.

Inside an extensive corridor, I'm taken to a small room, while Sam is led to another and Willa and Rodrick head into what appears to be a surgical bay. Tía Ines stays with me, and I'm grateful that despite all the time that's passed, she still seems to care about me in a way that no one except Rico has in years.

As we wait for the doctor, I change into a hospital gown, and tía Ines finally asks the questions whirling through her mind.

"¿Tu mami?" There's a hopefulness to her inquiry.

I simply shake my head and fight the urge to cry the way I've perfected over the past years since she died.

My tía isn't as able to contain herself. She's surely lived with daydreams of a potential reunion with her sister. Tears spring from her eyes in two sad cascades as her lips turn down into a disappointed frown. She blinks to no avail. I should console her. But there have never been the right words for what happened to us. Pain is constant and normal if you were born outside the Oasis.

There's a knock on the door, and a man walks in. He's so impossibly clean. Even in my hospital robe, I'm out of place, my hands and feet dirty, and goose bumps scatter across my body in the ventilated room.

"Vice President," the doctor says to my aunt, who wipes away her tears with the backs of her hands. She smudges her pink makeup into circles around her eyes.

"This is my niece," she says, and I still can't get over the fact she's the vice president of this place. "She has a twisted ankle and hurt shoulder, and I want her to receive the best care possible." The doctor replies with a slow nod.

He doesn't say much else as he checks my body for other injuries. By the time he's done, he's set a wrap around my ankle that nullifies the pain in seconds and given me a shot on my shoulder that heals the cut there almost instantly, and I'm ready to sleep for a thousand years.

"We'll need to take some blood to test for the Sibervirus and you'll be good to go," he says, offering me a warm smile. "The ankle should be healed by the time you get home." The wrap tingles as I marvel at it and wonder how they have this type of technology.

I grin back, though I turn away when he takes my blood.

"Let's get you cleaned up and take you home," tía Ines says once the doctor leaves with the ruby-red vials. There's that word again . . . *home.* It fills me with uncontainable joy akin to when Rico first told me he loved me.

Tía Ines leads me to a door in another part of the infirmary that has a showerhead placard on the outside.

"Is that what I think it is?" I ask, giddy.

She nods, pushes on the wall next to the shower, popping open a closet, and pulls out a pair of leggings and an oversized T-shirt I welcome. "Take all the time you need. Literally, stay in the water for an hour if you want. I'm going to go check on Willa. I'll be waiting for you back here."

I enter fast, undress quickly, careful not to damage the radio on my protective suit, and turn on the water. At first, it's cold, but in a matter of seconds, I take my first warm shower in years, and everything about it is heaven.

I don't rush. I take my time. I use extra soap and shampoo and—*oh my Diosito*—conditioner that leaves my hair silky smooth, and then I sob underneath the water until nothing else comes out of me. Seeing my tía, as happy as it makes me, is also a really hard reminder that I am not the little girl she knew, and everyone else who I've loved is gone. Except for Rico, I remind myself. Rico is still alive. All I have to do is figure out what I can do to get him here. Tía Ines is the vice president of California for crying out loud . . . Perhaps there's a way to at least check and see if Rico *is* blacklisted.

If they don't even remember Mictlān, he wouldn't have to worry.

As I stand underneath the water, a new determination blossoms. My fingers wrinkle. I stay for another five minutes. Once I'm out of the shower, I'm like a new person, frayed at the edges, but cleaner now, fresh, like I am on my way to being whole again.

My tía waits for me as promised, now joined by Sam, who smiles when he sees me.

"Sorry to keep you waiting," I tell them sheepishly.

"Don't apologize," Sam replies. "I took a long shower, too."

"Willa?" I ask next, already too concerned about my new cousin.

"She's okay," my aunt replies, with an assured calmness. "It'll take a couple of weeks for the wound to fully heal. But we have state-of-the-art medical equipment here. She'll be fine, thanks to you two and Rodrick. I owe you both a huge debt."

"You don't owe us anything," I reply. Though the fact that they have the medical supplies people in San Francisco need so badly makes my belly turn sour.

"Willa saved us, too," Sam adds.

Tía Ines claps and says, "Now, let me show you to your new homes. As a thank-you, I've made some quick housing adjustments so that your apartments are in the same building as ours. And I'll give you a tour of the North Shore on the way there."

We follow her out of the infirmary and into another tunnel. This one leads somewhere very special.

The surface.

The Masterdome is even more mesmerizing from this vantage point. I crane my neck up as we walk. Its shimmer reminds me of a soap bubble. The mountain has been carved out, and an entire city has been built up top in between the trees. There are sleek buildings that look like trees themselves, their windows refracting the light so that they give off a slight golden tinge onto the concrete roads and footpaths that have been paved through the forest for cars and pedestrians. I can't see much beyond the skyline of the buildings, and I can't wait to.

Tía Ines then leads us to an extra-large parking lot filled with cars outside the hangar. They don't look anything like those of the Old Epoch. They're sleek opalescent pods. All three of us enter the back seat of one of the pods, which starts when the door closes. A robotic voice greets us.

"Welcome back, Vice President," the machine says.

The pod moves on its own onto the road along with many others. It takes us away from the entrance of the Oasis and toward the heart of the mountainous city itself.

"Production of the Oasis started right after the first wave of the Sibervirus. Ronald Burberry saw the need for a paradise. He was a businessman. He charged ten thousand people one million dollars per person to live in the Oasis and made ten billion dollars in a week. He used that money to hire the sheriffs and deputies in the three lower isolation cities to help govern. And in doing so, he became the first president of California in the New Epoch," tía Ines says, as if this is a history she's talked about a lot and has memorized. "The Great Earthquake of 2065 changed a lot. Ron died, and his son, Hunter, took over as our leader. He began the lotteries so that the Oasis was no longer only for the rich. And now Hunter's daughter, my good friend Maddison Burberry, is continuing his work. Today, the haven still houses ten thousand people. The Masterdome overhead keeps the temperature within it at a perfect seventy-eight degrees. We all have free healthcare and fresh water and all the food we desire. It's the flawless world that every human being deserves."

What the Burberrys did is miraculous. But the people outside this city don't have any of these things. Does that mean everyone outside the Masterdome is undeserving?

I'm about to say that to my aunt, but she continues on. "Keep in mind, though, making it into the Oasis is only the beginning. Everyone works. Everyone earns their keep. Some put in the smallest amount of effort necessary to maintain their spot; others give it their all to ensure the land remains a paradise. Not only for the people in it today, but for everyone who has yet to enter. How you spend the rest of your life is your choice."

"I want to help everyone outside," I reply as I think of Rico.

Tía Ines's eyebrows knit in the middle as if I've said something wrong. "I don't think I want you to leave. Look at what happened to Willa. If she hadn't made it, I can't imagine how I could go on. But perhaps there are other jobs that might help you feel like you're doing something for those you've left behind. We can talk about it."

I'm about to make my case to be sent out just like Willa

and become a representative when the scene outside the pod stops me.

There's a whole lake to our left, the road winding around it. I'd heard whispers of it, and of course, we're given fresh water at the lottery events, but I never imagined I'd see this much fresh water in one place. It's massive in comparison to the small island in the middle that houses a sleek and shimmering building. The island is tiny compared to the massive dam at the edge of the lake, which holds the reservoir in place, containing the water so it doesn't escape down the mountains.

Between us and the island, there are giant, alien-like robots that glide across the glistening lake too gracefully for their size. I nudge Sam awake so he doesn't miss the sight. He fell asleep and now startles. His big green eyes focus on me for a moment before he calms, remembers where he is, then sits up. I point to the lake. The robots are as tall as the skyscrapers that once graced the San Francisco skyline. Their metallic frames are illuminated by tiny lights scattered across their forms, and they're even more impressive than the dam.

"Those are water filtration pumps, one of the most expensive parts of the Oasis. They were built to ensure the water we drink is safe for consumption. Each one is over half a century old and has four metal appendages protruding from the pit of its stomach, long needles it uses to suck the melted snow water straight out of the lake and into its belly, where it's filtered," my aunt says.

"Couldn't you all just make more? For the Wasteland?" Sam asks. He licks at his lips as if he's thirsty.

Tía Ines shakes her head. "It's not that simple; that technology is long lost to us. The creator of the spigots died on the island and took his knowledge with him."

We arrive at another stop. The pod parks in front of a tall building that has vines all around it.

We enter the building. Then an elevator that takes us up to the twelfth floor. We step out and into a large hall. To the left is a door. To the right is another. To one side of the elevator is a fully stocked vending machine. I haven't seen one of those since I was a kid.

"I'm on the thirteenth floor, if you ever need me. Most days, I work out of my home office, unless there's a lottery." Tía Ines takes out two blue bracelets from her pocket, rectangular pieces of metal with the symbol of the Oasis at the center of each one. "These key fobs are for the two of you. As long as you keep your bracelets on, you won't have to worry about carrying anything else with you. These will identify you, let you into your home, and allow you to purchase whatever you want. Talking about buying things, I've also given you each ten thousand dollars to be able to purchase new clothes and anything else you might need. It's meant to be used, so don't worry about spending it on extravagant things. Next month, you'll get another ten thousand."

"Where does the money come from?" I ask.

"Truthfully? It's all just digital money that gets recycled. The idea was that to maintain order here, people would still need to work and be worthy of receiving their salaries. Things couldn't be free or the populace would lose sight of how important it is for all of us to still cooperate in making the Oasis a paradise for all."

Her answer irks me. Perhaps it's the idea that even in what we see as paradise, people are still controlled by monetary compensation. It unsettles my stomach.

Tía Ines puts Sam's bracelet on first, and he tinkers with it some before he reaches for the door on the right. The door clicks open but he doesn't go inside.

My aunt helps me with my bracelet. "I'm going to leave you both to get acclimated. There will be a welcome party for you tomorrow, so rest up. I'll have dinner delivered to you later, and either I or Willa, if she's feeling up for it, will bring you both breakfast tomorrow morning. Meanwhile, I'll be just upstairs. And if you press zero on your phones, it'll go straight to mine. Remember, I'm here for whatever you both need."

I go to the door across from Sam's.

It clicks open as well, but like him, I can't step inside yet. My heart beats so fast. This all seems too good to be true. Too much, too soon. And I don't understand how just hours ago I was in San Francisco scavenging the Scar.

Tía Ines gives me another hug and whispers, "You're safe now, Juliana. Enjoy your new life. You're allowed to do that. Welcome home, mi chiquita."

They're the words I need to hear.

I examine the fresh carpet, the warm ceiling lights, the vents blowing clean air into the room, until my eyes land on a camera in a corner. "Are we being watched?" I ask my tía.

She comes closer to us. "I'll let you both in on a little

secret: Ninety-five percent of the cameras in the city stopped working last year. The tech is too old, but just the sight of them keeps most folks from doing anything that could get them kicked out."

I can't help but stare for a moment longer. She gives Sam a small squeeze on a shoulder. Finally, tía Ines says her goodbyes and heads to the elevator.

Sam and I stand at our doorways and look at each other as if needing confirmation that all is okay.

Sam takes a deep breath in, exhales shakily, and says, "We have to try the vending machine before we go in, right?"

Excitement runs through me. "Oh, absolutely," I reply and join him where he's already pushing buttons on the machine. Once he's made all of his selections, he holds his wrist up to a small scanner, which beeps and shows him how much he has left of his $10,000 before it releases the purchases into a slot at the bottom.

By the time we're done, we've each got three drinks and more food in crinkly bags than I've had in days cradled in our arms.

"I guess I'll see you at the party," Sam finally says.

I nod, grin, and enter my apartment, shutting the door behind me. Sam is right across the hall and tía Ines right upstairs. It'll be okay.

Inside, everything is bright, and it holds everything I could ever want.

There's a small kitchen against one wall that includes appliances I haven't seen in ages: a stove, a refrigerator, as well as copper pots and pans. I could eat for a week in San

Francisco if I sold those to the Sheriff. I set my drinks and food on the counter. I take a bottle of water, which I quickly uncap. I drink the water as I examine the small living room connected to the kitchen, which has two leather couches, board games piled in a corner, and a view of the lake. I gawk for a while before I move on to the first room to the right, which is a bedroom with the largest bed I've ever seen. The duvet on the bed is a white so bright it almost hurts my eyes.

The second room is an office. Most of it is bare. But beyond the simple wooden desk, there is a bookshelf filled with what must be one hundred books.

In San Francisco, Rico and I lived with a hundred other people. We slept together and struggled among one another. I'm not sure what I'll do by myself. I haven't been alone like this in ages. I haven't been *myself* in just as long. The person I could be if the world hadn't disintegrated into nothing. It's nerve-racking until I realize, in my own apartment, I can do and say whatever I want and no one will judge me for it. Here, I am truly free.

"I'm home!" I scream, walking into my room. When nothing happens, I yell out again. I laugh and twirl and fall back on my bed, and the floor spins for a moment, but in the best way possible.

I fall asleep as I stare at the ceiling, smiling to myself, my water bottle firm in my grasp, and drift hard into a dream. No—a nightmare. The Masterdome is transparent, fragile like a soap bubble. I run its perimeter, unable to leave the Oasis without popping its border. Somehow I can see the Scar from inside. Rico runs in the thick of it as he searches for something.

Me? I scream at him, yell his name as loud as I can, but nothing comes out. My voice is gone, my tongue bound by tiny ropes to the bottom of my mouth. He doesn't see me. The sun appears, and Rico's protective suit begins to melt upon his flesh. Then he looks right at me—but his gaze goes beyond my body.

I wake up terrified when there's a knock on my door. It must be the meal tía Ines mentioned she'd have delivered to me. Still, I feel alone and with an ache and the regret that while I'm surrounded by so many comforts, Rico still fights to survive.

CHAPTER 6
Rico

Jesus stands at the door of Mictlān's bunker, already drunk or high on whatever new street drug is popular. His eyes are bloodshot and spastic, and he's dazed. His steps are sluggish. Despite everything, he seems genuinely happy.

I wish I could say the same, but seeing Jesus brings me back to the night he burned me and the pain he caused. Not just physical pain, but the grief at having the one person you trust most break your heart.

This is not a good or safe place to be, or any place I would have come back to on any other day, under any other circumstances. My throat is dry. My voice scratchy. My eyebrow a painful mess. All I've had to eat today are the noodles. All I've had to drink with everything going on was the allotted cup of water from the lottery. And I've sweated every drop out by now.

Jesus tilts his head at me, squints his eyes, and says, "As soon as I saw you give Juliana your winning buzzer, I knew you'd come, primito."

I can't say I'm surprised he was spying on me.

"Ven conmigo. We have rice, enchiladas, and warm home-made pan the way mi mamá used to make it. And plenty of it all to share tonight. Come inside. I'll get you some ice for that shiner of yours and get you stitched up." He holds out his hand. A year older than me, at nineteen, Jesus has always acted as if he were automatically in charge of me. I take a long breath and stop for a moment. If someone had told me that I'd start my day kissing Juliana and end it eating with my cousin, I'd have told them they were delusional.

Damn the Sheriff.

It's not until I move toward Jesus that I notice someone behind me. When I turn, I find Nadine Chen, my ex. It's a relief. I want to persuade her to be the other person to go in with us, if that isn't already the plan. I need her smarts and the way she's always been able to talk some sense into my cousin when I couldn't.

Her hand is wrapped around the Jian sword she inherited from her father, her most prized possession. When our eyes meet, there's fire there. The same look of betrayal Jesus had when I left the group. But I'm hoping it's possible to mend the relationships I need for the Sheriff's plan to work. I turn back around but remain hesitant as I tell the lingering doubt in my mind that there's no choice but to take Jesus's hand. We walk through the front doors, my cousin's arm now wrapped around my shoulder ever so tightly. Nadine follows behind us, blade at the ready.

Mictlān is the Aztec word for the underworld, and it's like I'm going into the belly of it now. Tía Linda hadn't meant it in that way; her goal had been the opposite for the organization . . . She said the Wasteland was an afterlife. And if there was one thing she would do for me and Jesus, it'd be to get us into paradise. The Oasis. That was her goal, and I thought it'd died with her.

Inside, the underground bunker stretches out to the width and length of several basic bunkers combined. Still, even with the extra space, there are too many bodies in here. More than there ever were when I was a part of Mictlān. Jesus has been busy recruiting. The electronic music is loud, obnoxious, and hard to hear around, making everything more claustrophobic.

My body tenses as Jesus leads me past the main chamber, where other members of the group dance or make out, until we get to a room in the back I remember all too well—the makeshift office that my aunt once led the group from, now my cousin's. It's much different inside. Graffiti covers the walls, showcasing my cousin's talent for art. Vintage and mightily expensive comic books are scattered everywhere, and it's hard to walk through the various knickknacks piled high around the office floor.

There's a desk that Jesus works at, two chairs in front. He sits in one and signals for me to take the other. I do my best not to crush any of his things as I take a seat.

I pretend I'm still comfortable when two more of his people come inside the office before the door closes behind us. How sure am I that my cousin isn't angry enough to hurt me again? Not very. But Nadine approaches, kneels down next to me, a first aid kit in hand. She opens it up, pulls out a small jar filled with clear liquid and a couple of cotton balls that are a little discolored, and cleans my wound.

I hold back a scream when the liquid touches my skin, catching a hint of a smirk on her face. I guess I deserve the pain after I left without saying goodbye. It wasn't like I had a choice, though. Jesus had been clear. If I left, I couldn't ever go near anyone in the organization again, including Nadine.

Still, perhaps I should have asked if she wanted to come with me. I'd been so terrified her answer would have been no.

Fortunately, it worked out. I met Jules.

I take another quick survey of the room. There are five guns, nine switchblades, Nadine's sword, metal knuckles—and those are the weapons I can *see*.

"I assume you spoke to the Sheriff?" Jesus says, then grins at me like this is going to be the best day of our lives. "I sometimes imagined this moment playing out in my mind. But in my dreams, you grovel on your knees and beg me to take you back. And now that you're here, I don't know. Maybe I'm wrong that we need you for our plan to work. Maybe I should have left the past in the past, you with it."

Nadine pauses for a moment, as if Jesus's words hit home too much. I've felt terrible for leaving. But I couldn't stay when I knew that my aunt died because I made a mistake. Despite all my tinkering with tech, all my lessons, all my learning and practice, I froze and tía Linda got shot saving my life.

And so, I say what I think will help. "I'm sorry." Something catches in my throat at how real and true the words are. "But it didn't give you the right to bring me into whatever it is you and the Sheriff have planned."

Nadine pulls out a needle. "Keep still," she warns, and I hadn't realized how much I missed her voice. Before Jules, Nadine was my best friend, and she and Jesus were my family.

Jesus laughs, sits back, and asks, "You think we had a choice either?"

"Didn't you? Or did you make a bad one like always?"

Again, Nadine pauses, string tethered from my eyebrow to where she holds a suture needle in her hand. This time, she doesn't continue but clicks her tongue as if she disagrees with what I've said. I fight through the pain and discomfort, and I imagine what I must look like to them. Can they even take me seriously?

"But since the old man came to me, I've realized he's right. Standing up against the Oasis's leaders is the way forward." Jesus reaches onto his desk, pushes papers aside to get to a tablet underneath the pile. He turns it on and slides it over to me. "What do you see?"

I turn the tablet around, then focus on the cracked screen. "I don't get it."

"I don't get it," he mimics. "The Sheriff gave me proof my mom, your aunt, the rightful leader of Mictlān, is alive and being held in the haven," he says, his face edging on seriousness. "He said it'd be easy enough for her to have an accident if we didn't help him. Or we could have her back, and along with it, when he becomes leader of the Oasis, we can either choose to stay as well, or he'll make me the sheriff of San Francisco."

I'm sincere when I tell him, "And you believe this photograph of her is real?"

He sniffs. "We had it tested."

I stare at him, then at the photograph, which shows a woman whose face is recognizable and whose body is wilted away. *If tía Linda really is alive . . .*

"Cuz, you thought she died. Turns out you left her to rot in a prison. It's your responsibility to help free her. You were her favorite, and I admit I've resented that fact, but if you fix the train, I can get to her, show her how I've kept her dream alive, not you, and make her proud."

Tears well in my eyes, and I bite my upper lip. I wouldn't be alive if it weren't for tía Linda. "Okay," I reply. "But it has to be you, me, *and* Nadine. You keep your word to the Sheriff, I'll break the codes to free your mom from wherever they've been holding her, and Nadine will watch our backs." I turn to meet Nadine's stare. She cuts the string on my eyebrow with scissors, packs the first aid kit back up, and sets it on Jesus's desk. She goes to his side and sits on the armrest of his chair. He glances up at her, and their silent exchange reminds me of ones I had with tía Linda, when I was her right hand. Nadine gives him a slight nod before Jesus turns back to me.

I should be angry at my cousin, but he's also right. Tía Linda forced me to abandon her and take the train back down the mountain after she was shot. And I had. I didn't think she'd survive. I'd been wrong, and it turns out my cousin's resentment might be warranted. I was the one who understood the mechanics of the train the best. I was obsessed with learning everything about the train's engineering and became the one who got the ancient behemoth to run the first time. Maybe it's time to try again.

"Okay," I repeat. "Let's do this."

Jesus grins fully. Even Nadine beams. So many words bottleneck at my throat.

He signals to the men behind me. "Now that the talking is over, let's celebrate!"

An alcohol bottle appears out of nowhere. Jesus pours us both a drink of the moonshine Nadine makes for fun, another thing passed down to her by her father, who used to supply it to those in San Francisco as a way of getting by until Siber-virus killed him. I think about how long it's been since I had anything like this.

Nadine pulls me out of the office and into the noise of the party, and I convince myself that everything is going to work out.

I wake up on an old futon mattress. The reek of mold and sweat invades my nose. Perturbed by the smell, I reach for a hand that I don't find. The previous few hours rush back to me, and I remember why Jules is no longer by my side. My head spins like it was hit with a hammer and broke in half. The blinding light of day shines in through the window and doesn't help. I squint with my good eye. Those half dozen shots of mezcal weren't such a good idea in hindsight. My other eye aches, and I touch my injured eyebrow gingerly, my finger coming away with fresh blood. Most of the stitches seem to be holding at least.

I'm not sure drinking moonshine is all I did either. I'd forgotten how heavy Mictlān celebrations go. Jesus wanted to toast endlessly—a tribute to my return. And that was just the beginning. Either way, blacking out wasn't part of my plan. The memory is a haze filled with nameless faces, drinking games, and someone laughing uncontrollably.

Perhaps that someone—Jesus, most likely—left a glass full of water on the floor. But I ignore my thirst and the throbbing that sends a shooting pain through my brain with every step. As I move to leave the room, the image of my back reflected against the half-cracked mirror on the closet door stops me. Ripples of scarred skin spread across my shoulders.

It has been years since I've seen it. Jesus did this to me. He could have simply let me go. But I owed Mictlān the rest of my life, my existence, for being my family. And Jesus needed to earn or keep the rest of the group's respect as he ascended to his leadership role. Scarring me was the only way I was getting out of Mictlān alive. We both made a choice that night. And I decided to come back. Does that make me a fool? Or so deeply in love I would do the wildest things to keep that love alive? And now there's tía Linda. Double the reason to join the plan.

I grab my pants along with the new black shirt Jesus gave me and hastily get dressed.

Outside, Nadine stands across the hall at another door, arms crossed at her chest.

"I thought you were going to sleep all day," she says.

"I considered it," I reply, except that wasn't my plan at all.

When we were younger, I thought I loved Nadine. But now, if I really sit with it, it wasn't the kind of love I wanted. The kind of love that isn't selfish. I expected too much from Nadine. Now, I think of what I can give to Jules. Nonetheless, Nadine and I have history I'm not ready to face yet, even though I need her.

I head toward the bunker's exit down the hall when I notice Jesus eating what appears to be cereal out of a large bowl in a side room.

"Rico, our resident Bella Durmiente! Get in here." I want to ignore him and the Sleeping Beauty comment and keep on walking. But, despite everything, I owe him for the food—and I don't mean cold, barely edible noodles. I ate better last night than I have in the past two months. The rice had chunks of real meat in it. I don't want to know what kind, but real meat that tasted of smoke and protein. The pan—delicious, *homemade* sweet bread. Jesus even gave me ice last night to bring down the swelling around my eye. I can see a thin sliver of light out of it today.

"Hey, güey, ¿que pasa? What's going on?" I tread to him and take the free seat across the table from him. Nadine sits to his right, one leg bent under the other, and Jesus passes her the bowl. She doesn't say anything as she eats, and there's a gnawing in my belly that wants nothing more than to taste the cereal, too.

He shrugs. "The plan, Cuz, is what's up. Tell me you're ready to fix the train."

"I need to go see it. See if that's even possible. It could be we're not going anywhere, no matter how much the Sheriff wills it."

"I can help," Nadine says, mouth full.

"I'll manage for a while. Finish breakfast and meet me there," I reply since I want to stop home before I head to the train depot.

Jesus raises his eyebrows. "Nadine will go with you now, and I'll be there later to check on the progress. Over the past few weeks, I've wrangled some supplies, which should be at the train station. Everyone knows they belong to us, so I assume they'll still be there."

I nod, then get up as I say, "Well, better get to it."

Nadine is like a shadow. She stands almost immediately after I do. She passes Jesus back the half-eaten bowl. I let her follow me as I get dressed in my protective suit, which I pull from a bin by the front door. Once she has on her suit as well, we head out into . . . the after-lottery chaos.

"What the actual hells," Nadine says as we walk down the sidewalk. Her voice is muffled through her own helmet, but I can still hear her disbelief.

There is a mess of glass and all sorts of debris on the street. We have to step over bodies to move forward. There are fires that nobody'll be able to put out.

We pass a scavenger, who searches the bodies lying dead, left for the birds, his suit barely holding on.

The scavenger gibbers on erratically, gone in his own sort of way. "Line after line after line, the days repeat, time after time after time," he says, his voice loud and callous. "You went to work. Came back home. Went to work and came back. Labor. Home. Repeat. The Old Epoch. A cycle. A dawdling death. Now, the New Epoch is plaguing us. Slower death. Work. Steal. Starve—no. That's wrong. Wrong. What's beyond starvation? The black hole. Thirst. Home. Repeat. And when you think the sinking can't get any lower, you go down, down, down, straight to hell!"

Unnerved, I walk faster, until I'm jogging. This kind of madness is why I needed to get Jules out of here. More and more people seem this far gone lately. If Nadine minds the increase in speed, she doesn't say anything but keeps my pace as we dodge everyone and everything.

I don't notice when she takes it out, but ultimately, I think her Jian sword is what keeps the people away from us, and I'm grateful for it, and her, after all.

"I need to make a stop on the way to the station," I tell Nadine, who grunts an acknowledgment, her eyes and ears on high alert.

A few minutes later, we're outside the bunker where Jules and I have slept since we started working for Sheriff Ramos. Located four blocks away from Union Square, it's the farthest from the Scar we've ever resided. The Sheriff got us into a safe bunker.

I give a nod to the bunker's security man, Gustav—a tall, burly guy who stands guard, machete in hand. At first glance, you can't tell the Norwegian man is all heart to the people who live here.

He notices someone's missing. "Is she—" he starts. His wild blue eyes search behind me and find Nadine instead.

I shake my head and smile as I tell him, "She won the lottery."

He freezes—stunned.

"Never thought giving up the lotteries for a place in this bunker would mean I'd miss seeing Juliana win."

Most people haven't met anyone who has gotten into the upper isolation city. He must have thought she died somewhere out in the Scar during the day. This building, like the Oasis, replaces its residents when they pass away. But here, it happens every day. People die of starvation, of illnesses that *can* be cured but are too expensive to fix and horrible ones that can't be, regardless of whether they're the richest person in the lower cities. Or people are killed for mouthing off to the wrong person.

Nadine stays with Gustav, exchanging stories surely, while I take off my protective suit's helmet and trail the bunker's halls. Down here, I've felt like I was nocturnal. Endless dark tunnels have been dug deep into the earth underneath an old warehouse that once held pointless and expensive kitchen appliances that helped people make pasta and silly knickknacks that helped them do things like squeeze lemons—like they couldn't use their fingers for that.

Section 4 of the bunker is a large area portioned into rooms by thick burlap and overcrowded with people and their families who work for the Sheriff—the Chernyukins, a family of four who mostly keep to themselves but share their food with anyone hungry; old man Mohammed, whose prayer mat is worn to fraying but still used every day; the Alvarez twins, who always bicker yet sleep with their backs turned to one another; and so many others I know so well and yet don't have the heart to say goodbye to.

A group of kids runs up to me. Despite our circumstances, they're all done up in clean clothes and perfect hairstyles. "Rico! What'd you bring us?" they ask. It's typical that Jules and I find things while we scavenge that are worthless to the Sheriff but endless fun for the kids in our bunker.

I lick my lips, check my pockets.

Before I can give them the bad news that I've got nothing, Nadine appears behind me, her helmet off now, too. She pulls out a handful of individually wrapped candies she must have made. The kids crowd her, make the candy disappear in seconds, and run off.

"I'll be right back," I say, and Nadine leans against the bunker wall to wait for me.

I wipe tears away from my face as I make it to the corner Jules and I share—*shared*. Jules's belongings are still here. They're mine now, I guess. There aren't many things, but there is a photo. It's of Jules and her family, and it's the object she cherished most. In it, Juliana, her three siblings, and their parents are at the beach. She sits on her mom's lap and leans happily against her parent, who holds Jules snugly across the shoulders.

I painted a Frida Kahlo–style landscape on the back of it: a sun and moon, with a tiny blue parrot embedded where they intersect in the middle—all hovering above a green field. We'd run across some of Frida's still-intact paintings once at some rich person's abandoned home in the Scar. Jules loved them. But two weeks later, they were gone, stolen or destroyed—who knows. So I did my best to replicate Frida's work. Ever since, Jules has taken turns displaying each side of the picture. She flips the photograph over every other day. She left the painted side up yesterday morning.

There is also the stuffed animal she's had since she was four, a birthday gift she got from her brothers. She wouldn't willingly part with this mangy old thing, even during the apocalypse. There's a gold bracelet we found on our first day at work in the Scar that I haven't let Jules sell because she loves it so much. And a succulent she's kept alive through the two-year-long drought. The thing seems to survive off tears and blood, instead of actual water. And her hand sewer, which has kept our suits intact. She should have brought the items with her to the lottery, but Jules never believed we would win.

Thoughts of Jules suck the air straight out of me, out of the bunker, air that was already thin to begin with. I'm stifled. The heaviness of her ghost is like a rock on my chest. I stuff what little belongings I have into my old leather pack, adding Jules's things in before I head back toward the exit.

"Rico?" Gustav stops me. He appears to realize I only came back to pack. "Be careful out there. I'll hold your spot."

I grin at him the best I can. I shake my head, replying in earnest, "I don't think you'll have to."

Nadine doesn't say a single word as she joins me but gives Gustav a slight nod before she puts on the helmet of her protective suit. I do the same, take a deep breath, then keep walking. Behind us, Gustav calls out, "Pay attention to that eyebrow! Don't let it get infected!"

I raise my hand to let him know I've heard him, determined to not forget the people I'm leaving behind.

At the underground train station, the supplies are piled high and in the kind of disarray that makes me want to pull my hair out. Deputies mill about, their machine guns and batons on full display to keep everyone away from the train and the trove of goods around and within. I don't let their presence slow me down. I get to work on the train that once ran from California to Chicago but now hasn't moved since I and other Mictlān survivors used it to get back down from the Oasis. I search through the parts, taking a mental inventory.

I assess the wheels and mechanics and factor in the sheer luck that the mechanisms aren't rusted stiff. I think we can fix it. All we need to do is get some of the thick rust off the wheels and replace some wires. And maybe we're looking at a twelve-hour turnaround time.

Back when I helped tía Linda, going underneath this behemoth had been one of my jobs—what made me fall in love with the train in the first place. I was the skinny kid she needed to reach the tight spots. Now, Nadine is beneath the metal snake. She removes the rust on the wheels as I give her instructions. It's going to be an endless night.

Eleven hours later, I jump off the train platform to the ground, having finished the last of the repairs on the engine. I walk over to Jesus, who has finally joined us, along with a few others, and ask, "Should we give the beast a whirl?"

"It's now or never," he replies, placing an arm around my neck.

"Nadine—we're going to turn her on. Come on out!" I shout.

She squeezes from under the train and stands next to me. Now, with her suit off during the coldest part of the evening, she has grime all over her hands and cheeks but smiles nonetheless. I stare intently at the train, which was named the Zephyr during the Old Epoch.

After a few minutes, the engine hums. "Beautiful sound. Beautiful roar. Our beast is alive!" Jesus calls out, laughing.

Nadine says, "You did it."

"Don't waste gas!" one of the deputies shouts, and I turn off the Zephyr. I double-check no one has stolen my protective suit from where I left it just on the edge of the platform, before refocusing on the task at hand.

Jesus, Nadine, and I stare at the train. I side-glance at them. I missed being with my cousin. And with Nadine. It's an odd sensation, similar to what I've felt with Jules, like being with someone you love makes not really having a home or parents or security hurt less. Here, with my cousin's arm wrapped around my shoulder, there's a familiarity that transcends all that we've lost.

But then I remember that Jesus let the Sheriff blackmail me with Jules's safety. And tía Linda might be alive but trapped because of me. We can celebrate when they're both okay.

"We've still got a lot of work to do," I say to Jesus as I shrug his arm off my shoulder.

"Don't ruin the moment, Cuz," Jesus says. "For now, let's enjoy this. Mami would be proud, you know? We're going to save her."

There's a knot in my throat. After my own parents died, tía Linda took me in. Gave me a home. Food. Clothes. Clean water. Maybe I should have stayed and helped to uphold my aunt's legacy. But if I had, I wouldn't have met Jules. And anyway, there's no going back. Instead, I plan to give tía Linda the victory she should have had three years ago.

PART II

THE ZEPHYR & THE OASIS

CHAPTER 7

Jules

The bathtub that Willa has filled for me to relax in before the welcome party is full of crystal-clear water. All I can do is stare at it. Willa added in a concoction of bath salts and scents, which have melted in the liquid and filled the bathroom with the smells of honeysuckle and lavender. Bubbles skim the rim of the tub. I hesitate to get in, staring at my buzzer on the sink. If I'd kept it in the Wasteland, I would have been tracked down and killed. Here, it's a memento I get to keep. I never thought showering and bathing two days in a row would ever be an option for me. What would Rico think of using so much water in one day? What would the thirsty people back home think of my waste?

I clutch a sky-blue towel to dry myself with. It's way too soft between my fingers and way too clean. It smells like nothing—as if no one's ever used it before. I set it down where I'll be able to reach it when I get in.

There's a small tray on my counter, filled with what

appears to be black licorice. My eldest brother used to love candy. None of us could ever figure out where he got it from. It gave him cavities, but there weren't any affordable dentists left by that time. He used to cry himself to sleep—his mouth pained him so much. I had a cavity last year that hurt so bad Rico had to help me rip the molar straight out my mouth. And every single minute that my jaw throbbed, I thought of my brother. I wish I could forget those memories. I throw the candy in the trash bin next to the toilet and instead pick up the toothbrush. I unwrap it from its plastic sleeve and apply mint-flavored toothpaste on it, brush my teeth until they're all smooth against my tongue.

I move away from the tub, toward the closed door, which has a full-length mirror on its back side. I want to ignore my body, avoid my image until I become fully human again, but I need to sear it into memory.

I study myself. I will never be this thin again. In a few months, I won't be able to count the number of ribs I have in my reflection. The ruby color of blood will diminish from my lips as the cracks heal. My hair will soften. The bruises on my body from being assaulted on lottery day will fade. The unbelievable amount of dirt stuck underneath my fingernails and on my face and the soles of my feet will be washed away. My scars—old and new—will be my reminder of my old life, each one there to show me I am more than a single moment. I am made of many instances that have turned me into the person I am today: a survivor.

I hate myself for getting the chance to do this while so

many others won't, but I step into the tub and wash myself of every bit of dirt that's still caked on my flesh even after my shower yesterday. I scrub with the sponge I found in one of the drawers of the vanity.

Willa still isn't satisfied with my appearance once I'm out and dry and dressed in the clean metallic gray tank top and purple shiny leggings I found in my closet—a closet with new clothing—both of which are a couple sizes too big.

"How long has it been since you cut your hair? It's a tangled mess," she says as she attempts to run her fingers through my waves, face scrunched into something like disgust. I stare at her bandaged leg, so she adds, "Don't worry about me. It doesn't hurt. Only itches now."

"I don't remember," I admit, answering her question about my hair. She takes me back to the bathroom, then grabs a bucket. She fills it with warm water, careful not to be wasteful of it. As if this whole experience hasn't been wasteful.

"Sit," she orders. I obey and rest at the rim of the bathtub. It seems to be in my cousin's nature to boss people around, but I don't mind. My older brothers used to do it all the time. There's another ache in my chest at the thought of them.

"Lean your head back," she says. I comply. She uncaps a bottle and massages a good amount of shampoo onto my scalp and hair as best as possible.

"You said you were born here?" I ask as she works.

"Uh-huh."

"Isn't it rare with population control?"

She dumps some of the water from the bucket onto my

head as I tilt it back, then grabs conditioner. She leaves the stuff in until she can easily run her fingers through the knots.

"One in a thousand chances of me being alive, really. But my mom was actually vice president before your tía Ines. My parents were big shots, and they were able to get approval to have me."

"What's it like being born here?" I wonder aloud, even when I don't know if I really want to know.

Willa sighs. "Do you want me to tell you the truth?"

I chuckle. "Of course."

She pauses and I turn to her, water dripping onto my shoulders. Her eyes focus on her hands as she says, "You would think that I would believe I'm the luckiest person, but there's this guilt that I can't ever get rid of that's boiling in my chest. That's why I signed up to become a representative. My birth mom hated my job. Dad even more. We had so many fights about it before they died, but I had to get out of this cage and do something worthwhile. And there's almost nothing in this world more important to me than helping people get to the Oasis. And if I hadn't gone down this path, I wouldn't have met Rodrick."

"Strange that even in this city you can lose both of your parents," I tell her, saddened by the fact that Willa has seen too much death already as well.

"We're all human in the end," she says, the glow in her eyes diminished.

"I think you and Rodrick are superhuman," I tell her and mean it. "You are two of the bravest people I know."

She blinks hard and fast and, finally, flicks a tear off her cheek.

"And now we get to be cousins," she says. "Let's have some fun tonight, okay?"

"Okay," I reply and lean my head back once more.

Willa doesn't stop once my tresses are untangled. She blow-dries my hair and cuts inches off with extra-sharp shears, until my waves are back to their natural radiance.

"I look like my mom," I say, unable to find the person who was just reflected in the mirror. Already, the creature I was before the bath has disappeared.

"You look like you belong here," she says softly. I try not to let her words rub me the wrong way, even though they do. "And like you're ready for a party!"

She puts things away and drains the murky tub while I continue to stare at my face. It's hard to turn away as my mind catches up to everything that's happened. With all the dirt wiped away from my body, I can see a bit clearer. It's time to save Rico. And that starts with making sure I can contact him.

I move to sit on my bed as I say, "Willa, can I ask you something?"

"Yeah, of course." She walks over to my bed.

I open the nightstand next to my bed and pull out the eye-sized radio I took off my suit.

Willa takes a step back when I show her, but she seems to shake it off.

"It's a radio," I tell her. "Not dangerous. I was using it to talk to my boyfriend. He was actually the one who won the lottery, and gave me his win. But I can't talk to him anymore without a signal booster. Maybe you can help me figure out where I could find one."

She bites at her bottom lip before she reaches out her hand. "Okay, wait, you have a boyfriend? I'll need all the details. But first, let me see this thing?"

I hand it over when she sits beside me. She examines it some more before she says, "I don't have much access to tech, but I know someone who does."

My body relaxes at the fact that she is actually going to help me. "Who?" I ask.

Her expression grows smug, and she gives a little shimmy with her shoulders. "Rodrick. And the party will help us get exactly what we're searching for. Now, let's get ready and we can talk boys."

Two hours later, I pull at the iridescent blue-green sequins on my party dress, fighting not to smudge the eye shadow Willa applied. Willa and Rodrick have introduced me to what must be a thousand other people. Everyone has been nice but they all have a million questions. And since I haven't seen Sam yet, I've had to try to answer them on my own.

Where did I come from? What did I do to survive? What's it like out there now? Has Sibervirus spread again? Who did I know in San Francisco? Do I know their friend so-and-so, who they'd heard was still alive somewhere out in the Wasteland? What do I like to do for fun?

Fun, like it's a common word in my vocabulary.

It's like being back in the horde at Union Square or fighting the cannibals in No Man's Land. Okay, maybe that's an exaggeration. It is nice to be welcomed, I guess, even if it all feels abnormal. Everyone I've met appears to be happy. I get hugs instead of punches. Handshakes instead of rocks thrown at me. Loss was all too common in San Francisco. You never got close to more people than you needed to. You didn't exchange more than a nod with a stranger. The risk for exploitation was too high.

My thoughts drift to Rico in between greetings. It's around the time we'd head to the Scar—that lifeless place. Rico and I inhaled too many fumes there. We'd come back half high, half gone, and we always reeked of burnt tires despite our protective suits. If I'm lucky, I'll never smell of ash and death again. It's late enough now that the sun has gone down, deep behind the mountaintops. The valley underneath the Masterdome is cool.

I wish I knew whether he was all right, but there hasn't been a moment to ask Rodrick about the radio, not with so many people around.

The welcome celebration is being held in a meadow that's way too perfect to not have been man-made, away from any buildings, in a more remote area on the North Shore. Although it's only five in the afternoon, the sun has already mostly set. I guess I'll need to get used to early nights in the mountain valley. There is a massive white tent filled with a wide array of food, more than I've ever seen in one place, on long rectangular tables.

A woman named Krista or Crystal who has been placed in charge of watching over me for refeeding syndrome effects like seizures—caused by eating too much too soon and too fast—guides me through the selections. Using her long acrylic nails painted opalescent orange, she signals to me items I "must try a bite of," like the salmon, asparagus, corn, and nopales—cactus—cut into squares like my mom used to make them. She helps me put the right amount on my plate and guides me away from what might cause me more harm than good. Despite the delicious food, I can't take being surrounded by people who act like all of this is normal. I set my plate at the edge of one of the tables and walk away, leaving behind Krista/Crystal, in her own shimmering dress.

There're a few empty tables at the far-left end of the party. I take a seat with my back to the boisterous crowd, with a hope no one will bother me here, and take the radio in my hand, my lifeline to Rico.

There is more food to eat within that stupid tent than the hundreds here can possibly finish. It's enough to feed two thousand easily. I hate myself for being one of the people who get to enjoy the spread. There are kids outside the Oasis. The cries of whom I can still hear echoing off the walls of our bunker if I close my eyes. Shrill and hungry. They need this more than me. Yesterday, I'd been ecstatic to eat salty noodles. Here, they have so much food I've never even heard of.

I remember my reflection from earlier and put my hands to my ribs. I count them with a tap of my fingertips.

Then something pops in the air. A spectrum of light fills the sky underneath the gold of the Masterdome.

I search for the word to describe what I see and land on it: *fireworks.*

All kinds of fireworks explode and transform into the most magnificent shapes like dragons and whales, things of fairy tales, before dissolving.

Willa waves her hand in front of me and brings me back to the moment. *Of course* she and Rodrick found me. I didn't hear them approach, distracted by how much I wish things were different.

Willa looks gorgeous in a gold-sequined short dress. Her face gleams gold in glittery makeup. Rodrick's ever so handsome in a button-up shirt and metallic vest, sleek pants tucked into shiny chrome combat boots.

"You okay?" Rodrick glances from my fidgety hands, which I hold my radio in, to my tense face, and then up at the sky as the next firework explodes.

With a twinkling gaze, he watches white and yellow sparks turn into a bird with long wings and a sharp beak—a phoenix.

"Of course," I say, and force myself to unclench the muscles in my body. I put the radio in my purse. "A bit much to take in, is all."

"Yes, I suppose it is." He skims the party, twisting at the torso. His gaze lands on the empty space in front of me on the table. "Skipped dinner?"

I nod, glare toward the tent, where I left my plate, feeling a tinge of regret.

"I know it's tough to eat while so many people outside starve. But not having to worry about going hungry lets us concentrate on the larger picture, lets us focus on making good things happen."

How can he say any of that and think I'll understand where he's coming from? I know he isn't a terrible person. He saved my life, at the risk of his own, more than once. But he seems to be forgetting that good things only happen within the Oasis.

Rodrick turns to Willa, his eyes beckoning her to add something that might make me feel better. Willa puts her hands on her hips and says, "Being here is a gift, and while we have food and water and shelter and a community, we also carry a tremendous responsibility. To our species. To help humanity *carry on*. We're the lucky ones. And I promise, there're thousands of people out there who would gladly take your place. Should I go find one of them to trade with you?"

My cheeks flush hot with embarrassment. "Well, no. I—I only need time to get used to all of this." I need to know there's a plan to help those who don't have hope, the people of the Wasteland; to help Rico. I need to figure out what part I can play in said plan. "Yesterday, I wasn't sure this place even existed. Forgive me if I'm not quick to stuff my face." I turn to the tent. I hate it and the wealth it represents.

Papá used to tell me that in the Old Epoch, affluence was measured in paper money and gold and how big your house was and how prosperous your neighborhood was and how educated *you* were. By the vacations you took and how far you had traveled and how well you knew wines and cheeses. Now, in the New Epoch, wealth and power are measured by how much food you have to waste. By having food to eat and fresh water to drink and being able to enjoy them while you bask in instead of fry under sunlight.

"You can be whomever you choose to be. You can take how little you want to take. You can give back however much you desire. You're free in here, Jules. From everything that chained you down before winning the lottery. You are free to make your own choices, but you *must* think about your longevity. We *must* do our part to help humanity live on, and if you're not willing to help . . ." She flails her arms, exasperated.

I nod, unable to meet her eyes. I get it. I do. All I've ever wanted was for Rico and me to live. And I'm ashamed of my inability to adapt to this ideal situation, still trapped in my old world, ridden with guilt for having come this far already, especially when Rico's supposed to be here, not me.

Willa pulls me from my seat. "C'mon, come sit with us."

They drag me six tables from where I was. There, we join Sam, who stares blankly at the people chatting away in front of him. Maybe he thinks this is all a dream. It wouldn't surprise me. There have been moments when I believed the same thing. Willa and Rodrick take the two seats to his right. I take the one across from them.

It's a comfort to see someone from the Wasteland, like I haven't yet lost home. He's got food on his plate. A giant pile of it. Too much of it. He'll be sick if he eats it all. Where's Krista or Crystal to help him?

Not like it matters. He hasn't touched any of it, so maybe he knows.

Sam's been cleaned up some more and wears clothes that fit him—a shimmering green shirt that matches my dress—and eye makeup that I assume Willa had a hand in, but his wavy blond hair still reaches down to his shoulders in a disheveled mess. I exhale loudly and his eyes land on me. He has a crazy amount of stubble on his chin and upper lip. I'm surprised he wasn't asked to shave. All the guys I've met in this city are clean-shaven. Or maybe he simply refused to conform.

"How are you feeling about the haven so far?" Rodrick asks him.

Sam glares at his plate full of food. "Getting used to it, I guess." I sympathize fully.

"You will," Willa says. "It's shocking for everyone born outside to enter the haven. It's a normal part of the process. Take the days one at a time and try to exist in the *now*. We'll all be here for you—for both of you."

The four of us sit and people-watch for a long while. Rico's face makes its way inside my mind again and I hold on to it. First, I recall the color of his hair, black and glossy. His toothy smile.

As I'm imagining Rico's neck, a pure melody nuzzles its way into my head, fighting for, and finally winning, my full attention. And I try to do what Willa said. Take in the wondrous present. I turn toward the sound, to a small group seated in a semicircle. It's *live* music. One of them strums an acoustic guitar. Another, a large man with a topknot, plays a violin. The third has a stand-up bass that's almost as big as she is small. The fourth uses what looks like a banjo, and his fingers move from muscle memory.

I've seen all these instruments before, but I've never heard anyone play them this well.

The music is sweet, lulling. Magical.

But it's not just the music. I stare as a stream of—I don't even know what to call it—aura, perhaps, escapes each instrument as they play, each a different color. The colors mix into the sky in a giant swirl up to the Masterdome. How the effect works, I'm not sure, but it's another mesmerizing display of the advanced tech here.

"This is nice," I say out loud, to my surprise. In my periphery, Sam nods.

Has Sam left someone he loves behind, too? Is being in the Oasis bittersweet for him as well?

Suddenly, Sam reaches out and takes my hand, like he did when we needed to get to the train station, as if the anxiety of being so alone is too much. Or maybe he's noticed my own discomfort. The stray tears that fall down my cheeks occasionally. He squeezes my fingers. I don't fight it. Whether it's for my sake or his, I'm glad to have a new friend.

I turn to ask Rodrick a question, but he and Willa are no longer next to us. Without being too obvious, I pull my hand away from Sam's to scratch an itch on my arm. I don't want Sam. Or anybody who isn't Rico. And I never will. I don't offer my hand back, and Sam doesn't seem to mind; the moment between us drifts away with the soft breeze of the evening.

"Did you think you'd be here yesterday?" He turns my way, taking in all of me. The way his eyes latch onto mine and don't let go makes me uncomfortable. People usually avoid eye contact in San Francisco, as if by doing so, they are able to hide the miserable things they've done to survive.

Sam's eyes reflect my own hurt.

"God no," I reply. I pause for a moment to clear my throat. "I thought it was rigged or a lie. I'm not even the one who's supposed to be here. My boyfriend, Rico, is. He gave me his spot."

He nods. "It's like a heat-induced mirage. Have you ever seen one of those? I keep on thinking I've passed away and ended up in heaven. And I don't even believe in heaven. But it makes more sense to me than accepting that I won the lottery. I wasn't going to go to the lotteries anymore. But I was so hungry, I couldn't stay away. I mean, look at it all." He sweeps his hand over the horizon of the valley—which is magical right now. Fireflies float in the still air, and the horizon is a mix of pink and blue light brought on by the aura of the instruments. "This can't be real. It's a painting, and if I reach out, the colors will smudge."

But they won't. "It's real," I respond with certainty. If we were in heaven, I'd be reunited with my family. "Heaven wouldn't hurt."

Sam grunts in acknowledgment and tilts his head sideways as if asking me to go on.

The musicians laugh, they're having *fun,* and it seems like I'm on a different planet or in a parallel universe. The lives of everyone outside, in the Wasteland's lower isolation cities, and of the group within the Oasis are vastly different in the cruelest way.

Our lives are separated by a dome.

Knowing just how poorly people in the lower isolation cities are living compared to those in the Oasis fuels the need I have to find a way to help the people outside. But how?

At my side, Sam says, "I wish I could share this moment with my little sister, Caitlin. She died last year. She—she was twelve. I'd taken care of her all on my own for five years, since my dad died. But then . . ." His voice cracks as if he's about to cry.

The realization throws me into a panic. There is no one else seated at our table. Maybe if there were, they would know how to console him. I've never been good at comforting people when they're sad. But most people seem to be making a line inside the food tent—again. Or are visiting other groups to mingle with. Sam's sadness turns furious. In his ferocity, he knocks a fist against his knee so hard I'm sure it'll leave a bruise. "If I'd been able to keep her alive for another year, she'd be here instead of me. But Sacramento collapsed so quickly during the last wave of Sibervirus."

And there it is. What has made this so difficult for him. I swallow hard, scared of coming up short in my response. Sam is in a ton of agony. I've been in his place. I lost three brothers. I lost my dad. I lost my mami, who I loved dearly. These are facts I've never known how to deal with myself. Except to forget them, push them out of my mind so it's as if they're someone else's memories.

Grief is impossible to get rid of; you just live with it. But I can't tell him this.

"Maybe you're here for a reason," I say instead. "Maybe you had someone looking out for you—up there. Maybe you have a larger role to play."

I flick my chin up to the sky.

It's always been hard for me to believe in God, when so many ungodly things have happened in the Wasteland. I've lived through so many days I thought would be *my last days*. But it is also hard for me *not* to believe in something greater when I experience moments in my life like this one. Moments when I can just be a girl enjoying a night out, when eating is as easy as walking over to a tent and picking out what I want from a table without working a single hour in the Scar for it.

"She would have loved it here," Sam says. He turns away from me toward the music. "She would have also told me the hard truth: There is no one looking out for us."

I place my arm on his forearm. "Only the strong make it in the Wasteland. Only the strong flourish here. We've got to be our strongest selves, now more than ever. I might not be your sister, but why don't we make a promise to look out for each other?"

After a moment, he holds up his pinky to me. I lock my pinky with his, like I did with my brothers so many times before, and we continue to watch the fireworks and music until Rodrick and Willa return a few minutes later. They each carry a plate of food. Rodrick sets a plate in front of me. They retake their seats and share the plate Willa puts down.

I grab a bright cooked carrot and take a small bite out of it. It's sweet, hard against my teeth. When I'm halfway through chowing it down, Sam starts to eat from his own mountain of a plate. We eat one vegetable after another, until the sustenance fills our shrunken bellies. After Rodrick and Willa are content with how much we've consumed, the pair takes us on a second round of introductions.

And just as I'm about to end the day exhausted, Willa holds my hand.

"Let's go," she says and leads us away from the party.

"Where are we going?" I ask.

She grins brightly. "To get you what you need for your radio, of course."

CHAPTER 8

Jules

Rodrick uses a small and circular metal device, which he says is powered by magnets, to remove the key fobs from our wrists. We leave them attached to a branch of a giant potted tree, then Rodrick leads us to a parking lot filled with what must be a hundred pearlescent pods that look like insect eggs neatly lined up. "Let us show you the real Oasis," he says as he spins Willa around. Her leg seems even better than earlier, and I'm sure she'll be out of the bandages sooner than expected. My ankle has already mended. What would it have meant for my family, to be able to heal almost instantly, instead of having died so painfully?

I try to not be bitter or angry, but it's hard when my belly recoils, my hands clench into fists, and my teeth grind at the thought.

The four of us get into the vehicle before anyone, aka tía Ines, tries to stop us.

"Where are we going to find the radio part I need?" I ask as the pod moves, ready to talk to Rico.

"We're close to my pop's office."

"Won't you get in trouble?" I ask.

Rodrick shrugs from the front seat. "We might be doing something that's slightly against the rules, but if we can make it back to the party in time, we won't have to worry about it," he replies. The moment reminds me of when we drove through No Man's Land, and I can't help but peer out the window every so often. I expect to see a car come out of nowhere to ram us. Instead, there are other pods driving at a nominal speed.

Our pod travels up and down the streets. Neon shop signs of all colors advertise their wares, and stoplights ignite the world in color. So different from the darkness of the Scar. After we round past the giant machines in the lake, we park behind another pod. We walk a few blocks down to a plaza that's lined with trees and has a large fountain at its center. It's all too clean compared with Union Square. I stare at the fountain made up of golden statues of naked babies with wings that Mami would say were angels but are strange to me. Do they use fresh water to run the fountain? There is so much going on in the city. I thought it would be serene, but all the colors and people and music and noise are overstimulating. The pitter-patter of the water is peaceful, at least.

There are people outside a corner café. Several tables are filled with people eating and drinking, dressed in elaborate outfits for a night out as we are for the party. I stare at them, and they stare back, whispering among themselves and fluttering their two-inch-long eyelashes our way.

Even dressed in their style, I don't fit in. I glance up at the

Masterdome, and for just a moment, I see a spark, a make-shift star.

"They know you're new," Willa says. She comes to my side and interlaces our arms. "Don't pay them any mind. In a matter of days or weeks, you'll blend in, and soon enough, there will be others who are newer. Maybe even your boyfriend."

I nod, unable to respond, my throat too thick with emotion when Rico is probably right that his involvement with Mictlān means he'll never be allowed in the Oasis. They did try to take over the haven.

"We'll explore more later on," Willa promises. "Take you to the movies, the outdoor shopping area, the swimming holes, so you can spend some of that currency my mom gave you. We're going to show you what makes this place so special."

Beyond the plaza, Rodrick signals us to the back side of a building. There's a metal staircase that leads up.

"Let's go," Willa says.

I anxiously go up the fire escape as my boots clank against the metal. When we reach the door, Rodrick glances around us to see if anyone is watching. Since no one's around, he puts a key fob against a small rectangular box on the side of the door that shines green. The lock clicks, and the door hisses open.

"Overheard my pop say something about the computer system being broken right now, so they won't know it was me," Rodrick says with confidence.

The lights overhead turn on as we enter, so bright I need to squint at first. Inside, the space is well kept and filled with technology.

"It's an office," Willa explains.

"Like where people work on computers?" Sam asks, walking over to where a line of them rest.

"Exactly!" Willa responds.

"This is my pop's office," Rodrick says as we reach another door. "When I got into the Oasis, I was too young to live by myself, so they put me with my pop. I had great parents in the Wasteland, so I was terrified. But Pop has been incredible. This is where he works. He's an engineer for the haven, does a lot of the city planning, and keeps the sewers and things like that running. I was here a ton when I was little, still know all the quirks of the place. This is his tinker room."

"Do you know if your parents are still alive?" Sam asks.

"No," Rodrick replies. His downturned gaze betrays his carefree tone. "But most of us don't."

We tiptoe into the room, so when I laugh, it garners me odd looks from the rest of the group, but I can't help it. This room is a mess. And by *a mess*, I mean there is more tech than I have ever seen in my life laid out everywhere—on the desk, on the floor, on the shelves that line the walls. Items hang from the ceiling or are piled high in all corners of the room. There are so many knickknacks and parts, Rico would adore being in here.

"We're looking for another radio that might already have a signal booster we can snatch," Willa says.

Rodrick searches through the parts, and I look at a random item and consider its worth in lottery tickets.

"Why is this stuff sitting here?" I ask out loud. All this tech, I could trade it in to the Sheriff's Station easily.

Willa and Rodrick stop and stare at me.

"What do you mean? They're old things," Willa says. She smirks at me like I'm the strangest thing to ever come out of the Wasteland.

But three of these *old things* would equal at least thirty extra lottery tickets for someone. Doing a once-over of the room, I find battery packs, cameras, utility knives, what looks like a giant bottle of soap, solar sunglasses, and more—objects beyond rare in the Wasteland, gathering dust.

"We don't have any of these things anymore in San Francisco. Couldn't you share some of it?"

Willa shrugs. "I guess? We don't make those types of decisions, though. We're representatives. We go out into the Wasteland and bring people like you home. It's worked out. If you push too many buttons, they don't let you out of the Masterdome, so we try not to. And taking any of this and giving it to people beyond our border would be breaking the rules in a major way, no matter how much we want to help."

"Sounds like the rules need to change," Sam mumbles under his breath.

"Yeah, maybe," Willa replies, tone sincere. "But nobody tries to do that here. We're all too afraid of being kicked out."

It's not the reply I was hoping for, so I grab the nearest thing on a shelf, a bulk of zippers I can use, and put them into my pocket, rules be damned.

"Here!" Rodrick says and hands me a computer chip. "There should be a slot on your radio where you can insert this, and voilà! You'll be talking to your boy in no time."

I hug him. "Thank you so much," I say and find the empty slot.

"Try it, try it!" Willa beckons.

"Rico?" I ask through the radio once it's ready. "Can you hear me?"

There's static for a minute, and a screeching whir that makes us all cringe, but then . . . there's Rico's voice.

"Jules? You found the part?" he asks, his voice alight, and I swear I could kiss the radio nonstop. His voice is like the song of the universe.

Willa and Rodrick high-five.

"I'll be right back," I say, giddy and in search of some privacy. I walk to a corner of the room, where there's a desk inside a cube-like space.

"Tell me all about the Oasis," Rico says.

"It's something else," I start. My heart beats so hard and fast I think it's going to burst. "But you won't believe who I found here."

"Well, tell me!" He laughs, and I close my eyes to imagine him beside me.

"My aunt, Rico. I found my aunt. She's doing so good. She's, like, the vice president of California. I can't believe it, but I guess she's never been on the lottery announcements, only Burberry. And I have a stepcousin! And now that I have the signal booster, we can talk all the time. It's going to be perfect."

"Hey, Rico. I kind of need you!" a girl's voice cuts in through the radio, and for a moment, my heart stops.

"Who—who is that?" I ask.

He seems to move away. It sounds like shuffling and the thump of a heavy door closing. "It's nobody," he replies. But it didn't sound like nobody when the person literally said his name.

I shake away my discomfort. I have him on a call, and this should be the thing that matters. "Enough about me. Tell me more about you. I know it's been one day, but I miss you. How are you? Are you safe?"

"I'm fine," he says with a sigh that tells me he's not. "Just existing." He sounds off—though maybe it's tiredness. But there's a knock on the other end like someone is trying to get him out of whatever room he's gone into. He takes a long exhale. "Listen, Jules. I'm really sorry, but I can't talk right now."

"What do you mean? Are you okay?" Confusion enters my body, and my hands shake.

"I swear, I'm safe, all right? I love you, and I'll radio you a little later."

I don't get to say anything else to him before he goes static on the other line. I fight back tears.

I exit the room. Willa and Rodrick toothily grin at me in anticipation. "How did it go?" they both ask.

"It was fine," I lie. "He's doing okay and said he'll call me back."

They make eye contact. As if they can see right through me, Willa says, "I think we need to have some real fun before we go back to my mom's boring party."

Willa drags me down to the bottom of the stairs, where Sam waits for us. He stares at nothing.

"Hey, Sam!" I wave him over. "We're going somewhere fun."

He exhales and nods.

I don't really pay attention to where Willa and Rodrick lead us, gnawing at the insides of my cheeks trying to figure out who Rico was with, until we're entering a tall building in a secluded part of the forest that has a large golden door. To one side of the door, there's a line of people waiting. They complain as a man standing with his arms folded across his chest guards the entrance and lets our group in before them, with a "Hey, Willa, welcome back."

"This is Club Oro, our favorite," Rodrick says through the sound of blaring music. We walk through a large hallway covered in multicolored laser lights pointing every which way.

At the end of the hallway, what must be over a hundred people our age fill a room. At the back wall, there's a screen that extends from the floor to the ceiling, and there's a wild array of abstract designs on it that shift—a dizzying effect.

There's also a stage, and two women on it wearing long, skin-tight bronze dresses with a slit down opposite sides of their legs. Swirling designs have been drawn on their faces and arms and legs in bronze ink. They're making circular motions on these big machines at the front.

"DJs," Rodrick tells me. "They create the beats and remixes of the music."

I nod. In the Wasteland, we never had the tech for DJs, but someone was always making beats. Willa pulls me to the center of the room, in between the bodies. She dances to the rhythm of the music, her arms in the air as she sways her hips.

There are so many people in here, and all I can think about is disease and how easy it would be for me to get sick. But no one else except for Sam appears to be worried about catching anything. I feel alien, like I don't belong, even when I know I tested negative for Sibervirus. But I want to fit in, so I dance, however awkwardly my body moves.

In the darkness of the giant room, no one knows we're the new residents. We're just other sweaty bodies. I try to mimic Willa, move my waist to what Rodrick calls synthpop music, and bring my hands up.

I remember my pinky promise and go to Sam, following his gaze to a boy dancing on the floor. "You should come dance," I say, beckoning to him. At first, he's reluctant, but then I take his hand, lead him closer to the boy he was making googly eyes at, who invites us into his circle with a welcoming gesture. Sam chuckles for what must be the first time in a long time, and even though my conversation with Rico didn't go great, giving Sam something to smile about is special.

We don't stop dancing until the lights flicker off and the music stops, the bodies still, red emergency lights come on. Willa and Rodrick exchange a glance I can't fully read. Sam takes hold of my hand, and I squeeze back.

"Not again with the glitches," someone shouts, and as if in reply, the lights return, the music commences, and everyone dances again.

"Probably a sign it's time to go," Willa says, and we weave through the crowd toward the exit, get back in the pod, and return to the welcome party.

When we arrive at the parking lot, tía Ines is waiting,

holding up our four key fob bracelets on her pointer finger. She shakes her head and exhales.

"They needed to have actual fun, Mom," Willa says, taking the key fob tía Ines hands her and setting it back on her wrist.

"It's fine," my tía replies, but her serious tone makes me wonder if it really is. "The four of you go rest. Juliana and Sam, you're meeting the President tomorrow morning, and you'll need to be on your best behavior." I missed getting this look of disappointment. Like there are people who have a vested interest in me making good or bad decisions. Here, I can have that.

Tía Ines and Willa as my family. Friends. A home. Fun.

But how long will Rico stay on the other end of the line?

CHAPTER 9

Rico

I head back into the cars of the train to find the electronics on the cabin door sparking as tiny flames fly all over.

Nadine tries to use a fire extinguisher, but nothing comes out. “A little help?” she screams. Despite the chaos and the awful rubber smell of the electrical smoke, I can’t stop thinking about how upset Jules sounded. When I see her, I’ll explain everything. For now, we need to make it into the Oasis alive and in one piece.

Jesus enters the cabin we’re in with another fire extinguisher. “We’re lucky this works!”

He douses the flames. And I rush to the engine room to continue driving the train, rubbing at my eyes as I sit down at the controls once more.

According to the radar on the computer, it’s another mile to the dome. And then, what?

We’ll need to sneak through the Masterdome and past anyone who is at the train hangar when we arrive, something tía Linda and I weren't able to do the first time we took the train to the haven.

I rub at my face. My heart's already beating fast when something appears up ahead in the window. There's a goddamn bedrock wall. I reach for the brake. The wheels give a deafening screech, but it's not going to be fast enough. I drop to the ground, grasp the lever on the floor for the emergency brake with all of my strength, screaming as I pull.

In the cabin behind, Nadine and Jesus both yell words I don't understand as the train finally halts what must be less than five feet away from the wall.

"What in the world? We almost crashed!" Nadine says.

"What is that?" Jesus asks.

The cavern up ahead has collapsed. There must've been a cave-in sometime within the last three years. I glance down at the gas meter. We have a third of our gas left, which isn't enough fuel to make it back home even if we wanted to turn around.

I swallow hard.

I grab the helmet of my protective suit from where it sits on the chair next to mine and set it in place. "Let's go take a look." I turn my visor's light on and head toward the train car exit, Nadine and Jesus following.

Outside, darkness has swallowed all the light in the tunnel, and it's like we're the only things in the universe. Claustrophobia rushes me as it often does; nausea creeps up my throat like I might throw up. I fight against the strange sensation and rest a hand on the train to keep my balance as I head toward the wall.

There isn't going to be a way for the train to continue, but after a quick inspection, I spot a crevasse below, a waterway that might lead somewhere and allow us to cross to the other side.

"I'll go first," I tell them.

Nadine grasps my shoulder. "You have no way of knowing if there's a way out of there or how long the tunnel is."

"That's why I said I'll go first."

"We don't have a choice," Jesus says next to me.

"I'll walk back if I have to," Nadine mumbles.

"We're too far away from the city. Plus, it's too dark. Better to die quickly navigating this tunnel than starve on foot," I say.

She squeezes her eyes shut and groans.

"I'll go first," I repeat as I shift to a crouch. I reach my hand down into the water to see if there's even enough room to swim underneath the rubble. I don't touch anything, so I slip in feetfirst. There's no bottom underfoot. I don't know if this revelation makes things better or worse.

When we were younger, Nadine, Jesus, and I used to love to swim in the ocean. We'd spend hours in the water. I know we can do this. I know *I* can. I've come too far to quit now.

I breathe deep. Perhaps my helmet will help keep the water out some.

Even with my light on, I can't see anything ahead when I'm fully immersed in the water. Terror seizes my chest, which is ready to explode. My eyes blur, and I resurface.

"You okay?" my cousin asks.

I shake my head at the same time as I say, "Had a false start."

Jesus doesn't respond as he pulls me out of the water, stronger than I remember him to be.

"*I'll* go first," he says and then adds in a murmur, "Still freezing like always."

I don't argue. I let him take my place and watch him disappear into the murky water.

He doesn't come back up, and I fight to level my breathing.

"Remember when we were little?" Nadine is watching the hole as intently as I am. "The three of us got into so much trouble. We never followed the rules, were always stealing candy and whatnot from the few remaining shops. We'd mess with people by taking their glasses and medicines and other things. We were brats, looking back on it. But I never regretted it because the three of us had so much fun. Do you think it's fun in the Oasis?"

"I do," I say as I take my first real good look at Nadine since the beginning of this arrangement with the Sheriff. She's changed. Her facial features are less round and older, more worn in a way I can't fully explain. She's grown up, like I have. We're no longer the orphans tía Linda took in.

"Isn't it weird?" she continues. "We've all seen terrible things happen to so many people we love, and yet we still are trying. Even when the memories haunt us in our sleep."

"I think hope is all that we can ever have."

She huffs. "But for what? What makes any of this fight, this struggle, worth it?"

"Love," I reply. "I'm doing this because someone I love is inside the Oasis."

"I don't love anyone. Not anymore. Not like I did you at one point, but you left me."

That's not fully true. She must love me in the same way that I still love her, even if it's like a sibling. The way I still love my cousin and my aunt, and she must love them in turn, too. Otherwise, she wouldn't be here. The worst thing in this world is thinking you're alone, even when you're not.

"Nadine—"

"Come on, there's a way through!" Jesus's voice echoes.

Before I can say anything, Nadine puts on her helmet and goes into the water. I wait, give her enough time to make it to the other side but also ponder her words.

For so long, all I thought about was Jules. I'd forgotten about Nadine and my cousin. But I can't heal Nadine's pain over it. Instead, I can do what I can to earn her peace inside this haven, if it's what she wants.

I ignore my own apprehension and slip into the water. I breathe in as deep as I can and follow the light that Nadine's visor gives off. The passage is long, and a few feet in, my body tenses as the darkness encroaches, and I can't focus anymore. I take another breath, sucking in any and all the air that I have left in my helmet. Ahead, Nadine's light disappears so I know I'm close, yet I can't seem to move anymore. It dawns on me that my foot is stuck. I use my arms to pull and push myself in the water, but I don't budge.

I close my eyes and picture Jules to calm myself enough to think through the problem. The way she tilts her head to one side when she's content. Her laugh and how her touch is everything to me. The comfort of her head on my chest.

I slip my shoe off my foot. The moment I do, there's a rumbling as debris shakes loose. I swim for dear life as the hole fills with bedrock behind me. Somehow I get to the other side. Nadine and Jesus help me out as the whole area shifts.

Relief floods me with exhaustion. After a minute, I shift my attention. Even though a collapsed tunnel means we can't turn back, it's worked in our favor.

This hangar has been abandoned. The cameras in the room don't even seem to be connected. There are spiderwebs and dust bunnies in every corner that make me sneeze, earning me a glare from Jesus. No one's been here in a long time.

"Breaking in can't be that easy," Nadine whispers, her stance at the ready, her face questioning. She's left her Jian sword with the Sheriff. And I think she and I both miss the weapon.

I go up to the door, one shoe down, and hold the bracelet the Sheriff gave me to a panel. The door opens to . . . nobody. No one is waiting for us.

The three of us laugh as we take off our protective suits. The Sheriff gave us clothes that he said would help us blend in with everyone else here, and thankfully, shoes to match. We remove our new outfits from our waterproof backpacks and put them on. Slick silks in silver and gold instead of worn linen. We don't look like derelict Wastelanders when there's no lottery happening, and we won't be expected.

We stuff our gear into itself, the suits converting into second backpacks that we leave behind by the door along with our old clothes. Once we're all set, I go first for real, eager to get in and find the Sheriff's granddaughter and tía Linda and Jules. The door leads to a platform of sorts, an underground tunnel. But when we come up the stairs, all we need to do is ram through another door, and we're on the streets.

Two girls stare at us but shrug. They cackle as they pass each other a long cylindrical cup.

"I swear," one of them says, "I'm never getting this drunk again."

The three of us walk without really knowing where we're going or how we're going to find the Sheriff's protégé, Viola Hershall. For now, I take solace in not having encountered any of the Oasis's deputies.

I've seen photographs of what San Francisco and other places used to look like in the Old Epoch. This is it. Clean streets, people walking and talking without protective suits on. Streetlights that work. The sound of laughter in the distance instead of screams. Life aboveground instead of below the surface.

It's still nighttime, but we don't see the stars that I'm so used to. There's a gold shine from the honeycomb dome that protects the city. Tía Linda told me about it, but I never thought the Masterdome would be this huge. The color gives everything a slightly yellow hue.

For what seems like hours, we explore the haven as we search for an indication that we're in the South Shore or of how to get there.

"Oh my God, look." Nadine points to the strange metallic

beasts that sit in the middle of the lake. "The water filtration systems."

Jesus whistles and sets his forearms against the silver rail that surrounds the lake. "They must be a hundred feet tall."

"That's what the people of the Wasteland need," I reply, a new determination building inside me at such an astonishing sight.

We watch the beasts for a long while, then we walk until our feet are beyond tired, but our minds are too awake and alert. This place . . . it's unlike anything I dreamed of.

We cross the street, heading toward apartment complexes growing out of giant trees, ones aboveground rather than in bunkers, to see if we can find a place to sleep or food to eat, when I hear my name.

"Rico? Is that you?"

CHAPTER 10
Jules

Even though tía Ines told me to rest, I can't sleep. I toss and turn in my clean sheets until the powdery floral smell of them makes me want to puke. I throw them off, clutching the radio, beyond eager to hear Rico's voice again. I slip out of my apartment window and sit against the metal grate of the fire escape. The eclectic sounds of the city center radiate even here in the outskirts and occupy my thoughts as I try and fail to find a single twinkling star in the sky.

A group appears in the alleyway. I watch them. Did they win a spot in the Oasis or were they born here? What would that have been like? To begin life in a world where you never had to worry about the sun, of all things, hurting you? To Willa, it's burdensome.

But when the boy at the front turns around, my head spins as if I'm in a dream. I recognize every beautiful feature.

"Rico? Is that you?" I call out.

The boy faces me. *It's him, right?* Not a mirage like Sam

mentioned. But how can it be? His eyes lock on me, brightening.

"Jules?" he says and hurries toward me and up the stairs. He takes them two at a time as I frantically wait for him to climb to the twelfth floor.

"How is this possible?" I ask, heart racing, mouth wide in shock. Still unsure if I'm dreaming, I reach out to touch his face first. His cheeks are solid and warm underneath my fingertips.

I'm not imagining him.

"Surprise." He smiles as his eyes take me in. I recall Willa and Rodrick talking about rules, and there's something in Rico's unsure gaze that tells me he's broken the most important ones in the Oasis. He shouldn't be here. But he is.

"How?" I ask again, kissing his lips and his chin and his cheeks. "And what happened to your eye? Are you okay?"

"It'll heal," he says, then, as if he remembers something important, he shifts and looks down, but the people he was with are gone now. For a moment, I think he'll run after them. But he doesn't. "Maybe it'd be smart to go inside," he says instead. "And I can explain everything."

I nod and pull him in through my window, head still spinning.

"Wow," he says when he takes in my new home. I see myself in his tense posture and how he's frozen in the middle of my sitting room, as if he's scared to move and make the furniture dirty, even when he's dressed to fit right in. "This is . . . something else."

"Yeah, I'm still getting used to it," I say as I pull him toward my bedroom and onto the bed with me. "Just kiss me." There's the sting of tears welling up as I'm overtaken by an incredible emotion that must be bliss.

He laughs, a pure, unguarded sound. He kisses me, his lips so warm against mine and so perfect. I never want to be apart again. Never, ever again.

"I'm really not dreaming, am I?" I ask him.

"Nope. Definitely not dreaming," he says as I rest my head on his shoulder. I hug him so close, the familiar lull of his heartbeat welcome.

After I've gotten my fill, I study him and say, "We should shave your face, so you fully fit in."

He sighs but relents. We move to the couches in the sitting room. I bring a razor I found in my bathroom cabinet and a small cloth, some soap, and clean water.

"Don't nick me too much, okay?" he asks.

"You're in the safest hands," I promise and kiss him. His lips make my belly turn happily.

I take my time as I shave his face clean, extra careful around his ears and scars, suddenly shy. Rico barely blinks, eyes glued on me as I carefully shave around his lips. When our eyes catch, my stomach fills with swirling butterflies. A few minutes ago, I was sulking. I believed that Rico had already gotten over me. The way he stops me suddenly, pulls me close to him, and kisses me tells me everything I need to know.

He'll forever be mine.

When I'm done, I nuzzle the side of his neck and ask him, "How is this even possible? What did you do?"

"Well," he starts, then pauses before he continues. "After you left, I found out that the Sheriff rigged the lottery so that I would win. Giving my win to you wasn't part of his plan. Long story short, he blackmailed me into coming here and doing him a few favors. He said he'd hurt you if I didn't. And I also found out my aunt is alive and has been a prisoner this whole time."

"Oh, Rico," I tell him. "Is he the one who hurt your eye?"

"No," Rico replies quickly. I wipe his face gently with the cloth to remove any soapy residue. "It was during the lottery and worth it to protect you. He didn't harm me, just threatened me."

"What does he want you to do?" I wince as I try to figure out how injured Rico's eyebrow is. The stitches at least are straight, and someone who knew what they were doing helped him.

He pulls something out of the pocket of his pants: a photograph of a little girl.

"Apparently, his granddaughter lives here, and I'm supposed to find this person, Viola Hershall, his disciple or something in the South Shore. She'll help me find the girl, get her to safety before . . . I don't know, honestly—all I've been thinking about is keeping you safe and finding my aunt."

I sit on his lap, kiss his eye. He holds me by my waist. "I know. And who were those people that you were with?"

He hesitates, and I already know I won't like the answer.

"My cousin and—"

"The girl I heard on the radio?"

"Yeah, when you called me we were on a train up here. I won't lie. The girl is Nadine . . ."

"Like your ex-girlfriend, Nadine?"

His expression stills, waiting for my reaction. Relief floods my veins, not jealousy.

"It's okay," I tell him, then ask, "And no one saw you three come in?"

"A couple of very drunk ladies, but the Sheriff said the key fobs we have are special. They'll keep us hidden in some way," he says.

How can that even be? I think of how Rodrick's pop's office security camera hasn't been working. Did the same thing that's affecting the cameras make it easier for Rico to slip in undetected? Maybe not a thing but a person is at fault—the Sheriff?

"So what happens next?" I ask, unsure how to keep him secret in my apartment forever.

"I don't know," he responds. "I do what the Sheriff wants and you stay alive."

I sigh. "I should have stayed in the Wasteland, should have given my win to someone else." What do they do to those who come into the haven without having won?

Rico pulls me in for a tight hug. "I don't regret my decision."

An idea sparks. "What if I tell my aunt? She's the vice

president, Rico. If there's anyone who can allow you to stay and protect us, it's her."

Rico shakes his head. "Jules, you know you can't do that, right?"

"Of course we can," I protest. "All you need to do is tell her what you know. Share your intel with her, and I know she'll pardon you. Screw Sheriff Ramos. If he blackmailed you, this is the way you get back at him. This is how we stay together."

Rico's eyes narrow. "And what about everyone on the outside? I know the Sheriff maybe didn't go about it the right way, but he's trying to create a new haven, Jules. One where everyone is accepted, like my tía wanted. Plus, Burberry is holding his granddaughter and tía Linda hostage. What wouldn't you give to have a family member back?"

I still. "Or he's lying to you. You and I both know peace and a family reunion are not all the Sheriff wants. What is his full plan, Rico?" He lets go of me, glances toward the window. "You've never really cared about anyone else but us . . ." And it's true. Since we met, we've only had eyes for each other, and we've focused all of our energy on making sure we were okay.

"You're the most important person to me," he starts, "but there is a real opportunity to help those in the Wasteland and get tía Linda back. I can't let her die in a cell, can you?"

"I'm sorry if your aunt has been imprisoned this whole time, but we can't fight the leaders of the Oasis. Nobody ever has," I reply, *successfully* lingering on my tongue. "Rico, I *need* to tell my aunt and get us out of this mess. Perhaps if we tell her, she'll free your tía. And you need to remember what happened the last time you tried to break in." I regret the words as soon as I've said them. The hurt expression on Rico's face is enough to make my throat shrink, the air harder to breathe.

I move off his lap, sit next to him, my elbows on my knees, my hands running down my face.

Rico takes my hands in his. "Promise me that you're not going to tell your aunt. If you tell her, they'll hurt me and Jesus and Nadine. And they're—"

"Your family, too," I reply. My thoughts run at a million miles an hour. But in the end, he's right. I can't risk his life.

"Give me a few days to figure out what's right or wrong."

He goes over to his bag, which he left by the window, and takes out a few things I recognize. He sets my succulent plant on top of the coffee table in front of the couch and places the photo of my family next to it, my gold bracelet beside that, and the hand sewer that I used to create and mend our protective suits. Finally, he throws my old stuffed animal at me. I take in the mangy sheep with a hug.

"Thank you," I say. The faces of my family make my heart swell. "Okay, so you have a bracelet key fob, but do you know where this Viola Hershall is?"

He rubs at his temples. "She's in the South Shore. But do we have to worry about it right now? For tonight, can we live out our dream?"

"Yeah, I guess we can." I pull him back to me. I'll never let go again, even if at the end of this, I'm forced to go to my aunt for his own good.

CHAPTER 11

Jules

I startle awake before my alarm clock rings to the realization that I didn't imagine things. I take in Rico's face, listen to the lull of his breathing. He's so handsome, and I don't want to leave him. But today's the day I'm supposed to meet with the President, and neither she nor anyone else can suspect I'm hiding someone from the outside. I have to act like everything is normal.

It sucks to get out of bed, away from Rico's warm skin, but I slip out, dress, and leave him a quick note on my pillow.

I have a meeting. Didn't want to wake you.
I'll see you in the afternoon.—Te amo, Jules

When I'm ready, I tiptoe out, careful the door barely clicks.

"Hey—" a voice says from behind me in the hall. My arm goes up to my chest as I gasp. Sam's eyes go wide. "I'm so sorry," he says, face pallid. "I didn't mean to scare you."

"You're fine," I reply and push my unruly hair back

behind my ears. The elevator door opens. "I'm just nervous about today."

"Yeah, me too," he says. But he doesn't seem anxious. In fact, he's shaved since I saw him. I'm about to tell him that he looks good, when the elevator dings.

"There's nothing to be uneasy about," tía Ines states as she steps out of the elevator toward us. "You both are already doing wonderful—you're right on time. And all is forgiven from yesterday."

If tía Ines knew . . . would she forgive me for *everything* that happened yesterday?

Would she understand how much I love Rico and persuade those in power to let him stay? Or is it wishful thinking that I still mean that much to my tía?

I want to ask, even though Rico told me not to. If I can't confide in my aunt, there's no one here I can trust—except maybe Willa and Rodrick and Sam. But how much do I even know about any of them? Not enough to make a confession of such magnitude.

I don't stop thinking about Rico as we get into the pod waiting for us outside the lobby. I'm so distracted that I don't realize for a moment that it's daylight. The Masterdome is incredible. But even more amazing is the forest that surrounds us. Lush green trees line the mountain range, the air smells like rainfall, and the sound of nearby birds fills the morning sky. I don't think I'll ever get used to not having to wear a protective suit when the sun is out. Still, I make a mental note to fix my suit as soon as I get the chance. You never know.

We ride in silence as we head farther into the forest, deep into the North Shore along an impossibly long, winding road.

"We want to introduce you two to someone," tía Ines says, her tone excited, as we arrive at a mansion in the middle of the forest. It's a huge, three-story house complete with white pearlescent columns and sky-high glass windows on every side of the building. I'm fully confused about how something so out of place could exist here. But then again, isn't that what this place is supposed to be? A world so luxe everyone would die for the opportunity to be a part of it.

Everyone in the Oasis has much more than those in the Wasteland, and eons more than the groups in No Man's Land. Still, President Burberry seems to have so much more than all. It doesn't quite seem fair.

But what in this world *is* fair?

I hesitate to get out of the pod.

Sam must feel the same way, since he reaches out to me. He squeezes once, a reminder that I'm not alone and the pact we've made to have each other's backs stands.

I think about what Willa and Rodrick asked of me and Sam at the party . . . They want us to get used to all of this glitz overnight, as if we're machines instead of humans.

I'm forced to let go of Sam to leave the pod. As I do, I take in more of the quiet forest while we head toward the door. I keep in mind I'm not in the Wasteland. I don't need to find an exit route in case something goes wrong. At least, I don't think I do.

The door is answered by a bald man, his head so shiny it's like the sun is reflected on it. He's dressed in all black, and I take note of the weapon at his side—some kind of sleek metallic blaster I've noticed on other soldiers here. It's similar to the ones that Willa and Rodrick used in No Man's Land. This type of technology isn't in the Wasteland. I can't imagine how much worse the violence would be if everyone had laser blasters.

"There she is," the man says to tía Ines. They hug, and then the man shakes my hand and Sam's. "I'm Paul Burke, the Oasis's Sheriff. You kids can call me Sheriff Paul. Come in, come in. It's nice to have visitors. We haven't seen anyone in months."

"Tell me about it," tía Ines says with a bit of fire in her voice.

The man waves his hand as if swatting away a fly. "You know how it is when she starts a new project."

"A top-secret new project that I want to one day learn all about."

"Hey, even I don't know what she's doing . . . but you know it'll be splendid like always. But anyway, enough lollygagging—get in here!"

Tía Ines lets the man take her hand and pull her inside. It doesn't escape my notice that as he takes a whiff of her hair, his face relaxes.

Sam and I exchange a look before we walk in after the pair. He must see something in my expression, since he enters first. I glance back at the tall trees and a squirrel that scurries up on one. I'm skittish, that's all. Everything is as normal as can be.

The foyer of the mansion is beyond words. There are twin

stairs that lead to the upper levels. Red carpet runs on both sides of the stairwell and is way too valuable for our muddy feet to walk on. The chandelier that hangs in the middle of the entryway could be made out of a thousand diamonds.

Tía Ines removes her shoes and leaves them in the foyer. I follow her lead and slip off the sneakers that Willa gave me since we're the same size. The clean tiled floor is cold on my feet. The whole area is free of dirt or dust or ash.

"Ines!" President Burberry comes into view from the right as she descends the stairs with grace. It's as if she's floating toward us. "I haven't seen you in person for so long, darling!"

The two women practically run to each other, and I can't help but smirk at the sight.

This is who I was nervous about? On-screen, the President usually has her hair in a tight bun and wears a pearlescent suit. Today, she's dressed in an oversized black sweater, actual blue jeans, and fuzzy bright pink socks, her hair in loose curls. She seems perfectly normal. And very much unlike her citizens, who mostly dress in silks and metallics.

When they let go, tía Ines gestures to Sam and me. "This is my niece and her friend I messaged you about. They won the last lottery."

"Welcome, welcome. I heard that it wasn't an easy trip here. That we lost one group along the way. Very sad. But I'm glad you both are all right." The President doesn't wait for us to reply before she yells upstairs, "Sidra, darling, come! We have guests!"

"I'm coming, Mom," a small voice echoes back.

It's several more seconds before a girl makes her way to

the stairs from the left hallway. She skips down them as an orange cat trails behind her, and the bell on its collar rings their approach. Unlike her mom, Sidra is dressed in the latest Oasis fashions, a pearlescent miniskirt over shiny black tights, a short-sleeve shirt cut at an angle at the shoulders that shimmers sleek silver, and bright pink eye shadow.

I thought after Rico won the lottery, after I survived the perilous journey from San Francisco to the Oasis, after every miracle inside the Masterdome, that nothing would surprise me anymore.

But my breath hitches as I mentally compare the girl in the picture Rico has to the one in front of me. President Burberry has Sheriff Ramos's granddaughter.

"This is my adopted daughter, Sidra. Sidra, this is Juliana and Samuel, our newest members."

"Hi." Sam grins and gives the girl a small wave.

"Hey," I manage to add, my mouth too dry.

I take in the kid's coal eyes, so massive they barely fit on her thin face. Her skin is an olive tan, the same as the Sheriff's, and contrasts against Burberry's pale white skin. Her lips are naturally bright red as well.

The girl hugs the President's hip. Bile rises in my throat. Is this why the Sheriff grimaced whenever the President filled our broadcast screen in the Wasteland? Not jealousy, like I believed, but true hate. Does Rico know that the President is the one who has the girl? He must—he didn't mention it to me, but was that on purpose?

I force my smile to stay put, but it's a struggle. I reach for

Sam's hand again, but he's too far away now, and the air's suddenly colder.

The cat purrs as it weaves around Sidra's ankles, until the girl picks up the furball and it nestles against her cheek. "This is Checkers," she says, laughing. "He's the neediest and only cat in this city." She scratches under his chin, and I can't remember a time when I saw an animal in San Francisco. Unless rats and flies count.

"We don't normally allow animals since we have limited resources, but I had to let Sidra have a pet," the President says. She kisses Sidra on the top of her head before she signals us into another doorway to the right. "We were about to go make some pancakes. Come join us."

I can't keep my eyes off the girl. Her nose and face shape are exactly like her grandfather's. I never had any real affection for him, but he's kind to Rico. He got us into a safe bunker. And he is the one who sent Rico on this mission. He's the one who got him here, to me. No matter what the reasons were, no matter what's at stake, I'm grateful for that.

Sam seems to be more drawn to the cat than anything else, so Sidra ends up handing the feline over. It's the first time I've seen Sam excited, and he's way too cute walking and sweet-talking Checkers.

"Vamos," tía Ines says. My tía reaches her hand out and I take it.

Together, we move from the foyer down a hallway filled with photographs of the Oasis and of Sidra and the President, and I'm left even more confused. A photograph of them hiking. A photograph of them cooking. One of them simply sitting together, as they stare out of a large window at snowfall. Their smiles are large, sincere. At least the President has given her adopted daughter a good life. Could it be that true fondness is what has kept President Burberry from giving the girl back to her grandfather?

We're led to a kitchen that's as big as my whole apartment. The ceiling is high, and wooden beams traverse it. The roof is filled with windows that allow the space to be awash in natural light. There is a large table at the center made of rock and four ovens against the far wall.

"You can sit at the stools around the kitchen island," the President says. "And enjoy while we host you."

The three of us grab seats.

Sidra and Burberry cook pancakes like daughters and mothers should, laughing as flour goes every which way. The eggshells fall into the mix, and they need to dig them out. Soon, the whole kitchen smells of flour and chocolate and cinnamon and strawberries.

It's the scent of everything sweet that makes my stomach churn. I recall a time when Mami and I used to cook rice pudding with cane sugar and canela, which smelled like heaven on earth.

Paul comes forward and hands tía Ines two tablets.

"How exciting," she says, taking them and scrolling through.

"What is it?" I ask.

"Every resident who is older than seventeen is usually

given a job, but because of the bravery you two showed in saving Willa, I wanted your career-choosing day to be special. So I thought, why not a breakfast with the President herself? And instead of choosing your career in my boring office, you get to do it here."

Despite how the day has started, there's a bubbling in my belly. Excitement at the idea that I have the option to form a life in the Oasis. In front of us, Sidra flips a pancake again after seeing it's ready, giggling once more and adding it to the growing pile.

"Good job, honey," Burberry says to the girl, and something like pride twinkles in her eyes.

Sidra stops flipping pancakes long enough to give us a small salute before she goes back to her batter like she's an actual chef.

Tía Ines passes the tablets to me and Sam.

"There're more jobs than I thought," I say. "Why not bring more people in to fill them?"

When I look up, President Burberry's smile strains at the edges.

"Some of the jobs aren't necessary," my tía responds, tone flat.

The job listings include things like post office worker, retail shop clerk, florist. I stop at the position that stands out the most.

Caretaker to Sidra Burberry.

"See something you like?" Sam asks at my side, sliding the cursor up and down the list.

"Yeah, actually." Before I know what I'm doing, before I even think about whether or not it's a good idea, I say, "I can be Sidra's caregiver."

Tía Ines and Burberry smile conspiratorially, as if it was their plan all along. But it's my choice to take the bait.

"We were hoping one of you might be interested in that," Burberry says. "But we must admit, we were hoping it might be you, Sam. Since you had a sister."

Sam tenses. He sits up straighter as if the topic is the last thing he wants to talk about. He doesn't want to think about his sister any more than I want to think about my family, about all that we went through, about how they all . . . died.

"I did," he responds, his tone hesitant. "But—"

"I had three brothers and was very close with tía Ines's daughter," I say, cutting in, determined to do this for both Rico and Sam.

"That is true. She'll do great," my tía adds.

"I agree," Sidra says as she goes to the cabinets and, using a stool to reach up top, takes out some white plates that she juggles with her tongue slightly sticking out. She hands us each a plate. Her smile is so big, her eyes so bright. It's the face of someone who has never had to struggle or see death up close. And perhaps this place, and being by President Burberry's side, is the best thing for her.

Should we take her away from what seems to be bliss? For a life in the Wasteland?

"Okay, the job is yours," Burberry replies. "I trust you to watch her, teach her, guide her. I've been cooped up for too long and have too much work to do. It'll be a good change."

Tía Ines places three pancakes on my plate and the same number on Sam's. Sidra rummages around in the kitchen some more before passing out forks. She goes to the massive refrigerator and pulls out a can of something she says is called whipped cream. She adds the white fluffy stuff to each of our plates.

It is a feast that any kid in San Francisco would fawn over.

I wish I could take the train back down the mountain and make pancakes for all the kids of the bunker Rico and I lived in. Could you imagine? Their faces when given the sweet bread, whipped cream, and fresh strawberries.

But nobody who comes into the Oasis ever returns . . .

I used to think it was because no one would ever dream of leaving it. What if people *had* wanted to return, though? What if I want to visit? Could I do so without being a representative? Or would that be against another rule?

"In return for taking care of Sidra, I'll let you choose a specialty to pursue. When Sidra is eighteen, you'll be able to learn about that specialty from an expert in the field. And of course, you'll have access to this mansion, giving you every comfort imaginable."

Tía Ines adds, "Teach Sidra what's outside the haven in case what's outside ever breaks in. We want you to watch over her. And prepare her. Train her to survive like you did in the Wasteland. She's our future."

She's our future.

Another reason why Burberry's refusal to send Sidra home to San Francisco and her grandfather makes sense. I'd never thought about how a president gets chosen, and how they aren't chosen by the people anymore. Never gave a second thought to the fact we're truthfully living under a monarchy. They are preparing Sidra to take over for the President one day. But shouldn't the citizens of the haven get to choose who they want to be their leader? If the Oasis is meant to be reminiscent of the Old Epoch, wouldn't it be a democracy? And shouldn't everyone, including Sidra herself, know that she has a family on the outside who wants her home?

I swallow hard.

"I could use another good deputy," Paul adds, staring at Sam. "Someone I can teach to keep this house, the President, and her daughter safe. If you're interested?"

Sam licks his lips, looking around the room, but his gaze ultimately lingers on me.

I don't want to say anything—this needs to be his choice.

But I'm flooded with relief when he says, "Okay, I'm in. Thank you for this opportunity, Sheriff Paul and President Burberry."

As President Burberry's face settles into a smug acceptance, I can't help the gnawing guilt in my chest. Sam has no idea how important these jobs will be.

And I have no idea what I've gotten myself into.

CHAPTER 12
Rico

The moment Jules is out the door, I sprint from her bed. I told her I wouldn't do anything until we talked more, but if I don't find Viola Hershall or Jesus and Nadine, they'll surely send word that I've gone rogue, and who knows what'll happen to us.

In the bathroom, I wash my face with actual clean, warm water and soap, then give myself a once-over in the mirror. I cringe at the scars on my skin that can't be scrubbed away. I don't know what I dislike more, the number of scars I have or the clothes I have to wear to blend in with the people here. "The latest fashions," the Sheriff called them, almost with a chuckle, like he really enjoyed the idea of Jesus and me squirming into our hard metallic tops and skintight, sleek pants.

I shake the insecurity off my shoulders. I am here—by force, yes—but Jules is here, too. So now I need to fulfill the Sheriff's request to find Viola Hershall.

I exit out the window I came in. After making sure no one will see me, I jump off the final stretch of the fire escape and make my way around the building and onto the street, where people are walking outside freely, like the sun wouldn't scorch us all if it had the chance.

It's unreal to be out in broad daylight. I can't remember the last time I felt the warmth of the sun without it burning my skin. What would it be like if San Francisco had its own Masterdome? If everyone could be protected? I could very well get used to being out like this. And maybe if the Sheriff succeeds, it'll be possible to stay.

After a long time of staring up at the Masterdome, I snap out of it. I need to be back in Jules's room before she returns, especially considering I didn't think to leave her a note like she did for me.

The first thing I need to do is find the train that'll take me to the South Shore, where Sheriff Ramos said I'd find Viola Hershall. From what tía Linda taught me, the haven is split up into four shores. Each one is in charge of something different.

The North Shore, my current location, is the entrance. The North also contains the city center, where there are shops and restaurants and clubs, and where everyone is allowed to live a life that some would call fun. As well as half of the housing and the Security Depot. The West is mostly fields, where food is grown. The East has the Technology Center, including the main power grid station. And the South Shore, well, most importantly, it's where Viola Hershall lives. But it also includes more houses, a bookstore and library, a pool, and many other recreational community buildings.

I follow a footpath that eventually changes to a motorized walkway flanked by guardrails. I join others, who all wear their key fobs on their wrists as we're taken from one part of the North Shore to another. When people want to exit, they simply walk through one of the breaks in the railing.

Eventually, I see a sign for *Train Station—South Shore.* I follow behind a couple holding hands and kissing even as they exit the walkway, as well as a woman and her small child, the latter doing seemingly everything they can to get away.

The trains are nothing like the Zephyr. They look like a longer version of the vehicle pods and are three cars long. They must only hold like thirty people each. A mass of people waits for the train. But the crowds don't really bother me that much. After all, the ones in San Francisco were far more dangerous, filled with people who wanted to take what you had and were willing to end your life for it.

I scan my key fob at the entryway, copying what the people in front of me do, then I wait for the train to arrive.

I sit next to the woman and the little girl. During the ride, the mother pulls the girl's hair into two identical and adorable pigtails. The little girl sticks out her tongue at me, and I make a silly face that makes her laugh.

I can't imagine what it's like to grow up here, to not worry about your child having enough to eat or about the Sibervirus making her too sick. I've heard they're able to cure almost every ailment here.

And still, I get the sense that the safety is manufactured, by the way the adults all seem to constantly scan the area around them.

I don't know how long this trip will take, so I relax and slouch back against the soft mint-green and cushiony passenger seat, taking in how serene the forest looks. Eventually, I turn my attention to the television screens, where a host in a colorful suit shares today's news. Thankfully, none of the stories include video recordings of my cousin and Nadine getting into trouble, or any of us sneaking into the Masterdome.

The train takes us around the lake with the giant water filtration system until we get to the South Shore. An announcement on the train tells us we're approaching the station.

The little girl and her mom head for the doors when we're close to the platform, and I follow their lead. Before the train stops, the doors snap open. As they do, the little girl loses her footing. I move fast as a cat, catching the girl an inch before she falls out of the train while it's coming to a halt.

"Thank you," her mother says, face mortified, staring at my still-swollen eye for a few seconds too long before pulling the child into a tight hug. "That's never occurred before."

"Accidents happen," I say, pointing to my eye.

With the train fully stopped, the three of us get off, the little girl now in her mother's arms, eyes toward me. She gives me one last funny face that I return. As I shift back around to examine if there's an obvious glitch visible on the train, I bump into someone. When I turn around, I come face to face with a group of deputies making their way into the car. The deputy I bumped stares at me with disdain.

"Watch where you're going," he says, pushing me back so hard I fall onto my butt. Where the deputies of San Francisco had a soft spot for me, those here know nothing about me.

The little girl screams. Her mother notices I'm on the ground, but she quickly takes the little girl away from the scene without offering a word to help—unfortunately, proving that the Oasis is not so dissimilar to the Wasteland after all.

I don't know anything about the deputies here. I don't need to know anything except the fact that there are five of them and one of me, and I might be fast, but I'm also rusty when it comes to fist-fighting, having not needed to brawl since we began working for Sheriff Ramos. Not to mention my sight isn't at one hundred.

"I've been waiting for you," a woman says from my right. She approaches and helps me to my feet. The deputy takes her in and flicks at his nose with his thumb before he turns around and gets on the train.

I leer at him until the doors close, and the locomotive leaves me and the woman standing alone on the platform.

I turn and the woman flattens out her long floral skirt and straightens her pewter belt methodically. It's the way she smirks that tells me immediately she's Viola Hershall. And I didn't have to go searching far for her—she found me.

She must sense the recognition in my features since she

doesn't introduce herself but simply says, "Ricardo Villanueva. Let's talk."

Where Jules's apartment has an almost sterile, unlived-in feeling to it, Viola Hershall's apartment is warm and smells of honey and vanilla. Every crevice is inlaid with some kind of lush plant. Sunshine illuminates the space from large windows, including a rectangular ceiling window that reminds me that it's still early in the day. She has a small bookshelf with old paperbacks. Fairy lights hang from the walls, and she turns them on as she takes off her shoes and puts on fluffy white slippers.

I follow suit and remove my boots.

"Don't be shy," she says and leads me into a tiny mint-colored kitchen, crammed with a small, two-person wood table that's been painted green.

The moment I sit, though, the weight of my body doubles. I didn't sleep much yesterday, but that's nothing new. My stomach churns with a new kind of stress. I want Viola to tell me more about the Sheriff's plan, so I can deal with it and finally rest.

She turns on her stove, fills a teakettle with water, and puts it on to boil.

"You're a long way from home," Viola says when she joins me at the table. Concern is etched onto her face. Whether it's genuine or not, I'm not sure. "Is this the farthest you've ever traveled from San Francisco?"

"I mean, yeah. No Man's Land isn't exactly safe for road trips. There are raiders everywhere," I tell her, then add in, "This is a nice home."

She glances around her kitchen, looks off into the living room, and nods. "It's the Oasis. Everything is *nice*." She emphasizes the word bitterly.

"At least you're safe here," I reply, anger creeping out of me. Who would complain about having good things?

But she snorts as if I've said something foolish. "None of us are *safe*. That's an illusion. The Burberrys have simply had a shared talent of giving the populace a false sense of hope."

The teakettle whistles. Viola stands and pours hot water into two mugs with tea bags inside.

"Honey?" she asks.

"Sure," I say. I can't remember the last time I drank tea. She squeezes a large amount of the sugary substance from a plastic bottle shaped like a bear into one of the mugs before she hands it to me.

I take the cup gingerly in my fingertips, bring it to my lips, and even though the water scalds my tongue, the honey tastes like sunshine.

"I'm safer inside than outside the dome," I reply after another few sips.

"Yes, of course," she responds, weighing my words as she sits down with her own mug, her array of silver rings calling my attention. "I fear far too many in the Wasteland won't survive the harshness of summer next year."

I swallow, a lump forming in my throat. "If only someone

would do something about it," I retort and bore my eyes into hers, meeting fire with fire.

I got blackmailed into coming here and meeting with her to enact some big plan, after all.

She stares at her cup as she tells me, "I've stepped outside this dome more than most when it was an easier thing to do. Believe me, I *did* help back when I could. I was the very first representative. But I'm not allowed out there anymore, not after I started asking too many questions the President didn't like and got too close to Sheriff Ramos. And I'm afraid that Burberry tracks me far too much to ever let me travel outside again. But I still want to help. That's why you're here. It's why Edgar trusts me. And perhaps you." I'd never heard anyone say the Sheriff's first name before. Edgar Ramos.

"What is it that you both want from me exactly? All he told me to do was find his granddaughter with your help. What role do you see me playing in your takeover?"

"Once upon a time," she says, "all was in chaos, and humanity was lost. I don't mean earthquakes or fires. I mean we literally lost the ability to be humane. That loss led to events that nobody could stop, except for those in power. Those in power solely wanted to profit off the chaos. And I saw the United States fall. Some people called this the land of the free, the home of the brave, the place where any dream could be achieved. It was arguably once the most powerful country on Earth. But then we started to destroy the planet. Waging wars upon endless wars because those in charge wanted more power and more money. Too many people died and were killed in the most miserable ways. And then came the Sibervirus."

"People are killed every day in the Wasteland," I say.

She smirks. "You think you know suffering and pain? You've endured a great deal, but there are so many worse things than death that can happen, my dear boy. You haven't been alive long enough to know the half of it."

I sip my tea, a quip at the edge of my tongue I'm sure would get me in trouble.

"Two things occurred that would shape society today," Viola continues. "The first was the monetization of survival. People began needing the protective suits used in the Wasteland to outlast the summer heat and to evade Sibervirus. Manufacturers could charge an arm and a leg because they knew people had no other options. Contractors soon began to offer to build bunkers, and people used their life savings to buy their way into darkness, thinking that they'd be all right if they could hold out until a new future began.

The second was the decimation of democracy. The wealthy offered American families a chance to live at an exorbitant cost. When all of those elected government leaders died from the Sibervirus, the Burberrys had the most money, the most resources, owned the most land, and had already started building the Oasis. And so people flocked to them as their new saviors, even though that family didn't have citizens' best interest in mind. Our President Burberry isn't any different from her parents, or theirs.

"She uses the people of the Wasteland to keep this city

running. Saving those in the lower isolation cities would change the current social hierarchy. Burberry can't afford that. But Edgar and I, we're not going to let the Burberrys continue to govern. Paradise shouldn't exist for a select few, and we shouldn't hoard valuable resources."

I swallow. "What would that mean for everyone already inside the Masterdome?"

Her smile is condescending. "Does it matter when it means more outside would survive? The lottery system isn't fair. It wasn't designed to be. One person dies in here; another takes their place. But this haven could easily hold five times its current population and grows enough food and has enough water to keep them all alive. We would just need to build more housing and get Burberry out of power. The lottery wasn't simply designed to be exclusive—it was designed to keep people motivated after the Great Earthquake of 2065. If you can work hard to earn enough lottery tickets and increase your chances of winning, then who wouldn't work to the bone? And who would ruin their chances of *staying* once inside? But things shouldn't be this way, and I want to help ensure that they don't get worse. If everyone in the lower isolation cities dies, the Oasis dies as well. It's what Burberry doesn't understand. We're symbiotic."

"I don't want to hurt anyone," I respond after a moment. Because that's what this all comes down to. From the history my tía taught me, no real change in society has ever happened peacefully.

"Who said anything about hurting people?" But not even

the tone of Viola's voice can hide her laughter. She knows exactly how far Sheriff Ramos would go for revenge.

"Rico—what do *you* want the future to look like?" Viola continues, her dangling earrings rattling as she takes another drink of her tea. "Has anybody ever asked you?"

I swirl my almost-empty cup. No one cares about what I want. No one ever thinks about the way I'm screwed over by the decisions they make. "I want things to be fairer."

She nods and says, "I want the same thing. Edgar and I have a vision, you see. One where you and I, and everyone currently within the haven and outside it, can live together, can share the remaining wealth of this land. But we can't achieve that without—"

"Where does his granddaughter come into all of this?" I interrupt, eager to get to the point.

"President Burberry is using Sidra as a human shield," Viola replies plainly. "She pretends to love the child with full knowledge that the girl is the only way she can keep Edgar under control. I can't get close to the North Shore, though. My fob doesn't work on the trains anymore. I'm stuck here. Alive, sure, but a prisoner."

"Okay, so President Burberry has Sidra. And tía Linda? Where is she being held?"

"In the West Shore. That's where they keep supposed agitators. I've got spies keeping an eye on her who will let us know the best time to strike and get her out. Like I told your cousin and Nadine yesterday, we do plan to give you what you want."

I nod, taking note that Jesus and Nadine have been here already. "As long as you and the Sheriff both keep your word, that my family, Jules, and I will remain safe, I'm here to help."

"Edgar was right to trust you. And your cousin is fine, awaiting next steps with the rest of my people somewhere safe." She gleams, her eyes shiny. With tears of relief maybe? She pours me more tea. "You know, time is funny. It's the one thing that matters in the end," she continues. "Maybe the people outside will finally have their time to live a little in a Third Epoch. Because you helped give it to them. Edgar told me that you're the best techie in the Wasteland."

"I wouldn't say that," I tell her, straightening as I know what's coming: the moment she'll tell me what else they want from me besides rescuing Sidra. "So, after we get his granddaughter, then what?"

"Your aunt taught you how to hack the Masterdome?"

I shake my head. "I never succeeded in getting through the system. And if you can hack some of these key fobs to make me fit in, how come you can't control the Masterdome?"

"Because my best coder died after he made those for me."

"Died or was killed?"

"Let's say Burberry isn't as innocent as she seems on camera. We need you, Rico, and maybe it's time for you to fulfill your own destiny, the way your aunt wanted you to."

"I don't know if I can," I reply honestly. She knits her hands together.

"I trust you'll figure it out," she says. "We need to be able to control the Masterdome after we've taken over the Oasis.

You and your cousin and tía, once she's free, can do this. The Wasteland needs hope, and together, we're going to give it to them."

This plan of creating a different world for people like me *should* be a new beginning. Something positive to work toward because that's what this truly is. But I remember Jules, and how she wants to confess to her aunt what's going on, and my stomach turns sour.

Will she be our biggest obstacle?

PART III

THE ISLAND & THE TRUTH

CHAPTER 13

Jules

"What do you think?" Sam asks on our way home after spending all day getting a tour of Burberry's mansion and mingling with Sidra, or in Sam's case, getting the rundown from Sheriff Paul. We're in the back seat of the pod we've been given to get to and from Burberry's house. Tía Ines stayed behind, so it's just us two. Still, I don't know how much I can say out loud. There could be a camera in the pod, or a voice recorder. Even though Sam is the person I currently trust most outside of Rico, I can't confide in him in this place.

I ponder, attempting to come up with the correct thing to say. Unsure if I'm being paranoid, or if there truly is something to mistrust about my aunt and the President.

I shift my gaze from a serene sun setting outside the Masterdome to Sam. "I think I'm getting used to living in paradise."

His eyes narrow. I tilt my head, and it seems to dawn on him what my issue is.

He nods and says, "Paradise doesn't come easy."

"No," I respond as I turn back to the window, "it doesn't."

I see a store come into view with exactly what I need, but it passes by in a rush. "Stop!"

The pod doesn't come to a screeching halt. Instead, it remains on the road until it can safely pull us aside, and parks at the sidewalk.

"You wanna come with?" I ask Sam with an excited grin.

He tries to see what pulled my attention. "Where?"

"To that store!" I exit the pod and walk back a block.

"A fabric store?" Sam asks when we're in front of the building, which has a neon sign with a giant thread and needle at the end that reads The Good Stitch. "Like to make clothes? Do you know how to sew?"

I nod, holding the door open for him as we enter the store, which is filled with what must be a million yards of fabric all stacked on shelves and piled high on the floor in a wild disarray. "My mami taught me how to sew," I start. "She worked at a factory for a while making protective suits for people until it burned down. Then she made them from a storefront in Union Square. She was really popular in our area because she made the best suits that didn't melt. But it takes a special combination of fabric."

I don't face him as we walk past velvet and silks. Talking about Mami, remembering things about her, hurts the most. But it's true, because of her, I was able to create strong protective suits for Rico and me. And if nothing else, maybe that's what I can do here in the city—make solid suits that

Rodrick and Willa can take down with them the next time they return to the Wasteland to give to the people who don't have them.

A woman finally comes out of the back.

"Hi, you two," she says. "Sorry, we don't have a lot of customers usually. I was in the back sewing. Can I help you find something?"

"Do you have a piece of paper?" I ask.

When she hands me paper and a pen, I write down all that I need: a brand-new sewing machine with all the add-ons, Kevlar for the underlayer, Tyvek, rubber, anti-radiation materials, electromagnetic field fabric, and a couple of other things that come to mind.

"Impressive selections," the store clerk, whose name tag reads *Maggie*, says.

"Thanks. My mami taught me how to sew," I reply, blushing. "I'm really excited you're here."

"And I'm really excited *you're* here! You might be my biggest customer this week."

When Maggie's done ringing me up, I've spent over $1,000 on materials and couldn't be happier.

By the time we leave the store, Sam is carrying the machine while I'm holding what must be twenty pounds of fabric. I'm not going to waste my time. Everything happening with Rico might be confusing, but he is right that being in the Oasis gives us the time and space we need to think about the people we left behind. I'm going to save those in San Francisco. I won't turn my back on them.

Rico is gone when I return to my apartment. I can't say I'm surprised, but my skin prickles at how cold the space is without him in it, and part of me wonders if I dreamt him. I lie on my bed face-first and try to find his smell. I can't. There's only that of clean sheets. Where did he go? Is he safe?

Or did I actually make him up as a way to cope with so much strangeness?

I find my radio hidden in between the mattress and bed frame and press the button to turn it on. "Rico, are you there?" There's no reply, just static. "Rico?" I ask again.

This time, the static and unbearable tension break. "Hey, Jules, I'm waiting for the train."

I sigh in relief. "Where did you go?"

"The South Shore. I'll tell you more when I see you. How was your day?"

I bite my lip, noting how it's not so chapped anymore.

"I'll tell you more when I see you," I mimic. "Just happy to be home."

That last word seems to come out so naturally, but Rico mm-hmms.

"Be safe on your way back, okay?" I add.

"Always, amor," he replies. "I'll be there soon. Don't wait up for me. I know it's late."

"You know I won't be able to sleep until you're home," I say. "So hurry."

"I will," he replies, then adds in more excitedly, "Oh, and

get this . . . did you know that the Sheriff's first name is Edgar?"

I laugh. "The things you learn here, huh?"

"I was thinking that it's so strange how we never knew his full name, even though we did everything he asked." He goes quiet, thoughtful.

"I love you. You know that, right?" I say to bring him back.

"I love you, too," he replies. "Be there soon." And then there's static again.

I turn off the radio.

I miss the sound of his voice as soon as it's gone.

Back in the Wasteland, I was never alone, and I never thought I'd miss being with others. But here, the loneliness is cold. After lying in bed for too long in the stillness of my own room, worrying and thinking about worst-case scenarios, which indeed include Rico never returning, I force myself to get up and grab my sketchbook.

Mami used to say that creating clothes for people was her best distraction from the harsh reality of life.

I spend half an hour sketching what I want the suits to look like, factoring in any improvements I can make with enough materials. I can use two layers of fabric with how much I have, which would allow the suits to withstand an extra ten degrees. I might even be able to add extra protection by giving them tight cuffs around the wrists and make them more fashionable with a cinched waist.

I need more measurements, though.

Since it's impolite to go over empty-handed, especially

when asking a favor, I make three grilled cheese sandwiches that come out perfectly. Then I call Willa by dialing 0 on a mint-green corded phone stuck to one of my walls. Mami would call it vintage chic. "I'm going over to Sam's. You want to come?" I ask.

"I thought you'd never ask! Let me tell you, I've had a day. Thank God it's Friday. Give me five," Willa says on the other side before she hangs up.

I unlatch the lock on my window in case Rico comes back and I'm still gone, then grab the sandwiches and knock on Sam's door across the hallway.

He answers after a few seconds. He's wearing pajamas like I am, but my set is purple and his is a dark green so lush I almost get lost staring into the fabric.

I wish I could say he's happy to see me, but his eyes are questioning, tired.

I give him a tooth-filled smile, raising the plate up to where he can surely smell the cheesy goodness, and ask, "Want more company? I was hoping I could measure you for a protective suit."

At first, I'm not sure he's going to say yes as he glances back. But he moves out of the way and signals me inside, replying, "Yeah, okay." And as if something snaps inside him, he perks up and adds, "Actually, this is great. I know you're excited about the fabric but let me show you what I found."

"Oh, do tell," Willa replies, appearing next to me, a giant grin plastered on her face. "Did you both miss me? Because I missed you."

I laugh as Sam brings us into his apartment, which is an

exact replica of my own. The one thing that is different is his sitting area, which has been filled with books of all sorts and sizes along with maps and old papers.

I set the plate of grilled cheeses down onto the kitchen counter and make my way over to where he sits, holding one of the books. I move a few out of the way to find a place to settle.

"Where did you get all of this stuff?" I ask, curious.

He responds as if it's obvious. "I used some of the money from the Vice President to shop at the bookstore before the welcome party yesterday."

"I didn't know the Oasis had a bookstore." I try to recall seeing one on our ride over.

"It has a fabric store," Sam says. "Why not a bookstore?"

"Wait, you two went to The Good Stitch? I once wanted to learn to sew but realized it is not something I'm any good at," Willa says, sounding genuinely impressed. "But Maggie is so nice."

"We stopped there on the way home," I reply, when one of the books catches my eye. It has a dark smudge of ash on its spine. I pick it up and flick my pointer finger over it, wiping off some of the smudge. I bring it to my nose, the smell familiar, an unpleasant idea forming in my mind.

"What is it?" Willa asks.

"I used to trade books to Sheriff Ramos," I say slowly in a whisper. "In exchange for water and food. You don't think . . ."

Sam stares at me as if he's following my train of thought, and suddenly, he looks like he doesn't very much want to share his books with me anymore.

"Everything we have comes from the lower isolation cities," Willa says, eyes wide. "I thought everyone knew that."

I scoff. "No. I wondered what Sheriff Ramos did with the books, though. Never thought I'd come to discover that he sent them all to the Oasis. Guess I should be happy I'm lucky enough to enjoy them now." But it wasn't luck—it was Rico who got me here . . .

I know too many stories of people who died in the Scar scrounging around for these books, and for what? So lottery winners like me can have an in-home library and a bookstore?

I put on my bravest face, trying not to make a big deal out of it, but that all-too-familiar bubble of anger rises in my chest.

"This is what I wanted to show you," Sam continues as he holds up a different book. "Check out the bookmarked page. I've been digging through the books, to study, learn, and plan a way to create spigots by building a 3D printer to construct them."

I toss the other book aside and open his to a spread that shows the schematics of a machine.

"What is it?" Willa asks as she takes the book from me to get a closer look.

"Hope for the lower isolation cities of the Wasteland. I think it could be, anyway."

"It looks like a design for a weird tower machine thing," Willa adds in, handing me back the book.

"Not just any tower," Sam responds, leaning forward and speaking his next words slowly. "A water-*capturing* tower that

I think we can create in the Oasis for those in the Wasteland, similar to the spigots used in the lake. If everything that was ever collected by the people of the Wasteland was sent here, surely the haven has the tech that we need to make the 3D printer, which we could feed the schematics into to generate a spigot prototype. If it works, the printer uses plastic, something we have plenty of. The people of the Wasteland would be able to have water filtration structures, including those that desalinate."

"Where did you even learn this stuff from?" I ask.

"My dad. He was an engineer. He built something similar for our farm before we moved to the Sacramento isolation city. Sometimes I helped him. It was his dream to save others. I guess now maybe it can be mine. Maybe I can do something bigger for the people outside."

"Combined with my idea to help create protective suits, this might give the people of the Wasteland a chance to make it through the hottest season," I say.

Impenetrable clothing and clean water would change the lives of everyone else in California.

Willa frowns. "Burberry would never allow it. If people didn't need us for water, they would stop working. And if they stopped working, new books and other things would stop getting sent here."

When Sam and I don't say anything, Willa continues. "You don't think if she wanted to do something like this, she would have already? She has the time and resources. If there isn't water in the Wasteland, and ample water exists here, it's because the Oasis wants to keep it all to itself. They don't even let anyone outside the Masterdome if they're not a representative. And there're only thirty of us."

"But it's worth a try," I say, trying to piece together a plan, enthusiasm blossoming. "Even if we have to go behind Burberry's back. Would you and some of the other representatives be willing to take some protective suits and the 3D printer down the mountain?"

Willa doesn't say anything for a moment. "There're cameras everywhere. We'd get caught."

"What if we could save hundreds?" I ask, recalling what tía Ines told Sam and me about the cameras not working. Even if they were, it's worth it. I don't even care if I get kicked out of the haven. If we can offer a solution to those who have none, perhaps Rico doesn't have to do what he thinks he needs to.

"Okay," she finally says, though something gnaws at my belly. She wouldn't betray us, would she? Tell our plan to her mom?

When Willa doesn't say anything more, I add in, "And we can't tell tía Ines about this. Let's try to make it work . . . for those stuck in the Wasteland. This is how you ease your guilt, Willa."

"Okay," Willa says again, more confidently, her face softening until she's wearing her usual enthusiastic expression. "Let's do it!"

We spend another hour collecting and compiling information about 3D printers into Sam's tablet, which tía Ines let us take home from Burberry's.

By the time we're done, we've forgotten all about the grilled cheeses, but Sam's created a plan for us and a list of items we need to be on the lookout for to create a reliable 3D printer: aluminum, blind joints, a kinematic system, sensors, motors, wiring, a drive system, and too many other things I have no idea about but Rico will. I also take their measurements, which'll be helpful in sewing the first two protective suits.

Two hours later, we're lying in a now-more-cleaned-up area of Sam's living room, finally eating our microwaved grilled cheeses and also some strawberries Sam bought from a market. They taste like pure magic, and I sneak two into my pocket to take to Rico.

We stare out Sam's window. For once, the city is dark enough, and the Masterdome's shield is clear enough, that we can see the stars above. They remind me of how insignificant we are in the vastness of an entire universe.

We're truly the only ones who can save ourselves.

The ones who can save everyone outside the Masterdome.

When I enter my apartment, Rico is standing by the kitchen counter, six bowls of cereal in front of him. I laugh out loud at the absurdity.

"Did you know you have all these?" he asks, picking up one of the boxes and shaking it.

"Yeah, but I hadn't really gotten the chance to eat any of them," I reply, smiling through my tiredness. I set down the two books I've borrowed from Sam to show Rico.

Rico ignores the books and goes to the living room coffee

table, where he grabs a bouquet of colorful wildflowers and hands them to me.

"You got me flowers?" I ask, a smile wide on my face.

"And they're as beautiful as you are," he replies, kissing my cheek.

"Thank you, mi amor."

After I've placed the flowers in a drinking cup full of water, Rico slides a bowl of small brown beads my way. I take a bite, the chocolate flavor blissful, the coolness of the milk beyond delicious. "Oh, that's good," I mumble through a mouthful.

"Try this one next," Rico says, then proceeds to feed me a spoonful of each cereal like I'm a baby. My personal favorite turns out to be small square bites topped with cinnamon and sugar that Lucas, my middle brother, would have loved. Rico's favorite is Choco Pebbles, which he has two whole bowls of.

After eating what I'm sure Crystal/Krista would say is way too much, we slump down on the couch.

Suddenly, being this close to him, doing something so normal, overwhelms me with emotion. My throat turns heavy like there's something stuck that I can't get down. I sit in his lap and hug him around the neck. He wraps his arms around my torso.

When I've had my fill, I let go and search his body over. He's okay . . . besides the darkening bruise around his hurt eye.

He touches the spot gingerly, as if the memory is painful. "It'll heal," he says.

"Where'd you go today?" I finally ask.

He exhales loudly, so I already know I'm not going to like the answer before he finally lets out, "I'm sorry I didn't leave a note. Thought I'd be back sooner. I found Viola Hershall . . . or more like she found me."

I lean back. "Well, what does she want from you?"

Rico shrugs. "She wants me to lie low for the weekend, and I'm supposed to report back to her for next steps on Monday. How did it go with your aunt today?"

What I learned comes back to me with a jolt. "Rico!" I hit him on the shoulder as hard as I can with my free hand. He flinches, laughs, waiting for me to go on. "Why didn't you tell me?"

"What?"

"That President Burberry has Sidra, of course."

He sulks. "You saw her?"

"Tía Ines took me to Burberry's mansion in the woods. Sidra was there."

"I'm sorry I didn't mention it yesterday—"

"You keep saying you're sorry for things."

He runs his hand through his hair. "Well, I am. I don't want to drag you further into this, but if that's true, perhaps you're our in—the way we'll get Sidra away from Burberry. You can give me the lay of the mansion."

I shake my head. "Sidra's happy there, Rico. What if you're wrong? And what if the Sheriff was lying and all he's trying to do is take Sidra from Burberry to blackmail *her* instead?"

"We don't have a choice," Rico replies, eyebrows knit together. "If we don't do what the Sheriff wants, he'll have

Viola Hershall's people murder us. Some deputies and representatives are under her thumb."

I don't answer for a moment. Everything is so complicated. I don't want Rico to take Sidra from a happy situation, but I also don't want to get in the way of our own survival.

Why can't we have a third choice? Our choice.

I stand and grab the two books from Sam and pass them over.

"What are these?"

"*My* plan," I reply, and the way the words hit makes me choke up. Why do I need a plan separate from Rico's?

Rico scans the books, one of which is titled *Spigots of the World* and the other *The A to Z of 3D Printers*. "Even if the people of the Wasteland had water, it wouldn't stop the sun from killing them all."

I say, "That's where I come in. This city has all the fabric I need to create protective suits. I can help protect people in the Wasteland. I think we can persuade Burberry to let us use the skills that we have to aid—"

"You're talking like we have all the time in the world," he says, then his shoulders drop the way they do when he's sad. I hate it. I don't want to pile on to his stress. "We should follow the Sheriff's plan and make our lives easy."

"Easy? What about following the plan to take over the haven by force sounds easy? You're talking about starting a war."

"If it means that you and I survive at the end of it, I'm okay with that."

"I don't believe you. Maybe we could avoid fighting by showing the people of the Wasteland that they don't need the Oasis to survive?"

"And I'm sure President Burberry is going to let you do this out of the kindness of her heart."

"She might," I say, and I hate the way Rico looks at me as if I'm being naive. "And if not, we'll hide it."

There's a part of me that understands his point of view. I want to live just as much as he does. I want both of us to get a chance to live out our dream permanently. But haven't we seen enough death?

I breathe deep. "Okay, let's pause on this topic. Do you want to get out of here for a while?" I finally ask him, knowing that he's not going to buy into whatever I say to him about my plan. So I'll proceed the way I want, like he will with his own plan, and maybe we can meet in the middle. Whether Sheriff Ramos or President Burberry wins, something tells me that those who need help the most in the Wasteland will be forgotten either way.

He laughs a little. "And go where? You think it's wise to be seen with me?"

"Who cares about wise when we have a whole haven to explore?" There's a *while we can* on the edge of my mouth, but instead I say, "Besides, it's late. And I'm assuming your camouflage is working given you're still here. I actually know a trick to take off my key fob, so no one will know I'm gone."

Part of me expects Rico to say no. Out in the Wasteland, we were never spontaneous, never adventurous. Especially

Rico, who always seemed to plan our next steps and to be worried all the time. We had to survive, so that's what we focused on.

To my surprise, Rico shoots up to his feet, and even though his gaze is tired, he holds out his hand to me, which I take, laughing. We get ready. Rico washes his face, lingering on the warm water for a while and letting it simply fall through his hands. I watch him at the door, leaning my head against the doorframe and taking him in before I get into the only dress I have in my closet. At least for now, because tomorrow I plan to spend the entire day shopping. We look completely different than we did just a few days ago, and I can't believe this is really us, really happening.

We take off my key fob using the device that Rodrick gave me and lay it on my pillow to prevent tía Ines from tracking me. He says to not worry about his, so we leave it on, and we head down the fire escape. We walk hand in hand into the streets.

It's loud, of course, like every night is in this strange paradise. We tried to not call attention to ourselves out in the Wasteland. Here we do the same, not out of necessity or fear, but being so out of place we'd rather stay quiet. The city blocks are filled with people. There's a large group of women; one of them wears a sash that says *Bride to Be*. She's a little tipsy and giggling uncontrollably. And so we laugh with them. There's a band, rocking out in the middle of the square, and I can't help but think about the musicians who played at the welcome party. What must it be like to play with real instruments instead of the ones made of random materials, like in the Wasteland?

Rico must follow my train of thought because he says, "It really is something else inside the haven."

We continue aimlessly, not really knowing where we're going or having any sort of plan. But we still have his key fob and therefore an unlimited amount of ghost money apparently, which tops my $10,000, and so we finally stop at a place called Vicki's Ice Cream Parlor.

We stand stock-still, staring through the large window at couples and kids out way past their bedtimes, getting scoops and sundaes. In a trance, we don't move until a boy points at us and calls us weird before being whisked away by his parent, and it's in this moment, I wonder: Is the city filled with orphans like us and kids like Sidra? Have they all been adopted by other adults after winning the lottery?

"Shall we?" Rico signals me to the door. He holds it open. As we enter, the smell of sweetness invades my nose, and my mouth waters. My little brother, Antonio, would have loved the sugary treat. I fight not to think of him as I take in the smiling people and the workers giving everyone samples of the different flavors.

When it's our turn, we order an ice cream sundae with a scoop each of mint chocolate chip, pumpkin spice, and chocolate. The server puts whipped cream on top, along with multicolored sprinkles and cherries that are so red, they remind me of the color of blood. I don't take my eyes off it, and when it's ready, I hold the dessert in my hands like it's a baby.

Rico and I find a seat outside and don't hesitate to dig in.

I've never seen him smile this big. I fear his cheeks will hurt.

"Photograph?" a man says, approaching our table and holding out some kind of camera.

I nod quickly before Rico can say no.

We lean into the table and grin widely, then the man snaps the photograph. When a small image is ejected from the camera, the man hands it to us.

"Give it a few minutes," he says with a wink, and goes off to ask a couple seated at the next table.

The image has already started to change, and I wait patiently until Rico and I appear. I can't help but marvel at the fact that we look so ordinary.

"We're the cutest," Rico says, taking claim of the photo until I tickle him enough that he has to let it go to protect himself.

I don't want to be stuck in the middle of some war between Sheriff Ramos and President Burberry. I want to be free. I want to eat ice cream every day.

As I sit with the one person I love more than life itself, I know I need to focus my energy on making that happen for us. But this weekend, neither Rico nor I owe anyone our time, so I plan to spend every second with him.

CHAPTER 14
Jules

It's wild how quickly you can get used to living in a new place. But I guess paradise makes it easier.

"How much do you have to spend again?" Rico asks as we head to the shopping district by train.

"A little less than nine *thousand* dollars," I reply, and take his hand, intertwining our fingers. "I've only bought the sewing machine, protective-suit supplies, and some snacks so far."

He whistles as his eyes scan the train we're on for the fiftieth time. I'm not sure if he's being vigilant out of habit or is admiring the technology that makes the train zoom down the tracks.

"And I'm expected to use a good amount of it, so be prepared to carry a lot of bags," I say, calling his attention to me as I crack my knuckles and grin.

When the train arrives at our stop, I stand, anxious to make my way to the exit. Rico pulls me back when I press my nose up against the window of the door. "Be careful," he says.

I take his hand and tug him out as soon as the train comes to a full stop and the doors open.

The shopping district covers a few crowded blocks with all kinds of wares being advertised in neon lettering. Where the buildings of San Francisco were vacant and falling apart, here they're shimmering multistory buildings that promise a new you, a better you. There're nail salons and hair stylists and everything else you'd need to be taken care of.

"Where do we start?" Rico asks, face a little pale.

"Everywhere!" I reply, my voice an octave too high because this is everything I've never allowed myself to dream of.

I point to a shop called Retroland—A Vintage Clothing Store and pull Rico its way. Inside, cool air blows against my cheeks.

"Hi! Welcome in," a man in a sleek velvet suit says. "What can I help you— Oh my God! You're one of the new lottery winners!" He squeals and takes both of my hands in his.

I laugh and exchange a look with Rico. "Yeah," I say.

"Okay, you *have* to let me help you shop." He squeals again and finally lets go. He takes my arm and drags me down one of the ten aisles of clothing. He shimmies. "My name's Heath, and you've come to the perfect place if you still want to feel like you're home but obviously be dressed in clothing that's a little more . . . chic."

For over an hour, Heath picks out clothing for me to try on. Shirts in bright cerulean and lime green, constructed out of fabrics other than linen, like chiffon and nylon. Dresses I would never in a million years wear outside in the scorching sun back in San Francisco. Some of the clothes are clearly used. Others are practically new.

Today is about having fun and assimilating, so even though shopping is a foreign concept to me—considering in the Wasteland, you shop from the dead—I try my best to do it with no remorse.

The AC kicks up in the building, and a cool breeze descends on me, sending chills down my spine as my sweat dries.

"We don't get in as much clothing as we used to," Heath chitchats. "But we make do. And since I'm the vintage store in the city, I get all of the good old stuff."

When my arms are full and burning from carrying all the articles of clothing, Heath leads me to a dressing room, Rico trailing behind us, a massive grin plastered on his handsome face.

I tug on every piece, and Rico and Heath give me a thumbs-up or -down as I exit the dressing room, pulling the drapes to one side in an exaggerated movement.

I come out in a plain white sundress next, and when I do, they both still.

"What?" I check the dress, trying to figure out if there's a stain on it.

"You're beautiful," Rico replies, staring at me as if I'm the only thing in the entire world.

I go up to him and hug him tightly.

"You two are too cute," Heath says. "I can't believe you

found someone within a week. Here I am thirty years into living in the Oasis and am fully prepared to be a bachelor until my last day."

Suddenly, it occurs to me that Heath might blab about it to someone. "We knew each other from before," I say, which isn't really a lie so much as an omission. "If you don't share it with anyone, I'd appreciate it. I haven't wanted to draw attention."

He raises his hand, places it over his heart. "Say no more. Now, why don't we go ring you up?"

Three hundred and forty-nine dollars later, I leave Retroland wearing the sundress and carrying a bag with two pairs of jeans, a gold-sequined tank top, and a printed T-shirt of a band from the Old Epoch.

"Well, that didn't really make a dent in the remainder of my ten thousand dollars," I say.

"Why don't we go there?" Rico asks, pointing to a store where the window is filled with all kinds of jewelry, from pearl earrings to sapphire rings to watches that likely cost way more than I have left.

I follow Rico across the way, fully prepared to dodge the people walking toward us lest they aim to take what we have. I always needed to stay ready in the Wasteland. Here, though, the people simply pass us.

Rico holds the door open for me, and I go inside.

This time nobody comes to greet us because the worker is helping a woman adorned with more jewelry than I've ever seen on someone.

Rico and I split up as we gawk at all the display cases.

I stare longingly at a monarch butterfly brooch with a $5,000 price tag on it. Mami used to have one like that. It's buried with her. I'll have to come back for it next month when tía Ines has said we'll get another $10,000.

When I search for him, Rico hasn't moved from the same spot.

I approach the counter he's glued to. "You find something?" I ask, tone playful.

When he doesn't reply, I follow his eyeline down, down, down, until I see what's there.

The ring we found. Just like the books, the ring made it here. And the price tag?

Ten thousand dollars . . . I recall what Sheriff Ramos's deputy said at the Sheriff's Station when we took the ring to trade. He said it was only worth one extra lottery ticket. Anger boils and bubbles within me in a way I hadn't felt even before the encounter with the deputy.

Done with the customer, the worker approaches us. The earrings she's wearing shimmer like diamonds, and I wonder if they came from the Wasteland, too. If they were also worth one lottery ticket. "That one caught your eye? We got it in the other day," she cheerfully tells us, obviously not reading our demeanor. "It's a gorgeous ring."

"We'll take it," Rico says with no hesitation.

The woman is left almost speechless, but grins and takes out the ring from beneath the case.

"Want to make sure it fits?" she asks.

I stick my hand out, and she slips the ring onto my finger effortlessly.

"Guess it was meant to be," she adds in.

"Guess so," I murmur.

Rico pays using his key fob, and he really must have an endless supply of funds since the payment goes through without a hiccup.

"Do you need a box?"

"She'll wear it out," Rico replies, tone cold.

The worker clears her throat and nods. "You kids enjoy."

And we leave, wordlessly, unable to express how odd it is that the items we scavenged are being sold for a ludicrous amount of money.

"I think I'm through shopping," I say when the door to the store closes behind us.

"Now do you see?" he asks with a sigh as we weave through the crowd again, toward the train station.

"See what?"

"Why this place needs change." His eyes are so focused, his body rigid. I don't know what to say. I still can't imagine a different world, nor do I want to imagine one without my aunt or the friends I've made here. And I don't see how this place changes without something happening to President Burberry and my tía, given that they've had many opportunities to help the Wasteland and they haven't.

I don't reply, but he's staring at the ring when he asks, "Can I see it?"

I nod, slipping the ring off my finger and handing it to him.

And then he does it again—he gets down on one knee.

A small crowd wearing metallics and sequins begins to

form, pointing and chattering happily at us. But Rico's eyes are only on me. His love mine alone.

"I love you." It's not a confession, yet the words hold so much emotion behind them. "I have since the moment I met you. I don't know what will happen to us. I don't know anything, really. But . . . Juliana, will you marry me?"

Tears brim my eyes, slip onto my cheeks. I chuckle as I wipe them away, recalling what I told him: *I'd say yes in the Oasis.*

"Yes. Okay. We figure a way out of the chaos, and we get married," I reply. I'm not even finished talking when he's up and hugging me so tight it's hard to breathe.

He whispers into my ear, "In this lifetime, and every lifetime after, I'll love you. I promise."

The crowd cheers and whistles, and that terrible rage that filled me at seeing the ring for sale goes away.

He lets go and slips the ring back on, then kisses me. His lips taste like paradise, like home.

Another round of clapping erupts around us as onlookers celebrate. They bring us back to the moment, to our current location. My cheeks flush, and even Rico's redden.

Holding hands, we keep walking to the train station. Side by side, juntos, we get onto the train.

"Hey, Juliana!" a voice comes suddenly.

It's Rodrick, walking to me. Instinctively, I try to move away from Rico, to hide him, but everyone is so close together, it's practically impossible.

Through my periphery, I take note that Rico has already turned around, though, and pretends to pay us no attention.

"You finally went shopping," he says, flicking his chin at the bag on the train-car floor between my feet and Rico's.

"Yeah," I say.

"Nice! And look at that ring!" he replies. "That's a great find! Been searching for one for Willa for a while but saving up isn't always easy."

I raise an eyebrow. "You don't get ten thousand dollars a month?"

He laughs. "I think your aunt is giving you and Sam special treatment, which is okay. You both earned it out in No Man's Land. But no, we don't all get that much. One thousand dollars a month. Between Pop and me. Most of which goes to food."

I nod, guilt writhing in me. It occurs to me that I won't have an explanation for my aunt as to how in the world I could afford the ring, and how the credits didn't vanish from my key fob, so I say, "It's not real or anything, just costume jewelry that reminds me of something I found once in the Wasteland. So I had to get it."

He must see something in my expression because his face turns serious. I fight not to shift to Rico, thinking I've been caught in my lie.

"I know it's been hard to acclimate," Rodrick says to my surprise. "But I want you to know how much we've enjoyed getting to know you."

"I appreciate that."

"Been able to talk to your boy any more?" he asks.

If he knew. "A little bit," I say instead of the truth, and fight off a smirk.

“He okay?”

I shrug. “He’s fine. Trying to figure out the world like the rest of us.”

Rodrick nods like he fully understands.

“Well, I’m on my way to see Willa, if you don’t mind the company home. And as long as you’re not going to do any more shopping. Which you should do, though. Lots of.”

I laugh. Shopping is the last thing I want to do at this point, but I can’t complain when Rico made things better like he always does. I’m a freaking fiancée now, after all. “Company would be amazing,” I reply.

When we come to the next stop, I watch Rico leave the train without a second glance back, taking my heart with him.

CHAPTER 15
Rico

"Didn't think we'd see you again till Monday," Jesus says, standing by the row of pods leading into an area that Viola has sworn is a safe zone for her and her revolutionaries.

"I got anxious," I reply as I get off the motorcycle that I discovered I could rent from the South Shore's train station. I set the helmet on the seat and try to sidestep Jesus, even though it is a relief to see him all right.

He grabs my shoulder, nails digging into my skin through my iridescent shirt.

"Well, you arrived just in time to come with me to deliver these," he says, holding out an array of small disks.

"What're they?" I ask, tone annoyed considering that the sun is going to set in a couple of hours. I'm exhausted from walking around with Jules. All I want to do is make sure Nadine is doing okay, and maybe see if there's some place to take a nap before heading back to Jules's apartment.

"Three messages we're going to deliver, Cuz," Jesus says,

too cheerily for my liking. He turns my body around to face the pods.

"And what if I'm not in the mood to work?"

"Viola's made me a promise—I do this, and the next job we have is freeing Amá. I could use the backup."

I sigh, touch my face, which makes my still-healing eyebrow twitch.

"What about Nadine?" I ask.

"She's doing something else."

"You think it's smart to leave her?"

"You think it's smart to tell Nadine she can't or shouldn't do whatever she wants?"

I pause. "Fine. As long as she's safe, let's do this quick," I tell him.

Jesus leads us to the very last pod in the row. Inside, its fresh leather smell takes me by surprise. The navigation screen lights up, and the radio turns on to heavy metal music. I turn it down so it becomes background noise.

"Where's our first stop?" I lean back into the passenger side, the seat reclining with me.

"A place called Club Oro," he replies, typing some coordinates into the pod's navigation screen.

The drive is strangely quiet and calm.

"You and Jules get into a fight?" Jesus asks after a while.

I grunt since I'm not about to tell Jesus that Jules and I are officially engaged. My relationship with Jules is the last thing I think Jesus cares about or that I want to talk of. I don't open my eyes as I reply, "I thought it'd be different here."

"Paradise isn't always paradise when you're living with baggage. People here pretend that the past didn't happen. After everything we've seen, been through, after everything my amá taught us, this type of ignorance is equivalent to hell."

I look over at him now. I hate how if there's one person who gets me more than Jules, it's my cousin. The most beautiful girl in the entire world, who I love more than life itself, just said she would spend the rest of her life with me. I should be thrilled, celebrating with her, but all I can think is that I have no idea how long we have together.

The pod parks us around the corner from the club before I can reply. Jesus gets out, and I follow.

A line of people wraps all the way around the square-shaped warehouse building.

"This is going to take all night," I moan.

Jesus grins at me as if I'm a chump.

"C'mon, Cuz, get your mind right," he says. I trail him to the very front, ignoring the ugly stares from those we pass.

"We're here to see Marisol," Jesus tells the guard at the door.

The guard stares us down, lips tight. "Password?"

"Violeta," Jesus says, tone bored.

The guard's eyebrows quirk up in surprise, but he nods and lets us through. As we enter, the people behind us make disgruntled groans that I know Jesus is way too smug about.

Inside Club Oro, it's impossible to hear over music I haven't listened to since I was a kid: synthpop. It blares from speakers near the two women who stand at a platform—DJs dressed in long iridescent dresses, crowns that shimmer red on their heads, their nails long and painted gold, visible even from here.

"Which one are we here to see?" I ask.

Jesus points toward the DJs and heads straight to the bar. "Both of them. Let's wait until they take a break."

"Drinks?" someone behind the bar asks.

"Please. Whatever you recommend," Jesus replies, with a toothy smile that makes the bartender blush.

"Now who has to get their head in the game?" I mumble.

Jesus shrugs, and once the bartender comes back with our drinks, he turns to watch the DJs at work. They're as captivating as the music they create. Angelic in the way where you can't take your eyes off them.

"I was expecting these to give us a buzz," he says, taking a gulp of his drink and looking a bit disappointed. "It's some fancy soda."

I eye my cup with interest now, pick it up, and take a long sip.

It tastes like cherry cola, something else I haven't experienced since I was maybe six.

After ten songs and too many drinks later, the DJs finally take a break.

"Let's go," I say, rapidly scanning my key fob against a payment station set up at the bar to pay our bill. We follow the DJs into the back of the building, into a hallway where it's only the four of us.

"VIOLETA!" Jesus calls out. The word makes the pair turn around. As he raises his voice, my hand goes to my neck, to the burn marks that will never fade. He screamed that night, too—he'd been so angry that I'd chosen to leave. It's hard to cope with the memory, with how much hurt was in his voice, and how much agony it brings me now.

The DJs approach with no hesitation.

One of them holds out her hand. Jesus places one of the small metal disks containing the messages onto her palm. Without another word, they turn and continue on their way as if they never ran into us.

I could throw up from the uncertainty of this encounter.

What do the messages say? Are they battle orders? Are we going to war soon, like Jules thinks? Does Jesus know, and would he tell me the truth if I asked?

We weave through people who continue to dance. The guard gives us a slight nod as we leave the club and return to the pod.

"Where to next?" I ask once we're back in the vehicle.

"Already put the address into the pod. You're going to love it."

The pod comes to an abrupt stop in the middle of the road. I bump my head on the side window, eyebrow and eye hurting.

"What in the world—" I say as I look around.

The pod starts up again as fast as it stalled.

"That was weird," Jesus says, shrugging. You would think he'd care more about what happened, given that tía Linda taught us all about system glitches, some of which we were planning to enact ourselves once we broke into the haven.

And when the pod comes to a stop a couple of minutes after in front of a store called A Seat at the Table Books, he exits without another word about it.

A small bell dings as soon as we enter. The bookstore has a few stray folks inside, but we go straight to the cash register and wait for the person behind the counter to stop reading. "Arden?" Jesus asks.

Arden glances up and responds, "Yes?"

Jesus slides the message across the counter, and Arden doesn't verbally acknowledge it but covers the disk with a hand and says, "Take a book on me."

Jesus walks out without grabbing anything, but I reach onto one of the shelves and pull off a book I think Jules will enjoy, with a warrior girl in a mask illustrated on the front, a hidden hero, like we'll be at the end of this. Hopefully.

Jesus and I don't talk as we ride to our final location. Along the way, we see several of Burberry's deputies climb out of four black pods before they enter a squat building. Moments later, they're pulling a man out of the building, head covered by a black cloth. Jesus and I look at each other but we don't stop until we head out of the city center and onto a secluded forest road. "Now what?" I ask when Jesus tells the pod to park in front of a grove of giant redwoods.

"The next message is for us," he responds. Jesus twirls the circular disk in between his fingers for a bit longer. It looks like a compact mirror. He finally pinches the device at its center. It clicks and Viola Hershall's voice rings out.

"My dearest revolutionaries, the time has come. As I

speak, things are moving into place. We're but a mere ten days away from the start of a Third Epoch. So prepare and be ready."

"What does she mean?"

"She means that the Sheriff is coming," Jesus replies with a smile. "She means it's time for us to take over the Oasis." If the Sheriff is coming, that means we're closer to the endgame than I thought.

"What about Jules?" I say out loud.

"Cuz, what about Amá and her dream? What about our destiny? I think you need to choose, right now, right here. Will you throw away who you're meant to be for a girl?"

There are so many things I could say. So much I could scream. But I hold no cards, zero.

I don't know what'll happen in ten days, but I know that Jules and I need to be on the same page before anything does. First, though, I need to free my aunt. Jules, I know is safe. But tía Linda has likely been starved and needs our immediate help.

"We have one last stop," Jesus tells me as we drive back toward the city shopping center. We cross the exact spot where I proposed to Juliana and head to a closed department store. Jesus holds his key fob to the scanner.

The door unlocks. To my surprise, upon walking through the door, there's a stairway instead of an open floor. We travel down three flights of stairs, the lights turning on as our movement triggers them.

"No way," Jesus says when a train comes into view. "Burberry really likes her secrets, huh?"

"What are we doing here?" I ask.

"We're sending Sheriff Ramos's ride down the mountain so he can break in."

The two of us exchange a knowing smile. We're really doing this. In a day, I've managed to get engaged and set in motion a revolution. And suddenly, it doesn't scare me. It's liberating.

Jules is going to be so angry at me, but I follow Jesus anyway as he boards the driving compartment and settles into the conductor's chair. I exhale as I take in the strange mechanisms. I manage to turn the train on with the push of a bright blue button.

I enter several commands, then figure out how to set the train on a ten-minute delay to head back to the station in San Francisco. We don't leave the station until we've watched the train steadily roll down a dark tunnel, off to pick up Sheriff Ramos and bring him to victory.

CHAPTER 16
Jules

Rodrick and I walk in a comfortable silence from the train station to my apartment.

"You sure you're okay?" he asks when the building's in sight.

I shrug in a less-than-convincing manner.

"Do you ever wish you hadn't won the lottery?" I ask, immediately wanting to retract the question, recalling the way I'd seemed ungrateful at my welcome party and how it hadn't been taken well.

But he chuckles and seems relieved that that's all I've got on my mind. "You and I actually have a lot in common," he starts, slowing down. "I didn't win my lottery either—my biopop did. I think most kids who are let in don't. It's their parents, or their grandparents, or simply a guardian outside. My win was a gift like yours was."

I still for a moment. "Willa told you what I said to her?"

He shrugs like it's no big deal that my cousin's blurting

out all my secrets. "Don't be upset; she tells me everything. She won't tell anyone else and neither will I."

"Can I hold you to that?" I ask.

His expression falls as if the sincerity of my question hurts him.

"I risked my life to get you here, risked my pop's career to help you talk to your boyfriend. I didn't have to. But Willa and I believe in the lottery and what it means to give people of the Wasteland a chance to live in the haven. I've never taken it for granted. Maybe we're not perfect. Maybe saving your life in San Francisco wasn't enough for you to trust me. But I'll earn your trust. You'll see. Meanwhile, you okay taking a detour?"

I eye him suspiciously, unsure if I want to say yes. But the idea of going home makes my belly recoil when on Monday I start my job at Burberry's, where I'll have to act as a double agent.

"If you promise that you're not taking me into the woods to murder me," I say, even though I follow him as he turns left.

He laughs, says, "Taking you to a surprise. Now, c'mon before it gets too late."

Rodrick leads us away from the foot-trafficked area to where there's a parking lot with two small rows of motorcycles. He scans his key fob next to a tablet on a pedestal near them. One of the motorcycles comes to life as soon as he does.

He passes me one of the helmets he takes from a glass box next to the motorcycle.

"I'm not going to die, am I?" I ask, the vehicle roaring.

His face turns stern. "I've only crashed seriously like three times, but I like to think the metal in my head helps during a fight."

After a moment, we both burst out laughing.

We get on the bike, and I'm barely on before Rodrick skyrockets us past signs and people, onto the winding roads similar to the one Sam and I took to get to Burberry's.

The world is a blur as we go, and I hold on tight as the trees become nothing but a line of green.

After about fifteen minutes, we stop at a sign that reads *Hiking Trail—Northern Entomology Loop.*

"I think I went on a hike once, when I was like seven," I tell him, glancing down at my clean sneakers with a frown.

"I promise it'll be worth it," he says, not minding his own clean shoes.

We hike down the trail, the sun above us beginning its descent.

After what must be two miles, we reach a clearing surrounded by trees that have been decorated with what look like forty award ribbons with names on them.

Rodrick pulls out a ribbon from his pocket. I approach as he pins it to one of the trees.

The name *Gregory* has been embroidered on the ribbon. It's the name of the representative Rodrick and Willa said was their mentor, the one who died with the other winner on the way to the Oasis.

"It's my way of honoring the representatives who have died since I became one."

"There've been so many," I say and place my hand on Rodrick's shoulder.

"Yeah. But at least I get to remember them in someplace beautiful."

He turns around with his arms wide open, and I don't know why he's so excited, considering he's doing something so sad, until a shift in the brush startles what must be a thousand butterflies of all types. I've never been inside a forest, so nature is surprising to me. The trees are singing giants, whooshing in the wind of the evening. The rocks are warm to the touch and covered in bright, spongy, and soft moss. The trees grew hot during the day and now release a perfumed smell I'll never get enough of.

"I love it," I tell him, grateful he invited me to this special location.

Rodrick sits down in the middle of the open space. I join him. And for a while, we're silent as the butterflies circle the grove. As it gets darker, I note that the butterflies begin to glow a soft pink.

"One day soon, things will be different," Rodrick says. "And we'll enter a Third Epoch, one built for everyone."

Before I can respond and ask him what he's talking about, a flickering above catches my attention.

"The dome's been doing that a lot lately," I say instead.

"What?" Rodrick asks.

I point behind his ear, to where the Masterdome still seems to be glitching out.

"Never seen that before," he replies, concentrating on the

spot. "I'll have to tell my pop about it. Seems like it's been harder to fix glitches lately. I don't know why."

I swallow. "There couldn't be something wrong with the Masterdome, right?"

He shakes his head. "It was built to last forever."

"According to whom?" I murmur.

"All the Burberrys," he replies. "There're glitches sometimes. Nothing's perfect."

I'm unconvinced.

We stand in the butterfly grove until it's hard to see in the dark, then make our way down the trail.

As we get close to the entrance, Rodrick suddenly pulls me to the ground.

"What is it?" I whisper.

He points into the brush, to where three deputies in glow-in-the-dark protective suits head deeper into the forest. I note the great design idea for later and focus on staying quiet.

"They're going to repair the glitch," Rodrick says. "Let's go before they see us. They don't like young people coming here."

I hurry after Rodrick, crouched down, until we're far enough away that we can stand upright again.

We ride the motorcycle home.

"Thanks for today," I tell Rodrick as we enter the elevator. "Who knew I really needed a hike?"

"Willa and I are here for you anytime, Jules. I mean it. I'll see you later," he replies when I get off. He heads up to go see Willa.

Inside my apartment, it's quiet, but that's a sound I now welcome. I get out of my clothes and into pajamas, brush my teeth and my hair, and lie in bed with the light on, waiting for Rico but managing to not think about him. I don't think of anything. I focus on my breathing, meditating the way Mami used to. I picture the butterflies, the flurry of magic in the forest.

The static from my radio brings me back. "Jules?" Rico says, his voice low as if he's afraid of being heard.

I pick up the radio from the kitchen counter and turn it on. "I'm sorry I took so long to get home if you were looking to get in."

"You're okay," he says. "I'm actually at Viola's. She thinks it's almost time to break tía Linda out of wherever they're keeping her. It may be a few hours or a few days before I see you again, okay? But I need to stay here for now."

"What? I thought we still had tomorrow. Will you be safe?"

"I know. I'm sorry. But I'll be fine," he says in the most unconvincing tone of voice ever. "I don't want you to worry about me."

"I'll never stop worrying about you. Are Jesus and Nadine going with you?" I ask, because even though I don't like the idea that he's spending time with his ex, if it means he'll come home to me in one piece, I'll take it.

"Yeah, it's the three of us." Before I can try to change his mind, he says, "I gotta go, but I love you—you know that, right?"

"Always," I respond. "I love you, too. Call me when it's over."

"I will," he says. "And, Jules?"

"Yeah?" I ask.

He pauses, as if he's scared of telling me. He takes a long sigh before he continues, "Something might happen soon."

"Like what?" I say, hand over my mouth.

"I don't know exactly," he replies, though something tells me he does. He doesn't want to confide in me. Or he wants to protect me for as long as possible. "Stay alert and prepare to run. Viola sent a message to some of her people to be ready in ten days."

I nod to the radio as if he can see me.

"Okay" is all I say.

But I want to swear. I want to scream. And now all I can think of is *my* plan, and how to make it happen even though I can barely think straight.

CHAPTER 17

Jules

Seven Days Later

"You're already getting better," I say to Sidra when she solves a maze in under thirty seconds on a piece of paper she received as homework from her virtual tutor. I hold my hand up for a high five. She slams it happily and closes her school notebook for the day, thank the Oasis for that.

Sometimes I hate being at Burberry's mansion as much as working the Scar because being around Sidra only makes me think of all the kids we left behind in the Wasteland. Especially since I have been asked to work on a Saturday, when even Willa and Rodrick seem to be resting, and haven't gotten a mental break. But on days like these when she hasn't stopped smiling since I got here, I can't imagine doing anything else. And part of me is terrified of getting too used to the comfort of luxury living.

I face the forest, staring out the massive window from the couch in the living room. The Oasis is paradise, beautiful and peaceful. But every day, I imagine that something terrible will happen because of something that Rico and Viola Hershall and Sheriff Ramos have done. Rico hasn't returned to my apartment in the past week, and the only time I hear from him is in the evenings when he checks in to tell me that he's still alive and needs more time. And to remind me that I need to stay on high alert.

Every day, after work, I spend the evenings sewing until my fingers hurt. But I've managed to construct six protective suits and am close to finishing a seventh. From the materials I have, I might be able to put two or three more together.

"Jules, tell me a story," Sidra pleads now, bringing me back to the moment, dragging my thoughts away from Rico. "I'm so over doing homework." She feigns fainting, and I catch her in my arms and proceed to tickle her. She collapses onto the floor laughing.

Before I can reply, Paul and Sam enter. I haven't gotten used to seeing Sam dressed as a deputy. The sleek suit. The badge. The slicked-back hair. At least we get to be around each other. At least I'm not the only one working this Saturday.

"I'm going to go run an errand," Paul says. He gives Sidra a tight squeeze when she skips up to the man and hugs him. "But Sam will be here."

He sends me a small salute and smile, which I return. Sidra rejoins me on the couch and leans her head against my shoulder.

Sam makes his way over to us the moment the front door clicks closed. He carries a leather notebook that he keeps with him at all times and that I know contains a list of all the parts we still need to find for our 3D printer. He sits with us, and the three of us end up with our legs and arms intertwined. Sidra laughs uncontrollably. The sound reminds me of my brother Antonio's laugh. Infectious. From the belly.

Don't cry, I tell myself as I turn toward the window again. A monarch butterfly dances among the trees, dark orange and black, and I focus on it until I stop wanting to burst into tears. Until Antonio's smile fades from my memory, until the sound of his final breath vanishes, and I can take in air again. I might not have my family, but right now, at least I have butterflies.

"Jules is spaced out. Will *you* tell me a story?" Sidra asks Sam.

"Have I told you about the time I stole a horse and almost rode to Nevada?" he asks, drawing my attention.

"No, and as fabulous as I'm sure that adventure was, I want you to tell me about the people outside the Masterdome. The ones who have tried to break in. All the things my mom would be pissed if you told me." She smirks.

"Why do you want to hear about the revolution? It's part of the past," Sam questions.

I hadn't ever heard what Rico and his aunt did—or tried to do—called a revolution.

Of course, when it happened, everyone outside the Oasis knew about it. I remember the way Mami's eyes gleamed when she heard news that Mictlān had possibly made it in, and the way she visibly shrank when she found out they'd failed and that the woman she'd so admired had fallen. She died shortly afterward, as if Mictlān's failure had sped up her decline.

A year after, I met Rico and he told me intimate details about his tía Linda, and Mictlān, and what had occurred.

Sidra shrugs. "It's going to happen again. One day, when things are desperate in the lower isolation cities, another group will be at the entrance of the Masterdome, and we'll have to defend ourselves. My mom says I should learn as much as I can of our history and how the haven was built. That it's the most important subject I'll ever learn. She says most people ignore it and don't learn anything from the past. But she also only tells me certain things about the outside, like she wants to protect me from something she can't talk about. I don't know what gives."

"Well, she might be right. History has a way of repeating itself," Sam says. He stares as if asking me to help him veer the conversation in a different direction, one that won't get us into any trouble with Sheriff Paul.

Sidra sits upright and hugs her knees. "From what I've read, wars repeat themselves with different people for different reasons but end the same: thousands dead and one set of victors. I hear Mom and Vice President Ines discussing it. When a new war starts, we might be on the losing side this time, which is why I want to figure out what it takes to win."

"You don't have to worry about these kinds of things. The Masterdome is impenetrable," I tell her, tickling her. She lets out a loud chortle.

Distractions.

We're always trying to keep ourselves distracted from the reality of things here.

I don't tell her about Viola Hershall or about Sheriff Ramos. About the boy who once tried to get inside the Oasis by force and how he made his way in again years later. About how there are things happening that might affect everyone in this city.

I concentrate on what I can change in this moment: Sidra's fear.

And focus on my own tasks: getting what we need for the prototype and sewing protective suits. Things that, despite everything, might change everyone's minds about having to go to war for survival. If Sam and I can make living worthwhile in the Wasteland, there'll be no need for an insurrection.

"How about *you* tell *us* a story?" I ask her, backing off and sitting cross-legged on the couch.

"Have I ever told you two about the island in the middle of the lake?" Sidra asks, catching her breath, her tone excitable.

"Nope," Sam replies, raising his eyebrows at me. I give him a small shrug.

Sidra turns to Sam. "Well, it's haunted. That's why nobody goes out there."

I don't believe in spirits or ghosts. "And whose ghost is haunting this island, exactly?"

"The Mad Scientist. One of the ones who created the spigots that recycle the water at the lake. He was a genius. But he went insane, hence the addition of *mad* to his title."

"Okay, so tell us his story," I say.

"Once upon a time," Sidra starts, "there was a scientist who was brought to the Oasis by my great-grandfather. This scientist was the one who ran a crazy-cool program called Project M. On *that* island. He designed the spigots. He made them work. He wanted a cure-all for diseases. So, for years, he ran his experiments.

"As the years went by, he grew obsessed. He wouldn't sleep. He barely ate. He got older and grew angrier. Anger ate him up inside. Anger took his very soul, until finally—" Sidra claps her hands together, pauses for excitement. "Bam. He went bonkers. Kicked out his helpers. Lived out there by himself doing who knows what and wouldn't let anyone near the facility. By the time my grandpa died and Mom took charge, he'd perished. She went to the island once with seven others. But she's the only one who came back."

"That automatically makes it haunted?" I reply.

She rolls her eyes. "Well, yeah. Duh. The rest of her crew was totally killed by the ghost of the Mad Scientist."

"That doesn't make any sense." I cross my arms. But . . . something occurs to me. If that's where the Mad Scientist designed the spigots—might there still be materials there or schematics that we could use for our printer?

"What if we went to see if his ghost is still there?" I say. Sam tilts his head at me as if I've lost it, until I double tap on his notebook, and his eyes widen. "Is there a way onto the island?"

Sidra perks up, the edges of her lips rising slowly. "I'm not really allowed outside the house without Paul," she says, holding up her hand so we can very much see that she has a fob and is being tracked like us. "Mom says maybe when I'm fifteen I can venture out more. But since I'm twelve, she wants me in the house at all times when I'm not at school. Especially with the recent wave of glitches—she doesn't want anyone to approach me about them. It's happened before. People get scary."

"What if I had a way to remove our fobs?" I ask, knowing all too well how fearful an aggressive crowd can truly be. "Plus, Sam and I would never let anything happen to you."

Sidra eyes Sam and me for a moment, then jumps off the couch and hurries to her room. She returns within minutes dressed in shorts, a long-sleeve shirt covered in sunflowers, sunglasses, and a giant sun hat. She's got her backpack on, ready.

"Let's do this." She reaches into her pocket and pulls out a key card.

"What's that?" Sam asks.

"It's the magic way inside the lab. Took it from my mom's room," Sidra says, smiling from ear to ear. We shouldn't do this. Or I should say, *We need to make sure we don't get caught doing this.*

I walk over to her and rub the sunblock she's haphazardly applied across her face, noting the fact that Sidra was easily able to enter Burberry's room.

"I'm going to run to the restroom and then we can go!" I say, walking toward the corridor to the restroom located near the entryway. I open the door, close it, and tiptoe up the stairs. My heart pounds in my chest as I hurry to Burberry's room.

The door is slightly ajar. I go in quickly and look for—I don't know what. Proof that she's a horrible person?

Her room is almost bare. The drapes at her windows have been pulled closed, but I don't want to touch anything.

I go to her desk and open a notebook, urgency making my mouth dry.

What I see makes me take a step back. They're evacuation plans of some sort. A location. A list of items she needs to take with her like weapons, medicine, and maps. Is this the top-secret project she's been working on that not even tía Ines is privy to?

I close the pages, hurry back down, open the bathroom door quietly, then flush the toilet and pretend to wash my hands.

"You sure?" Sam asks when I rejoin them.

"Yeah," I tell him, aware time is ticking and we need a win sooner rather than later.

After I've gotten all three of our key fobs off, we're free to do what we please.

Sam doesn't say anything as he pulls open the front door.

One of my favorite perks of this job is the fancy pod that Sam and I share to get to Burberry's mansion. The three of us get into the vehicle and direct it to the docks, where according to Sidra, there is a special submarine meant to take us from the shore to the island.

When we arrive, there're plenty of people gazing at the water filtration spigots. Besides the Masterdome itself, they are truly the most impressive man-made things in the city.

The lake itself is a deeper blue than the sky, surrounded by green in all directions—living, breathing, lush trees, visible from this far away. The machines that suck up and filter the water to ensure it is drinkable are like metallic beasts from here.

The island has a block-like building at its center, where I'm assuming we need to go.

"You're sure you know how to get to the island?" I ask.

"Absolutely," she replies, taking my hand and pulling me to the right, to a building labeled *Modern Museum of the Lake*.

All the museums in San Francisco have been turned into bunkers, but I recall one time when Mami and Papá took me to see one of the last remaining science museums. My brothers were alive then, too, and we'd been enthralled by dinosaur skeletons. How such magnificent creatures had existed once on our planet. Seeing the dinosaurs had left me wondering what would replace humanity when we humans were all gone.

This museum isn't empty. On the contrary, it's full of people learning instead of surviving. There are so many displays featuring ancient machines and old construction schematics and building parts that Rico would fall in love with.

Each machine part has a story behind it. And every story has one name attached to it. *Burberry.*

"Sometimes Mom closes down the entire museum for the two of us," Sidra says, staring at one of the bronze placards. "She loves looking back on our family's legacy. She tells me one day the Oasis will be mine to lead."

Sidra doesn't sound excited at that idea, though. And for

the first time, seeing her confused over her future, I truly consider telling her about her grandfather, assuring her that she has options.

"What do you know about your biological parents?" I ask suddenly.

Sidra shrugs. "I know they're dead, and that my mom took me in and took care of me afterward. I'm grateful to her for giving me a home. For really loving me even though she isn't my birth mom. To me, she's everything, so I want to protect what she loves the most."

"You?" Sam asks.

"The Oasis."

We stare at one another until she sniffs, then keeps walking past other people, straight to the back and up to a shiny gold door.

I want to tell her that one of her grandpas isn't dead and that he's outside the Masterdome doing whatever it takes to get her back.

But still, I stay quiet. Instead, I wonder if anyone will stop us, but nobody even bats an eye. Here, people don't stand out the same way they did in San Francisco, where you were looking at everyone constantly to see if they were planning to rob you or worse. In here, we all blend together. A group of people who don't do anything bad . . . ever.

And yet war is coming to them.

It makes my heart squeeze.

Sidra takes out the key card and scans it over the door, which turns completely silver, then unlocks. She goes in without a word.

"You sure we won't get kicked out if we're caught?" Sam asks.

I grab his hand and drag him with us, fairly certain there is no way that tía Ines would let either of us be kicked out simply for taking a closer look at the museum.

We enter a very narrow hallway, barely wide enough to fit one of us at a time.

Sidra laughs from the front of our line. "We're almost there," she says, giggling as she hurries through. "This always makes me feel like we're in a tube of toothpaste getting squeezed."

We arrive at a platform, and a sign above that says *Submersible Ahead—Authorized Personnel Only.*

"There are stairs at the end of the platform that lead into the submarine. It works with this card. C'mon," Sidra says.

She signals us to the end of the platform, which literally looks like it disappears into the water. I don't know how to swim. Never needed to learn, so I stare as something in my chest tightens and tells me that I should run.

We enter the submarine anyway, and Sidra turns it on with her stolen key card. Excitement literally radiates off her. I relax a little. If a twelve-year-old isn't afraid, I shouldn't be either, right?

The submarine turns on with a hum, the orb-like lights surrounding its edges coming alive. Sidra tinkers with the control panel, Sam hovering over her shoulder. I sit back, watching them, realizing that I have to trust them with my life.

The submarine begins to move suddenly, and I take hold of the railing behind me. I thought we'd be able to see more, but it's pitch-black outside as we sink farther and farther down into the oblivion of the lake.

Luckily, we move so fast that I don't even have time to stress. After a few blinks, we're out of the water, on the far side of the island, away from everyone. I exhale with relief as the submarine docks at another platform.

Sidra turns around to me, smiling big.

I shake my head, laughing, and say, "Okay, let's go exploring!"

The island is a lot larger than it appeared from the shore across the lake.

From up close, the Mad Scientist's old building is a giant concrete cube ten times as tall as I am. Out of place in between so many trees, it has no windows. Only one visible door directly to our right. Sidra takes my hand as we near the entrance. "I've been to the island so many times, but Mom's never taken me inside the building."

"You don't have to worry. You're with us," I tell her.

The three of us walk in a line up the stone steps. Sidra pulls out the key card and places it against the rectangular pad on the left side of the door. I almost expect it not to work, like our luck will run out. But then the pad turns green and the door clicks open.

Sam pushes it wide. As he walks in, he mumbles, "Let's hope they don't have security cameras."

I look up, but not at the walls—at the Masterdome, wondering exactly what makes the border between worlds work.

I take out the small flashlight I like to keep in my pocket, too used to carrying a light from working the Scar. Sidra pulls one from her own backpack, a giant thing that barely fits in her hand. The building is split up into several rooms, with this one large area at its center. It's darker than I thought it'd be. The air tastes like dust and rock powder. It's hot but not a dry heat. It's humid and smells dank. Like no one has been inside this place in ages.

"I saw solar panels on the roof. It's midday, so maybe the lights will work," Sam says.

Sidra runs over to the light switch and flips it on.

They're blinding LEDs. I shield my eyes until I can see without squinting.

Everything is white. The walls are white. The floor is white. The large screens and computers set up all over the place are all frost colored. There is more technology here than I've ever seen in one place, even Rodrick's pop's office. Sidra rummages through the scattered papers on top of the computer system, which runs along the entire left-hand wall, lifting gunk into the air that causes her to sneeze. Straight ahead, there are three giant screens, all turned off, their displays as black as a starless night. To the right, mechanical parts, both small and large, are scattered without any type of care. Rico would gawk at the piles. He would be able to build so many things out of these materials. At least Sam and I might be able to find the parts we need for the 3D printer. If we could even complete one spigot prototype this year, it would be a step forward.

"Now, where do you think the Mad Scientist's ghost is

looming?" Sidra asks as she moves her flashlight throughout the room. "Not a lot of places to hide around here." Sam creeps up on the kid, startling her when he grabs her shoulders. She jumps and shoves him back. "That wasn't funny, Samuel. Not cool," she says, flustered.

"Sorry," he replies, still laughing at himself.

"How do you put up with him?" she asks me.

I shrug. "He grows on you." He teeth-grins at my words, bats his eyelashes.

I was once in Sidra's shoes, when my brothers would scare me. Back then, I thought they were annoying bullies. But I know now it was their way of goofing around with me.

I return my attention to the array of papers. They're all schematics and numbers that make no sense and have no rhythm to them, so it's good Sam's with us. "There's no ghost here, Sidra," I say. "Look at this place. There's no such—"

"Oh my God," Sidra cuts in. She signals me to come over. I join her and peer through a pane of glass.

Skeletons.

A row of them lie askew on the white floor. They've all got their hands tied behind their backs, holes in their skeletal foreheads, indicating that they're not science dummies—these are real skeletal remains. Of people who have been murdered. A ghost couldn't do this. The fact that there's been no light or moisture until now has likely kept them intact.

Sidra moves to open the door. Sam pulls her back.

"Don't," he says.

"But they were—"

"I know."

"This is what my mom barely escaped," she says, as if that would explain this much death.

The kid believes that. I don't. I count eight people. Sidra said seven came here with Burberry, which means the eighth, the one still draped in what looks like a doctor's coat, must be the scientist. There's something valuable in this place. A secret. Burberry's secret. How else would she be the last person standing?

"Go check out the machinery over there," I say to Sidra and point to the piles on the opposite side.

Sam hands her a sheet he's pulled from his notebook, which he's taken out of his backpack. "Here, see if you can find these parts."

The kid examines the names and sketches to go with them, then goes without batting another eye at the dead or asking what in the world we need the materials for, hurrying over to rummage through the mountain of parts. I'm not sure if I should find her reaction alarming or not.

I turn back to the skeletons, studying them to see if there's anything I can glean from the bones without going inside the room.

"Hey, Jules," Sam says. "Come look at this."

Sam moves to a computer and leans over a desk. It's cleaner than all the rest. I sit down at the desk chair in front of the computer screen.

My throat tightens.

It's a log of errors, from lights glitching to pods halting suddenly to the train losing power.

Sam scrolls and the list keeps going, on and on and on, until he finally gives up.

"There are over fifty dated from today," he says. "That can't be normal, right?"

I shake my head and swallow hard. Something's off here, and it isn't just the log.

Sam touches my hand. "Let's search through everything as fast as we can before anyone notices."

He walks away, but as I roll back, something tucked in a nook to the right of the desk catches my eye, some kind of leather bag. I yank it out and wipe spiderwebs off it, then stuff the thing with papers that could be useful. As I'm pushing in a paper with a giant spigot sketched on it, I notice there's something hard as a book within the satchel already.

It's a journal.

I open it and stop at a page that reads:

RESULTS AND UNQUESTIONABLE FACTS

SPIGOT CAPACITY: At a maximum

CHANCE THAT WATER WILL SOMEDAY BECOME DRINKABLE ON ITS OWN: None

CHANCE THAT WE'LL BE ABLE TO CREATE A VACCINE FOR SIBERVIRUS: *None*

RESULTS FROM CLIMATE CHANGE TESTS:
Temperatures have risen above predicted percentages, causing an early deterioration of the dome's alloy.

THE OASIS'S CURRENT POPULATION: *The maximum 10,000 people that the spigots can produce enough water for.*

LONGEVITY OF THE MASTERDOME: *Undeterminable if Burberry continues to refuse to see the problem for what it is: the beginning of the end. We need to plan to build a new Masterdome. What'll be the final outcome of this cover-up remains to be seen.*

I turn to the next page, the final one with text on it.

All it says is *Channel 19*.

But I don't know if it means a channel on the television or a radio or something completely foreign to me.

Sidra glances over my shoulder. "What is it?" she asks, trying to get a better view of the words on the page. I quickly close the journal. My cheeks burn hot. I try to call to Sam, but he's too busy searching through another pile of parts.

I focus on Sidra. "Nothing important. You find anything?"

She stares for a few lingering seconds before holding up pieces of metal I don't recognize but must be among the parts on Sam's list. I give her a thumbs-up and open the satchel for her to stuff them in. I add the journal to our haul, trying to ignore my growing unease as I put two and two together. The fact that the Mad Scientist knew the Masterdome was failing, and so did President Burberry, who likely killed him to cover it up. Coupled with what I know of her evacuation plan . . . My stomach squeezes as a thought occurs to me that is too terrible to speak out loud.

How close are we to the end?

Even though it hurts to talk, I manage to say, "We should get back before Sheriff Paul or your mom gets home."

Sidra turns toward the skeletons. "What about them?"

"We can't do anything about them; they're already dead. Just don't tell anybody we came here."

She purses her lips.

"We could get in major trouble for snooping," Sam adds in, rejoining us and handing me more parts to add to the satchel. "They might even kick us out."

Sidra's eyes go wide before she finally nods and says, "Okay, I won't tell anyone."

As we're hurrying out of the building, I spot something else, a small transceiver sitting awkwardly on one of the tables all alone, set to the number 19.

It can't be a coincidence, so I place the heavy device into the bag as well.

The submarine is even more claustrophobic on its return route. The three of us remain silent this time, the water so dark it's like we're ants in a universe that is too large, too hectic, too frightening.

Sam takes my hand, squeezing tightly as if he's reading

my mind again, or maybe we have the same thoughts. I don't make eye contact but squeeze back.

Luckily, no one bothers us as we leave the museum, and only a few people stare at Sidra as if they recognize her, proving why the little girl really doesn't leave the mansion often.

Once we're in Burberry's driveway, I leave the satchel in the car, hiding it from plain sight as much as I can. Inside, the three of us put our key fobs back on and fall onto the couch.

Burberry might be able to tell if she tracks the pod, but I'm hoping that we'll be in luck and she doesn't.

We're not inside for ten minutes before the door opens. Burberry walks in and grins when she spots us on the couch, all of us with books in hand. Tía Ines enters behind her. Lately, they've been inseparable, and I wonder what exactly they do all day.

The Mad Scientist's journal said the Masterdome was unsalvageable—that it's failing. He didn't see a way things would get better. But then there was channel 19 . . . Perhaps Rico is right: Maybe new spigots aren't enough to save people.

I don't know what happened in the Mad Scientist's lab. But one thing I do know is that if word got out that the Masterdome is failing, it would cause mass panic, both within the haven and throughout the lower isolation cities. The violence directed at me in Union Square would be amplified by a billion. Worse still, if Burberry's not doing anything to try to fix it, what does that mean for everyone here living in ignorant bliss?

Burberry approaches us and hugs Sidra. The moment the two break apart, a high-pitched alarm rings through the mansion.

Sidra and I raise our hands to our ears, but it doesn't help enough to drown out the sharp sound. Sam cringes.

"I'll go," tía Ines says to Burberry, then turns to Sam and me. "An alert that we're needed at the Security Depot. Sam, can you stay until Paul gets back? Juliana, why don't you come with me, and I'll take you home afterward so Sam can keep the pod."

Without any choice, I nod, following tía Ines and leaving the satchel behind—with all its answers.

CHAPTER 18
Rico

Viola Hershall will never be someone I can fully trust, not in the way that I did my tía Linda. And not in the way I grew to trust Jules. But I do admire Viola's determination and her willingness to help us free tía Linda. Enough to have been here all week instead of with Jules to guarantee I'm ready to go when Viola gives us the necessary information.

Every time Viola talks, there's a fire in her words I can't help but be inspired by. She and the Sheriff are risking everything to take over the Oasis and give the people of the Wasteland true faith that we can survive the apocalypse. And even more, to allow us this one chance to rescue the woman who became my second mother.

"Are you listening, Rico?" Viola asks me now. Nadine, Jesus, and I are in her apartment to plan the biggest night of our lives—the one in which we get my aunt back. My nerves are on high alert; my body shivers with anticipation, even though it's warm and Viola's fairy lights give the room a calming effect. "You need to pay attention. You three will have one opportunity to get Linda out of her prison. You can't mess this up, or you'll put the entire operation at risk."

I focus, nodding as she pushes my tea closer to me across her multicolored rug. She seems to think tea is the cure to everything. And maybe it is. When I take a long drink, the heat of the chai makes my chest relax, my muscles untense.

"They're keeping Linda in a warehouse in the West Shore, like an object. You will need to break into the warehouse by knocking out the deputies on guard. Rico, you'll be in charge of hacking the computer system to get the warehouse doors open. Once inside, you'll need to access the warehouse data center, where you'll be told what part of the building your aunt is being kept in. Remember, you'll be alone. I can't risk getting any of my people or myself caught this close to Edgar joining us. We're only three days away from our future. And now is the time to act."

"What happens if we're caught?" Nadine asks, her eyes wide in admiration for Viola.

Viola brings out three plastic boxes the size of my thumbnail from her skirt pocket. She passes one to each of us.

I open the box. There's a single pill inside.

"We cannot risk the three of you being interrogated—"

"So we take the pills and die if we're caught?" Jesus says, eyes narrowing.

"I think if you're willing to give up your life to save your mom, you're willing to give up your life to keep her dream alive, too."

"We'll make sure it doesn't come to that," I say, interrupting before Jesus erupts. I place the pillbox in my pocket.

Jesus and I lock eyes. His are a fuming revolt. I give him a small nod, and he repeats it back to me. Whatever animosity we've felt for each other, Viola is right about one thing. To succeed, we need to be a team. Even if we pretend that we're absolutely ready to swallow a death capsule if needed.

"That's the spirit," Viola says, placing one hand on Nadine's shoulder and another on mine. "The three of you can do this. Don't hesitate and don't get caught. If you can pull this off, you'll have Linda back and one less thing the Burberrys have over us."

Viola looks at her watch and notes, "It's time."

Nadine, Jesus, and I have matching watches so that we're breaking in exactly as the guards are changing shifts at nine.

As we stand, Viola goes into a part of her apartment I've never seen. She returns with a large velvet purse, which is a deep purple, and pulls out three dark gray blasters. They're old, the metal scarred, but they'll work in a pinch.

"Don't lose these. They're valuable . . . and fully charged," she says.

I take the blaster with a sharp exhale, the jitters running through my chest. I'm not in a tight spot, but I'm still claustrophobic.

Viola hugs each of us as we leave her apartment.

"I'll see you all in a few hours," she says.

Nadine and Jesus walk down the hall to take the elevator.

Viola grabs my forearm, pulling me back to her.

"What's wrong?" I ask, taking her in. Her face doesn't hold its usual light. Her words are more measured.

"I promise," she starts, "that at the end of this, your aunt will be free. Remember that when you're inside."

"I will," I say, then run after Jesus and Nadine.

We board the pod we've been given to travel to the far edge of the West Shore near the Masterdome's wall.

My leg bobs up and down at a million miles a minute as we roll onto the city's main road. Nadine sets her hand on my thigh. "Be still already," she pleads. "You're making me nervous."

Jesus leans back as if he's got no worries in the world. He turns my way. His piercing brown eyes question if I'm ready for this. Like with the waterway in the tunnel, I relinquish the lead happily, so when Jesus starts spouting off the plan, I don't interrupt.

"Nadine will distract the guards by pretending to be some lost and stranded girl asking for help," he says with a smirk. "She will take out the guards at the front with her charade, while I'll take out those on the left, and, Rico, you'll take those on the right before they can act. We'll reconvene in the back. Once they've all been knocked out, we'll tie the guards up. The main goal will be to do this incognito. To ensure the cameras never capture us, we're wearing these face masks."

He hands Nadine a masquerade mask with an elaborate moth design, me one of a black cat, and he'll wear one that's of a wolf.

"Where did you get these?" I ask.

"I made them," he replies with a slight blush.

"They're cool," I say. He smiles until his mask hides his expression. I follow his lead and set my mask in place.

I take a deep breath when the pod comes to a halt along the edge of a hill.

We exit the pod without a sound and crawl until we can see the warehouse, located at the bottom of a weaving road. From here, it's practically hidden from view.

Nadine makes her way forward without even saying goodbye, as if there's no shot that this goes wrong. I watch her go down the hill, and I wish I had said more to her.

Jesus slaps my cheek in a painfully playful way. "She'll be fine. Vamos. Let's go have some fun and save my amá."

Before I can say anything to him, Jesus leaves, too. I wish I could shout out to him to be careful, but I'll have to simply pray that we'll be celebrating instead of mourning at the end of the night.

I weave through the large redwoods and other trees and bushes on the hill, toward the valley, to get to the right side of the warehouse undetected. I have to fight to not get distracted by the wondrous gold shimmer of the Masterdome above us.

When I'm in position, I check my watch. We need to be in sync. Otherwise, the noises will warn the others and our plan won't work. My watch flashes for a split second, and I act as stealthily as tía Linda taught us to.

The first guard doesn't see me coming before I take the end of my blaster and hit him in the back of the head. Unfortunately, the other two guards on my side are facing me when I do.

The first one fires their own blaster at me, which I evade but barely. The second guard fires, but this time, the ammo scrapes the side of my body. I fight. Push the limp body of the first guard into the second and use that time to attack the third, who puts his blaster away and comes at me with a baton. The baton, though, is electrically charged, and it touches me once.

Once is enough for me to spasm and stumble.

It also becomes obvious that they aren't trying to kill me—they're trying to capture me. Like they did my aunt. Something I want even less, given that Viola Hershall's death pill is heavy in my pocket.

But I don't have time to worry about that, not as a fourth guard rounds the corner. He comes at me and knocks me to the ground. He is so heavy, I can't breathe.

Then his blood comes squirting at me as something metallic slices the guard's throat.

I swear, not at him, but at the grotesque situation, then at Nadine when I manage to push the limp body off me and stand. Tía Linda taught us how to fight, but Nadine was never this good—or so cold-blooded—when I was a part of Mictlān.

We weren't going to kill anyone. That wasn't part of the plan. We were to only incapacitate them.

"Why?" I ask, voice breaking.

Nadine rolls her eyes at me. "You're welcome," she says as she hurries away.

I run after her, not knowing how many other people she's killed today, aware of truly how much she's changed in the last three years. The Nadine I knew growing up would keep bugs as pets instead of getting rid of them, would offer her meal for the day to an elder, and definitely would never purposefully hurt anyone.

My legs burn, my side aches from the pain of being electrocuted and bloodied, and my eyebrow has been in constant discomfort. On the other side of the building, Jesus is grinning as he knocks the teeth out of one of the guards, who falls to the side, passing out.

As my cousin turns around, a hard fist meets his face, and he's thrown back. Nadine and I are on the guard before he even has a chance to register us. I push the guard, then Nadine knocks him out with a swift kick to the side of the head.

In our disguises, we don't have to worry about being identified as people who shouldn't be inside of the Oasis. Even so, we have a few minutes before reinforcements come.

So I don't dither, aware that our lives are at stake if I do. I circle to the front of the warehouse.

To our luck, we don't even need to hack the doors. Two guards are exiting the warehouse. Nadine pulls the first one down, taking him by surprise. She rams his head into her knee, and he falls over, his body holding open the door. Meanwhile, Jesus holds the blaster in the direction of the other.

"Let's tie them up," I say. When I can read the hesitation through my companions' masks, I add in, "That was the plan."

I bring out the string from my pocket.

"Kneel," I say to the deputy who Jesus points his blaster at.

To my relief, the deputy listens.

To my disbelief, Jesus exhales loudly and simply comes over and hits the deputy with the edge of his blaster, knocking the person unconscious.

When I scowl at him, he shrugs.

"We don't have time for pleasantries," he says, then slips into the warehouse.

Inside, we wait to see if someone else has heard and is coming to fight.

The warehouse itself is a giant, dark space that looks like a black hole.

Thankfully, there doesn't seem to be anyone else inside the warehouse.

I run over to a computer system set up near the entrance. I slide into an office chair and over toward the keyboard. I type in commands and rummage through files. But there's no indication of where tía Linda could be.

"I can't find her," I say, fighting the desire to slip off my mask and throw it on the floor.

My heart is a drum, beating hard against my chest.

"We search on foot," Jesus says. He hits me on the back of my shoulder, a signal for me to join him.

"I'll watch the door," Nadine adds.

Jesus and I hurry through the warehouse. The lights aren't bright on the high ceilings, but we can see well enough. We hurry through the aisles from the middle and front of the warehouse to the very back, to find no cell or any type of holding spot for a prisoner. There are stacked boxes and tins with various things labeled like clothes, kitchenware, fireworks, and the like.

Without a word, we split up. Jesus takes the left side, I take the right, as we zigzag through every aisle, until both of us meet Nadine up at the front again.

"What is going on?" Nadine asks us.

"We've been tricked," I reply, barely audible as my throat squeezes shut.

"Son of a—" Jesus says, rubbing at his face below his mask. "This can't be happening. The photograph."

"Maybe Viola got the wrong information," Nadine says.

"Or maybe she simply *gave us* the wrong information," I reply, remembering her hesitation earlier. "We need to get out of here, like, yesterday."

The three of us move in tandem.

Only, the moment we step out of the building, there's a pinch at the skin of my shoulder and the sound of a bullet hitting its mark.

CHAPTER 19
Jules

This is my chance to tell my tía the whole, entire complicated truth before the ten days are up.

I can tell tía Ines about Rico and how he's been blackmailed by Sheriff Ramos. How Sheriff Ramos and Viola Hershall are planning to take over a crumbling paradise.

About the dead scientist's island and what we've discovered.

But there's a reason why I haven't. Because of the gnawing fear she knows that the Masterdome is failing and still hasn't said anything to help save the people here. Hasn't done anything to help those outside who depend on the Oasis for hope in the Wasteland. My heads spins. I turn the air conditioner on and face it toward me, then lean against the window, the coolness of it welcome against my forehead.

"What are you thinking about?" Tía Ines asks me while we're in her pod.

"Truthfully?" I ask. "Antonio. Ever since I started watching Sidra, I think about my little brother nonstop." It's a half truth, since I have thought about him. But I keep pondering even more about the books from the Scar, about the ring I have at home, about the bodies on the island, about where Sidra really comes from, but this answer is one I know my tía will believe without a question.

Tía Ines's hand lands softly on mine. "I'm truly so sorry for what you have gone through. You'll never have to suffer like that again, querida."

"The Masterdome," I question, eyes turning to lock on tía Ines's face. "It'll really protect us for as long as we live? We really won't ever have to go back to the Wasteland?"

Tía Ines doesn't skip a beat before responding, "Never, ever again. I promise." Her eyes are so sincere, her facade unfaltering. Is it that she's so good at lying to herself that it's nothing to lie anymore, or is she truly ignorant of the fact that the Masterdome is getting ready to fall?

Or was the Mad Scientist the liar? But why the secrecy? Why the skeletons?

"Tía? How much do you trust Burberry?"

She laughs some, as if it's a silly question.

"I trust President Burberry with my life. She's the best person I know."

The pod stops before we can continue our conversation.

I step outside and ask, "Where are we?"

The Masterdome looms rather than comforts tonight. From this close, its shimmer is almost blinding.

"We're at the edge of the North Shore, near the wall of the Masterdome," she replies as we head toward the padlocked door of a building that's a lot like the one on the island, a small fortress in the middle of nowhere. We go through three security zones: one where she scans a key card, one where she scans her retina, and another her thumbprint. Wherever we are, whatever's inside is top-secret.

Inside there have to be at least a hundred people typing away on computer screens, all in a few neat rows. They don't pay us any attention as we pass, so I can't get a closer look at their faces.

We cross the computer room to get to another door that takes us down a long corridor. It's empty and noiseless. The sound of nothingness is so damn eerie, I'm glad for tía Ines's heels click-clacking. Eventually, we come to the end of the hall.

Tía Ines knocks on the door but doesn't wait for a reply as she scans her key card again.

The room is about half the size of the sitting area in my apartment, and there's one man inside. He wears this strange contraption over his head and is swiping at the air in front of him as if he's seeing something we don't. Tía Ines clears her throat, and the man finally realizes he's got visitors.

"What's happening, Cody?" she asks the man when he takes the machine off his face.

He holds it gingerly on his lap and almost hesitantly says, "We have survivors outside the Masterdome . . ."

He flips some kind of switch on his desk, and six medium-sized screens lower from the ceiling, displaying various sections surrounding the Oasis. There must be hundreds of live cameras around the perimeter of the haven. Working ones.

I spot the people he's talking about on the bottom-left screen.

"That's amazing," I whisper. Where did these people come from, and how far did they travel to get here? By their tired faces, hunched shoulders, and dirty skin, it must have been a grueling voyage.

Cody stares at me, quirking his head to the right, noticing that I'm present, and now gives a *why-is-a-stranger-here* kind of glare to tía Ines.

"It's okay. She's my niece," tía Ines responds.

Cody nods slowly, pursing his lips. He says, "There are almost fifty people. From what I can count, at least half of them are children."

I expect tía Ines's next words to be *Let them in*, or *That's incredible*. But all that comes out is "Let me check with Burberry."

"Wait here, Jules," she says, then steps out for a moment.

Cody's mouth moves slightly as if he wants to tell me something, but he doesn't actually say anything. We stare awkwardly at one another until tía Ines returns.

My tía glances at me once, her face neutral, before simply shaking her head at Cody.

Cody swears under his breath, and I'm lost.

"What's going on?" I ask tía Ines. "What did President Burberry say?"

"Go wait outside, Juliana," she tells me.

"Why? What is it?" I repeat, my face warming, noting how she emphasized my full name.

"Tell her," Cody says, a dark edge to his voice. "If you're

willing to give the order, you should be willing to own up to it."

Tía Ines's expression shoots daggers at Cody. But there's also something else in her eyes—understanding, like she knows he's right.

"Tell me," I say.

She sighs. "The Oasis functions on a delicate balance. We don't know who these people are. And there are too many of them. We can't afford to let them in. We need to sustain the balance. We need to protect this haven from those who might do us harm."

"What are you talking about?" Even if this city is failing, if we don't let these people in now, they'll die.

"Wait outside, Juliana," she repeats, forcefully now.

I huff but leave as tía Ines turns back around. I glance at Cody, whose eyes shift to the left in a too-obvious manner.

When I'm out of the room and see a door to my left, I realize he was giving me a signal.

I enter a makeshift closet and slowly close the door behind me.

There is a vent on the side connected to Cody's office, so if I stay really quiet and I hold my breath, I can make out what they're both saying.

"I'm tired of doing this," Cody says to tía Ines. "And tired of telling you that I'm going to resign and hearing I can't or the President will come after my family, Ines. This isn't why I wanted to do this job. I thought we'd be protecting the Oasis . . ."

"And you think I like it?" she barks back. "But this is the

job. Ready the blasters. We *are* protecting the Oasis. Ten thousand people are all the water filtration systems are equipped to help."

"I would cut my water rations in half if it meant helping more," Cody says. "And others feel the same." I hadn't even realized there was a water ration. Is being exempt from it another benefit of my tía's special treatment?

I close my eyes, trying to wrap my mind around what my aunt has asked for.

Tía Ines grunts, then she says, as if speaking into a microphone: "Citizens of California, you are unlawfully close to the Masterdome of the Oasis. Abandon your position at once and turn back immediately."

I can make out the voices on the other side.

"Please!"

"Don't turn us away!"

"Help us! You can help us!"

Their pleas are echoed when others join in. As if all of them connected their voices into one single cry.

A bitter taste makes its way to my throat. My head spins.

Turning them away isn't any better than killing them all on the spot. There is nothing but death and discord outside the haven.

Tía Ines goes on. "You will be given five minutes to retreat to where you came from, or we will open fire. We will not miss—we will not dither. We will aim to kill. And we *will* shoot the children. Understand it is with great difficulty that we cannot allow you all within our border. But it is the only way to ensure the haven continues to stand. Please head back toward the nearest city and participate in the lottery like all other Californians. You now have four minutes to retreat," tía Ines warns. She adds, "Please don't make us hurt you."

The begging continues outside. Tía Ines implores them to leave once more, her tone nearing its breaking point.

The voices outside sound even more desperate. I can tell they think my aunt is bluffing. They've made it to us from wherever they came from, a feat in itself. They think she's kind enough to accept them in on this fact alone.

I know in my bones that she is *not*.

I know now why the perimeter of the Masterdome isn't packed with people. Why the groups in No Man's Land haven't simply taken over the haven. Burberry and those who follow her are ruthless. And the cost of her maintaining order is high. Too high. In the end, we aren't saving humanity. We're not even giving people hope—we're slowly eradicating it in the name of temporary self-preservation.

"Your time is up," my tía warns. There's more noise, and people screaming. Then there's my aunt's voice, saying, "Fire at will."

I love tía Ines. I have since I was a little girl. I remember when she would come to visit Mami, the eldest, and spent time braiding my hair. I remember Mami giving her hugs and holding her tight. I remember her laughing when my parents and siblings were still alive. But the idea that she is taking the lives of others as if their existence isn't valuable just seems so enormously wrong and contradictory to the woman I once adored.

The first shot sounds. A wheeze releases from the center of my chest as I jolt back. It reminds me of the plaza and the lottery, of when Rodrick pulled out the gun to stop the crowd from killing us.

But this is different. These people aren't attacking anyone. They need our assistance, and we are turning them away. I count each shot, one by one, and imagine the body each blast hits. I think about what Cody said. Half of the people outside *are children*.

I walk out of the closet, slamming the door behind me, and move fast to find my way out of the building. I ignore the stares of those I pass, until I'm outside and throwing up on the concrete.

Tía Ines's heels sound as she appears behind me.

"Juliana," she starts, rubbing my back.

I reach out my hand to stop her, my palm facing up. "Don't." I move away from her and wipe at my lips. "Did you kill those people?"

"Not all of them," she replies, as if that's any better.

"What will happen to the ones who didn't die? What'll happen to the bodies of those who did? Are you going to bury them, or pretend they never existed?"

"What always happens," tía Ines replies, looking away from me. "The animals will likely get them. The bodies and the rest. It won't be a total waste."

"The animals will get them," I repeat, unable to even comprehend what she's saying, then scoff. "When did you become so evil?"

Her face contorts as if I've struck her. But it's the truth.

Good people don't do what she did. And suddenly, I know I can't tell her anything after all. Or trust her. The Oasis is dying in one way or another, and Rico was right. It's for the best.

But he needs to know that the Masterdome is failing and there's no point in Sheriff Ramos coming to take it over.

"I've done a lot of things since entering the Oasis that are not considered good. Those actions haunt me. But we are the chosen ones, Juliana."

"The chosen ones?" I want to throw up again, but there's nothing left in me but bitterness. "I wasn't chosen. I came here because someone I love gave me his spot. I came here because that someone thought I would be safe here. There is no such thing as *the chosen ones*. Fate doesn't exist. There are only the choices we make. And you made one that makes you inhuman."

I wonder if Willa and Rodrick know what goes on at the border.

I can't imagine they'd like this either.

Cody comes out and bickers with tía Ines.

"She can kill me if she wants," he says, throwing the device he had on in his office so hard that it shatters on the ground. "I'm done. I resign."

As tía Ines rushes after Cody, who is obviously way more important to her agenda than I am, I take the opportunity to run, so eager to escape, I don't even care if it's on foot.

I don't know where I'm going or where exactly I am. But I'll figure it out like Rico and I figured things out in the Wasteland. And like Mami and Papá taught me to do when things got bad. I'll figure out how to get through this because my brothers would want me to.

It'll be a long way home without getting a ride from tía Ines, so I take out my radio to call Rico.

I press the button. "Rico? Are you there? Tell me you're there. I really need you. I have to tell you what I found out today. Please, please pick up."

There's nothing but static on the other end. I'm left with being completely abandoned, alone. I haven't felt this way since my family members died, and I hate it. Because in the pain, I can't even be angry—all that's left is a hole of endless disappointment.

I didn't try to stop my aunt . . . That's the only thing I can think about in the hours it takes me to walk back home. Hours of walking in the night, my small flashlight guiding my way. Hours of putting one foot in front of the other, blisters forming on my feet.

I'll move past this moment, as I have many moments before.

I miraculously make it to my apartment to find Willa sitting in the hallway in front of my door. She grins at me like I didn't just watch tía Ines do the worst thing on the entire planet, and it takes all of me not to explode.

CHAPTER 20

Jules

Willa is the last person I want to see. I'm so repulsed by tía Ines and, by extension, her daughter. My gut is now asking me if I can even trust my stepcousin.

"What's wrong?" Willa asks when I don't return her smile.

"Your mom," I say as I move around her to go into my apartment to grab the protective suits and what little I can pack. I'm leaving to join Rico. Wherever he is in the South Shore.

"What?" Willa asks, confusion coating her voice, as she trails behind me. "What happened? Talk to me."

She grabs my arm, pulls me around, and I break, noting the genuine concern in her expression. A sob overwhelms me. I'm so tired from walking. And from failing . . . but I don't even know what I'm failing at. Life in general? I'm trying to be a good person, to make a difference, but I keep falling short.

Apparently, my crying is loud because Sam comes out

of his place. I'm thankful our other neighbors pay me no mind.

"What happened?" Sam asks, tone worried as he approaches us in the hallway, tablet and notebook in hand, along with, to my relief, the satchel from our pod.

He sets the items down to rub circles on my back.

"We should take her inside," Willa says.

So Sam picks me up, cradles me like a child in his arms, and carries me into my apartment. He sits me down on the fluffy rug in the middle of the living room.

"Start from the beginning," Willa asks, dabbing at my cheeks with her shirtsleeve like she's actually my friend. "I know my mom isn't perfect. I know the haven isn't either, but you're our family, Jules. My mom hasn't stopped talking about you, and I haven't seen her this happy since before my dad died. I've known your aunt for years, and there is so much she's kept from me about what happened to her and what her life was like before the Oasis, but she never forgot you or your mom. She loves you. So what happened today?"

"She killed kids," I blurt, pulling at the threads of the rug. It isn't even the deaths themselves. I'm used to seeing the dead. What I'll never get used to is senseless killing, or the fact that some people think their power gives them the right to decide who lives and who dies.

I need Rico.

Willa shakes her head; her chest rises up and down as she turns to Sam for help. Sam's eyes are on mine, though. And for a moment, my body relaxes because I know he is someone who will listen to me, who will understand. He'll keep his pinky promise.

I wipe at my eyes, try to talk, but continue to cry for a few minutes more.

When I can finally get words out, I explain everything. How tía Ines took me with her to the Security Depot, how there were people outside the Masterdome, and how Burberry made the call to end their lives, and my aunt executed it—them—like she was completely and utterly heartless.

"She wouldn't do that," Willa argues. Her face is blank as she sits back.

"I didn't think she would either, but I heard her, Willa. And she tried to justify it by saying we're the *chosen ones*."

Suddenly, there's a knock at the door, and I know immediately by the heaviness of it that it's tía Ines.

I shake my head violently at Willa. "Please," I whisper.

She stares at the door for a moment, then turns back to Sam and me.

Willa points to the fire escape, the one I'm so used to Rico coming through. She takes out one of Rodrick's devices that disconnects the key fobs and removes the three on our wrists quickly, then slips them underneath the rug in the room.

We move as silently as possible after. Sam picks up the satchel with the journal and transceiver, slipping his tablet and his notebook inside. When there's another knock, I hurry to stuff all my belongings, including the picture of Rico and me at the ice cream shop and my winning buzzer, into Rico's pack, which is still by my window. I don't forget the ring or the protective suits, no matter how heavy they are. We climb out the window, each carrying a few of the suits, and run into the darkness before tía Ines comes into my apartment uninvited.

From the shadows of the street, from the trees we're hiding behind, I see tía Ines's silhouette take over the window frame, and she peers down. But her eyes don't find us.

I sniffle, and Willa brings me in for a hug. "Don't cry anymore, okay?" she says. "We'll figure this out. I'll talk to my mom tomorrow." Willa takes my hand, adding in, "C'mon. I know the perfect place to crash."

We end up at Rodrick's two-story house, which has a vegetable garden growing out front and a picket fence all around that makes me utterly jealous of a life I'll never have. He lets us in, ushers us into his room.

"Pop's working so he'll be in the garage for a while," Rodrick says.

His room is a giant space in the attic complete with a massive bed, a gaming area, and endless comic books like those I used to sell to Sheriff Ramos and wondered why they were so valuable. More valuable even than a diamond ring. Two lottery tickets. Here, they're collector's items, endless entertainment for teens who get to have fun.

Willa plops down onto an oversized bright pink beanbag chair that I assume must be her usual spot, the beans inside squeaking against each other as she sits. She taps the space next to her twice, and I join her on the cushion. I rest my head on her shoulder, trying to figure out what more to say as she bites her fingernails. But I'm too drained, too tired. And my eyes keep shutting and reopening no matter how hard I attempt to remain alert.

"Let her rest," I hear Rodrick say to Willa as my eyes drift shut. "And tell me everything."

I awake to loud static echoing through the room, and for a moment, I one hundred percent believe that I'm back in San Francisco. I'm about to call out to Rico, but as reality comes crashing back, I sit up so fast the room spins. I fall back with a moan to keep my head from rattling.

"You okay?" Willa asks, popping into view above me.

"No," I say honestly, sitting up a bit slower this time. "Not really, but I'm glad I have you all with me." She takes my hand and squeezes.

I accidently knock my free hand into Sam, who is curled up next to me and doesn't stir. I move up the blanket covering him so that it goes over his shoulders, tucking it in slightly under his body and watching as his breathing relaxes afterward. I used to do the same for Manny, my eldest brother, because he bore so much of taking care of us kids.

I blink away the memory and take a deep breath. There are two more days until whatever Rico was warning me about.

"I can't believe you snooped through my bag," I tell them

both, walking over to where Rodrick is tinkering with the transceiver. "Did you find anything?"

"Well, Sam filled us in on your unsanctioned trip to the island and how he saw you take this transceiver, so we didn't necessarily snoop so much as we were informed. I've actually been waiting for you to wake up, because I need the radio we helped you fix before to fix this larger transceiver now. The signal booster, I think it'll help."

"Oh." I turn the other way, reach down into my shirt, and pull out from my bra the small radio that I keep with me at all times in case I need to get into contact with Rico.

I hesitate for a moment.

If I turn it over, how am I going to talk to Rico? But what choice do I have?

Rodrick stares at it for a moment before taking the piece and getting to work.

Willa comes up behind me and hands me a cup of orange juice. It takes me three long gulps to finish, and I'm already craving more. In San Francisco, there'd been plenty of times when my mouth was so dry, I'd resort to using whatever saliva I had to satisfy my thirst. Here, I've been able to drink all the water and juice and sometimes even a soda or two. And I pray to whatever gods there might be that I won't ever have to worry about where to get my next drink from again.

Suddenly, the transceiver speaker comes alive, and Willa and I shift our attention there.

"Try channel 19," I say to Rodrick, who returns the dial to that number.

There's actual recorded music on channel 19, which means . . . someone's running the station, playing the music. But who? It must be someone the Mad Scientist knew, right?

As if the world is trying to give me an answer, a voice cuts through the static.

"Hello, survivors of the apocalypse, my name is Ahmed Abu Nasrallah. If you are hearing this, then you're in what used to be known as the Golden State."

Instead of replying, Rodrick turns off the transceiver, his face stone-cold as he says, "We need to go somewhere that's not my house. I can't get my pop into trouble."

Sam joins us, having surely heard the man speaking through the transceiver. He's got a blanket draped over his shoulders. We make eye contact, his eyes burning with something like fire; this could be another way out.

"We can't all be gone at once. You should go back and pretend you don't know anything," I tell him.

"You're as close to family as I've got now, Jules, and I'm not turning my back on you," Sam says.

"No, she's right," Rodrick says, staring at the transceiver as if he's seen a ghost. He looks up at Sam. "We need someone on the inside. Pretend . . . like I've been pretending."

"What do you mean?" Willa asks, expression questioning.

Rodrick begins to pack up the transceiver. "We can't use this in my pop's house, but I know where we can."

"And where exactly is that?" Willa's voice has risen an octave, and it makes Rodrick halt. It seems I'm not the only one who has been keeping secrets.

"You all don't have to trust me. Jules, I know you don't. But this is the right move. We need to keep the transceiver away from Burberry and your aunt. So let's go."

Willa looks as if she's about to say something else. But then she starts to stuff an assortment of things into her own pack.

"So, I go to the mansion?" Sam asks the room.

"For now," I tell him. "When we have a plan, we'll come get you, and Sidra. I promise." I hold out my pinky to him. It's this gesture that makes his face soften.

He nods. "Okay."

Sam leaves Rodrick's first, sneaking out with a device that Rodrick has said will make his movement undetectable. I wonder if it's the same thing Rico has.

Ten minutes later, we head out.

There's something less frightening about walking around during the day, when the city is bustling with adults going to work and living simple lives that just involve catching the train on time.

The train station is filled with people laughing. And maybe Burberry made the right move in hiding the fact that the Masterdome is going to collapse one day, to not cause a panic. As we watch reporters on the television screens that play on the train talk only about good news inside the Oasis, I wonder where ten thousand people would even go. The Wasteland? They wouldn't last two days after the comfort they've lived in. Everyone would have it out for them.

"Did you read the Mad Scientist's journal?" I ask Rodrick.

He nods.

"But you didn't share it with Willa?" I gesture to Willa, who stands in line to buy us train tickets.

"I couldn't," he replies. "I keep thinking about it. On the one hand, we know what's outside. The life that awaits them if it all really does finally fail. But on the other hand, what if the Mad Scientist was wrong? What if nothing happens to the dome for a very, very long time?"

I put my hand on his arm. "I don't think we should tell her until we have to."

"Tell me what?" Willa asks, holding out two train tickets for us.

"Nothing," I say.

Willa eyes us warily but eventually shrugs. "We should get to our platform."

We take the train to the last stop of the South Shore, and I note that the only people who get off here are those similar to us in age. We all walk in the same direction, following a trail up a mountain. We trek north, where we arrive at a smaller lake, which is obviously a well-known swimming hole.

Several groups have claimed areas. A kid on the other side of us jumps in from about ten feet up, and there's wild applause from his group.

Rodrick hollers at them, too.

"Rodrick!" they yell out as a hello.

I can't help but laugh.

"What is this place?" Willa asks.

"It's an oasis within the Oasis," Rodrick replies. "Once we

cross the scanning point, no one can track us. It's like a glitch of sorts in the system."

We settle on top of one of the giant boulders surrounding the lake, far enough away from the others that we won't be overheard.

The sunlight that seeps in through the Masterdome has made the spot so warm. There's a lot we need to talk about, yet all I want to do is bask in the moment.

Willa nudges Rodrick. "What are we doing here? What are you hiding?"

"He's been hiding me." A woman sits down beside us. There's something about the way she grins at me in a familiar way that lets me know exactly who she is.

"You're Viola Hershall," I whisper.

"The first representative?" Willa asks.

"In the flesh," Viola says.

Willa turns to Rodrick, head tilted sideways as if she's waiting for an explanation.

Instead of meeting her gaze, Rodrick turns to me.

"I was the one who was meant to bring Rico to the Oasis. I've been Viola's go-between for a while. Gregory and I."

"You were going to let him in, even if he was a part of Mictlān," I state, before continuing. It's why he paused for so long at the lottery. Why he initially tried to take Rico even when I held the winning buzzer. "You've been working with Viola Hershall this whole time?"

"Well, Sheriff Ramos and Viola both knew Gregory, the guy we lost to the raiders. Gregory's the one who got me involved," he says. Now he turns to Viola. "I don't have good news."

Her eyes narrow. "What do you mean?"

"Tell her," Rodrick says, signaling to me. "What's in the journal. What you've discovered."

I take out the worn journal from the satchel, hand it over to Viola, open to the last few pages.

"The scientist who designed the spigots, and I guess the Masterdome itself, thought the Masterdome was failing."

"That's impossible," she says.

"Is it?" I ask.

"Stop!" Willa shouts. Her eyes are clouded by impending tears, and her face has turned red with embarrassment or anger, I'm not sure which one. Perhaps both. "You all need to tell me what in the world is going on. NOW!"

And so I do. I tell her what she knows: about Rico and how he gifted me his spot in the Oasis. And what she doesn't: about the Wasteland and the Sheriff who governs San Francisco. I tell her how Sheriff Ramos blackmailed Rico, and how Rico is in the haven without winning the lottery, and how he's been working for Viola, too, who is helping Sheriff Ramos take the haven over. And how none of it even matters if the Masterdome stops working. If what the Mad Scientist wrote in his journal is correct, we can't stay here. None of us. And lastly, I tell her that Sidra is Sheriff Ramos's granddaughter, and he wants her home.

Willa opens her mouth several times to speak but closes it again, pressing her lips together.

"The technical glitches," Rodrick finally says. "Those

started happening about three months ago and are getting worse, no matter how hard our engineers try to fix them. I think the scientist might be right."

"But what does it mean?" Willa asks. "How much time do we have?"

I exhale. "That's not the most pressing issue," I say, turning to Viola and giving her our full attention once more. "We're two days away from Sheriff Ramos entering the Oasis."

"You need to call this whole thing off," Rodrick says to Viola.

"I can't call it off with only the ramblings of who you all keep referring to as the 'Mad Scientist' as proof."

I take out the transceiver. Turn it on. "This device has an answer for us and will reveal more."

The music stops, and the man's voice comes through again. The words he uses are different this time, so we know he's really there.

Rodrick nods at me.

I grab the radio transceiver's speaker, click it on, and say, "Come in, come in. If anyone is listening, this is a survivor from California."

There's noise on the other end, a clicking of another transceiver coming to life.

"Hello? Who is this? Is Dr. Urreal with you?"

"No," I respond, assuming that's the scientist's name. "Dr. Urreal is dead. My name is Juliana Ramirez."

Viola's hand goes to her mouth, her expression one of deep concentration.

"Wowsers, I never thought I'd get a response from anyone in California again. Felt like you all fell into a black hole."

"We found Dr. Urreal's transceiver and his notebook yesterday. He had this channel written in his notes. Who are you? And what were you doing with him?"

"Well, Juliana, my dear, that's a long story. But to sum it up, I'm to the north of you, in Oregon. I've been trying to reach you folks for almost three years now. Started trying to when I was in my prime. I'm the president of Oregon now. Dr. Urreal would have found that both alarming and exciting, I think." He chuckles as he says this. "Dr. Urreal asked me to help him get people out of your city. We were working things out, but he went dark. Without any way to contact him again or anyone else, I thought the worst."

"Could that be done?" I ask. "Getting people out?"

"I mean, with a ton of resources, sure. When Dr. Urreal stopped calling and picking up my calls, I assumed it was too late. That the Masterdome had failed and everyone had already scattered, so I couldn't risk my people or what we'd need to use to make it to you. But it sounds like your dome is holding on, same as ours."

"*Our* dome? Same as *yours*?"

"You didn't think yours was the only Masterdome built, did you?"

"Kinda." I laugh. "But that's incredible. Could you still help us? We think our dome is about to fail."

"How many are you now?"

"There're ten thousand of us."

He exhales extra loudly. "I need to run some numbers,

talk to a few members of my cabinet. But I can tell you what I told Dr. Urreal. We have a compound surrounded by our own dome that was based off the Oasis. This compound is not in the mountains, though, but in the last viable forest in Oregon. Dr. Urreal helped me salvage our dome and extend it into two conjoined bubbles, to help more people. I owe him the lives of everyone I'm meant to protect. But he didn't have the parts needed for his own, and worse, I didn't have any extras. There is no repairing your Masterdome, and when we last spoke, we figured its failure would be imminent once the glitches started happening concurrently. But if you all can make it to me . . ."

"Dr. Urreal didn't mention No Man's Land? I don't think most of us can make it to you alive. Not with the raiders and cannibals. And the glitches have already been happening for months."

The line goes silent on the other side for a moment, and I bite the inside of my cheek as we wait.

"It sounds like it could topple at any minute, then. I meant what I said. I owe Dr. Urreal everything. He cared about everyone inside the Oasis more than his journal will ever tell you. And it sounds like he gave up his life for it. Give me three days to get you an answer. We have been working on a hovercraft, and we might be able to push its construction. Meanwhile, I know that Dr. Urreal isn't alive to hear this, but I am so damn happy that you all are surviving."

"Thank you," I reply as my mind spins in circles.

"And, Juliana, one more thing . . ."

"Yeah?"

"Dr. Urreal told me about the water spigots. He had promised to help us create some of our own—"

"We have his notes on them! We know what's needed. We started looking for the parts to build a 3D printer that could make some. We can bring what we have."

Ahmed laughs. "Wonderful! So, that's our plan. Make sure to bring any research you have with you, and I'll make sure to get you all out."

"Okay," I reply.

"I'll call back when I can. Stay safe until then, Juliana."

"Holy shit," Rodrick says once the line goes static, and we turn the transceiver off.

"They've told us there isn't any other place to go to." Willa stares down at her hands as if everything she's ever known is a lie. Perhaps it is.

"That doesn't prove anything," Viola says as she stands. "The plan must continue."

"Where's Rico?" I ask. He's always been better at dealing with people than I am. Perhaps he can persuade Viola Hershall to stop this madness now. "Last I heard, he was freeing his aunt."

She licks her lips. "And the last I heard, he went radio silent."

"What does that even mean?"

"It means that one incredible thing went according to plan yesterday, and two others did not. We're playing a waiting game now. But perhaps there's something you can help us with still."

I try to focus on the task at hand instead of whether or not Rico is okay. He always is, I remind myself. And always will be. For now, the best way of reconnecting with him is by staying close to Viola. "And what's that?" I ask.

"Sidra."

I close my eyes and send a prayer to Mami and Papá, who both believed in some kind of afterlife. If they're in heaven, listening, watching me, perhaps they can guide me in some way.

"Tell me what I need to do," I say. I thought being inside the Oasis and with Burberry was the safest place for her, but not if the Masterdome is failing. It's obvious she isn't safe with her grandfather either, someone who would blackmail teens to get what he wants. So, in the end, I'll agree to help free her, but not to benefit Viola or Sheriff Ramos.

"Go to the mansion and tell her the truth. I believe if you do, she'll leave willingly. Sneak out. Bring her to me," Viola replies.

"Wait. How exactly do you think you're going to whisk away the President's daughter without Burberry coming after you with all three hundred deputies in the Oasis and Sheriff Paul himself?" Willa rambles, crossing her arms.

"I don't know," I respond. "But I'll figure it out."

CHAPTER 21

Rico

My eyes are shut, but there is no darkness. Only blinding white light.

I'm not dead . . . not yet.

I stay this way for a long time. Lucid, like I'm living in ten different versions of my body all at once, and each one of them is fighting against something different. Fighting to be heard. Fighting to survive. Fighting to keep loving and be loved by Jules.

And all ten want to get up.

The warmth of a calloused hand on my forehead finally brings me back to reality. Nadine stares at me with delight instead of hate for the first time in far too long. I'd missed her not hating my guts. "I knew you'd wake up. You're too stubborn to die. Just wish you'd done it before sunrise."

I jolt as I remember I've been shot. Recall that we came here to free tía Linda only to find no one but deputies at the warehouse. The pain comes in a spasm, hurting so bad that I see white until I lie back down.

Gingerly, I touch my shoulder with a shaking hand. I'm not wearing a shirt. Someone, likely Jesus if he's still alive, has bandaged me up with torn strips of linen. I've been shot and my wound is bleeding through the bandages. Still, I guess I should be thankful knowing that my cousin didn't leave me to die.

I glance up. We're still in the warehouse.

"What's the verdict?" I ask as I gape at the soft ceiling lights.

"Well, it's morning and we're surrounded, but there's no way into the building except the front," Nadine says. "So at least no one can kill us unless we give them the chance to."

I try to turn toward my cousin, but his silence tells me all I need to know. Jesus never shuts up unless he's truly worried about something, and I guess this is worrisome.

"I think I can stand," I say. "It hurts, but luckily, I didn't get shot in the leg."

"Can you run fast enough, though?" he asks seriously.

I shrug, but it makes the wound ache. "If I don't, I'm probably dead, so I'm going to have to. You don't have to worry about me."

Jesus scoffs. "I've worried about you your whole life."

"You're a year older than me," I say, even though it hurts to try to laugh.

"We need some kind of distraction," Nadine says. She sits back and hugs her knees. Then she takes out a switchblade and brings it back and forth and around in the air, over and over again, deep in thought.

Part of me wants to give up. Pull out the pillbox.

But I won't give up as long as Jules is inside the Oasis. She'd be pissed.

I picture Jules's face and remember the melody of her laugh as she enjoyed an ice cream sundae, remember how warm and safe it felt to lie in an actual bed with her, remember the way she stared at the ring. Even though the taste of finding it was bitter, I know she was glad to have it back. It's enough to get me on my feet. Because I truly don't have any other options. I need to get out of this building and back to Jules.

Jesus perks up at the realization that I might not be a lost puppy. Just because I left Mictlān doesn't mean I suddenly became incapable of doing what needs to be done. I always have. And I always will.

"All right," Jesus responds, standing as well. "Let's go find a distraction. This is a whole warehouse; there's bound to be something useful here."

We search several aisles and bins for a few minutes before we find the perfect item. And even though I've been shot, something else has happened. The air between me, Jesus, and Nadine isn't as dense. They saved me when they didn't have to. They could have simply left me outside the warehouse, and Viola Hershall wouldn't have been any the wiser. They could have gotten rid of me but didn't.

"Fireworks?" Nadine asks, grinning, as she strains to carry over a giant box.

"Fireworks," I say with giddy excitement. I search through the contents of the box with one hand and find that the pyrotechnics aren't handmade, or for little kids. These are legit and huge.

"There're more of them, at least two other boxes," Nadine says, signaling for me to follow her.

Nadine carries while I kick-push three more boxes filled with fireworks over to where we've made our home base.

I jump, my shoulder smarting, when a loud knock comes from the warehouse doors. Then someone says, "Leave your weapons and come out with your hands in the air."

Jesus brings out smoke masks for us, ones he found elsewhere in the warehouse, along with what look like grenades, eighteen of them. I swallow hard, my mouth suddenly tasting metallic like blood as I recall the way Jesus and Nadine took out the deputies guarding the warehouse with no remorse.

I'm not like them. "No," I tell him, taking the mask he hands me. "We're not trying to kill anyone."

Jesus's face shifts from bemused to serious as if he has a retort on the tip of his tongue. Instead, he sets the grenades to the side and says, "Fine. We'll do this your way, Cuz. Only because I think I've seen enough blood for today." I shudder at the fact that he means mine.

We quickly sort through the boxes of fireworks, finding the largest of the bunch that'll really blow things up and cause enough smoke for us to slip by unnoticed. That's our biggest goal—none of us want to go out with a bang more than we want to actually get out of here alive.

Luckily, Jesus has two lighters on him, giving us enough juice to cause a stir, but we need to time things perfectly.

We make a line of fireworks, pointing them all in the direction of the entryway. Exactly how many deputies we'll face is an unknown, but we prepare for a fair number. Uncertainty sits at the pit of my stomach, probably fueled by the fact that every step I take makes my shoulder hurt so much that my toes spasm as if they've been hit by a lightning strike.

Every time I think I can't go on anymore, not without legitimate medical help, I remember Jules. Her smile. Her face. The smell of her skin and the taste of her lips, and I breathe in deep and keep moving.

The plan is for Jesus and Nadine to run through and light the fireworks and get out of the way. Meanwhile, I'll open the doors so we can escape. If we can do this all fast and smart enough, we can get out of here and no one will ever catch us.

We ready ourselves. Growing up, we got in trouble plenty of times. But the three of us always managed to get out of it, together.

I turn the radio on when the time nears. "Jules, can you hear me?" I ask.

There's static and I'm almost out of time.

Then I hear her voice. "Rico? Where are you? I'm so happy I got my new signal booster in time. I really needed you last night—"

"Hey, Jules," I cut in, ignoring the fact she needed to find a new signal booster but glad she was able to find one so I can have this moment. "I don't have a lot of time. I needed to call you really quick and . . ." There is so much to say that I'm unable to figure out a place to start.

"And?" Her voice cracks as if she senses there's something wrong.

"And I'm sorry, for all of this. No matter what happens, I need you to know that you've been my oasis."

"You're scaring me, Rico. What's going on?"

"Let's go," Jesus says, bumping against my shoulder and shooting daggers at me with his eyes. *Get your head in the game*, they tell me.

"I gotta go," I say to Jules.

"Rico, wait. I have to tell you—"

"I love you. Always."

I turn off the radio.

I slip my new multi-gas respirator mask on, blinking hard as I struggle to see clearly out of its scratched-up visor, but at least I'll be able to breathe through the smoke.

I can't keep still as we count down the last ten seconds.

But there are some things that will never change, like this ability Jesus, Nadine, and I have to move in tandem. We don't have to yell at each other for our plan to go right. At once, Jesus and Nadine strike their lighters, matching each other's speed as if they've done this a million times before. Perfectly in sync.

"Five, four, three, two . . ."

"Now!" Jesus shouts when they get to the last couple fireworks. The instant he does, I don't hesitate. I press the button to open the doors. I don't know if it's the moment, or the fear of what we're about to do, but the sound of the doors opening echoes fifty times louder than it did when we entered.

I run over as best I can to Nadine and Jesus, to the left of the door. Bullets fly past us, but they serve to cause a larger explosion as they hit the fireworks. They ring out, each one firing after the next until the whole entrance and the outskirts surrounding the warehouse become a smoke screen, thick enough to hide us, even in the daylight.

The bullets and laser blasts continue to fly; the sparks and flames of the fireworks bite as soldiers rush past us, shouting in confusion. And meanwhile, my cousin, Nadine, and I carefully slip out. I almost crash into one of the soldiers, but luckily, he has his back turned toward me, and I manage to skirt around him.

We escape back into the forest, to the pod Viola Hershall gave us for this job. The moment I'm inside the vehicle and we're far enough away, I scream, the pain of my injury too much, the adrenaline of the moment waning too quickly. My arm shakes, and Nadine holds me while I cry into her torso, wondering how I'm going to explain all of this to Jules.

"It's okay," Nadine says softly.

"No. It's not, Nadine," I shout back at her, the weight of everything crushing. It's overbearing. "Things weren't supposed to turn out this way. We were supposed to find tía Linda. And I'm so tired." I let myself cry, the way I did after I thought tía Linda died, and at some point, I pass out, either from the pain or disappointment. Hell, maybe both.

I stay asleep until we get back to Viola Hershall's place, and I honestly have no idea how they manage to get me out of the vehicle. They strap me down to a table and wheel me into some kind of plastic medical pod I can't break free of. I gasp, unable to breathe in the tight space. I hate the feeling of suffocating even when you're surrounded by air. And I hate the fact that Jules isn't here to lessen the constricting of my chest the way she's done whenever I've had a panic attack.

The pod whirls, and a bright beam slowly sweeps over my body and scans me. The machine tells me that not only do I have an injured left shoulder, but I'm also suffering from malnutrition. I want to completely destroy it after that. Even more so when a metal arm protrudes from the main mechanism and sprays some kind of pink disinfectant that stings across my shoulder.

I knock my head back against the board until I feel a pinch of something. Whatever is in the needle doesn't knock me out, but I do calm down enough to see that outside the medical pod, Nadine is watching me, brows furrowed. Whatever they've given me, though, I'm suddenly giddy and laugh uncontrollably.

I don't see her, but I recognize Viola's voice as she says, "He'll be himself soon enough."

The person she's speaking to comes into view, and I swear I see tía Linda, even though it can't be.

I keep laughing, but in my mind, all I can think about is that if I don't make it back to Jules with an explanation, I'll really be dead.

Hours later, I'm pulled out of the medical pod. Whatever the machine is programmed to do, it's done its job well. My arm isn't quite the same, but close enough that I can actually function without feeling pain with every movement. I'm supposed to rest, but of course, all I can think about is Jules. She's the only thing that makes the pain of living okay. And I desperately need to hear the reminder that it'll be okay from her.

I dress and sneak out of Viola's medical bay, eager to get back to Juliana and let her know I'm still alive.

"Wait," Nadine calls out to me, hurrying to catch up when I'm right by the door. "You shouldn't leave until you're better."

"I'm fine," I say, continuing on.

"No, you're not," she replies, taking a hold of my uninjured shoulder.

I whip around, ready with snakes on my tongue, but I take in the person who stands next to Nadine.

I wasn't imagining things after all.

Tía Linda is thinner; the medical pod would surely say she suffers from malnutrition as well. Her eyes are dull, opened wide, as if she's in shock. But she's alive, and here. She's safe.

"Hola, Ricardo," she says, wiping at the tears on her cheeks.

I run up to her, hug her tight. "How?" I ask.

The hallway fills with more bodies. Jesus, who grins, arms crossed. Viola Hershall, who has a smug expression. And others in her group.

"Distractions," Viola says. "I'm sorry that we couldn't tell you. But the real plan was that you three would distract the deputies and pull Sheriff Paul's attention to the commotion at the warehouse, while another team would get Linda out of where they were actually keeping her. It worked."

A part of me wants to swear. Yell. Argue. Ask *What the hell?* But mostly, I'm relieved that my aunt is safe.

"So now what?" I ask no one in particular.

Tía Linda sets her hand on my cheek and says, "Now, mi hijo, we win."

PART IV

THE MASTERDOME & THE REVOLUTIONARIES

CHAPTER 22

Jules

Willa, Rodrick, and I have been in Viola's secret underground compound for hours, hiding out from tía Ines.

This place is unlike anything I've seen. It's eerie and huge, at least thirty feet tall. And it's too quiet and cold. At least it is where we've been sequestered. The dim room we're in has a few couches, only one overhead light, an old television sitting on a small round table that none of us have even tried to turn on, and a refrigerator on one side, which Willa is searching through now.

She pulls out a soda but doesn't immediately open it. She rejoins me on the couch, facing the door, nails rapping against the can. Meanwhile, Rodrick lies on one of the other couches, bouncing a small rubber ball against a wall.

"How long are we going to be here?" Willa asks, breaking the silence.

"Till Rico comes back," I reply. Or they kick us out.

"What if he doesn't?" she asks, voice concerned.

"He will," I say.

Rodrick exhales. “Let’s just give it time.”

“Do we have time?” Willa asks, anger in her tone.

Rodrick stops playing with the ball. He and Willa exchange tense looks I can’t fully read but clearly show just how strained their relationship suddenly is.

“We have hope,” he replies. His words seem to settle Willa. She pops the top of her soda can and takes a long drink, closing her eyes.

Seconds later, the door opens and Viola Hershall enters, smoothing out her skirt.

“The group is meeting,” she tells us. “It’s time we all talk about next steps.”

“What about Rico?” I ask.

Viola doesn’t reply, walking away instead. Rodrick moves to follow her and signals me to come along. Willa hesitates when I hold my hand out to her. She stares at it for a moment, until she relents and takes it.

We head down what feels like a nicely furnished tomb, and eventually arrive at the end of a long corridor where the sound of people talking over each other reaches us.

“This is our meeting room,” Viola says, opening the twin doors leading in with both of her hands, which she raises once inside as if to show off what she and San Francisco’s Sheriff have created: a true revolution.

The crowd turns to take us in. There’re more people in here than I expected. At least two hundred jam-packed into the meeting room. Some of them clap; some of them cheer and call Viola’s name; others simply have expectant gazes.

I turn to Rodrick, who looks almost as smug about it all as

Viola. There's a light in his eyes that isn't there in Willa's. I recall what he said in the forest, about a Third Epoch. I should have guessed back then that he was a revolutionary. It makes sense. The Sheriff and Viola would have needed to have representatives on their side to send each other messages.

In between Rodrick and me, Willa scrunches her eyebrows in confusion as she takes everyone in.

I want to say something to console her, aware how betrayed she might feel. Did she truly not suspect what her boyfriend was up to? If I were in her position, I don't know how long it would take me to forgive Rico. But after giving it some thought, I know I would. Rodrick was trying to make life better. So I don't say anything. No words would help, anyway. She needs time. I just hope we have it.

I spot a familiar face in the crowd, and my heart skips a beat.

"Rico?" I shout, letting go of Willa. I leave our group, squeezing through a multitude of bodies.

He sees me, too, and stands to embrace me. He winces as he does.

"I was so worried," I say, giving him a glance over for injuries. I can't believe Viola didn't tell me he'd come back. The wound on his eyebrow continues to be worrisome, and it seems like he's favoring one shoulder over the other in the way he stands, but he's not so bad. "Are you okay?"

"It's a long story," he replies, but then turns to the woman next to him. She's staring at me. She's too thin, her cheeks sunken as if she's been starved, but there's an expression of hope that I recognize in Rico.

“Tía Linda?” I ask.

She grins. Takes my hand. “You must be Jules.”

I laugh, don’t even know what to say.

Viola Hershall whistles, calling everyone’s attention. Rico gives me his seat at the table and stands behind me, one hand caressing my shoulder.

“The time has come for a Third Epoch,” Viola starts, and the smile I had fades. After everything, haven’t they been paying attention? Listening? You can’t build anything new on a crumbling world. A Third Epoch isn’t going to happen in the Oasis.

I lock on Willa’s gaze from across the room, where she has remained by the door. She gives a slight shake of her head. Even Rodrick suddenly looks uneasy as he stares at an empty spot on the table.

The rest of the revolutionaries stomp their feet, though, fueled by Viola’s words. She should tell them everything: about the Mad Scientist and the Masterdome, so that they can make an educated decision. But she only keeps going.

“There is a lot to do. You all know what your assigned roles are. Know that if we pull this off, which we will, we’re going to lead this city within days. We’ve been working hard for this—it’s our destiny.”

There’s more stomping, and my heartbeat thumps with every vibration.

Viola continues to give everyone false hope. Or perhaps I’m overreacting, and she’s right. There is no knowing how soon the Masterdome will fail. Therefore, it’s not worth alarming anyone.

Then how come my stomach won't settle?

I don't know. If Sheriff Ramos were here, he might understand that the Oasis might be worthless in the end. He might be content simply having Sidra back. I could be wrong, though.

After Viola gives her speech, the others disperse and go back to doing whatever they were doing before.

I grab Rico's hand, lead him away from the rest of the group, even while his aunt eyes me suspiciously. I find a corridor that seems empty, at least for now.

He takes my face in his hand, presses me against the stone wall, and gives me a lingering kiss. "I can't even express how happy I am to see you," he says.

I kiss him again but then pull away.

"We need to talk. I need to catch you up on everything."

He presses his forehead against mine. Sighs. "Please tell me it's good news."

"It's not," I confess. "And Viola Hershall is making it worse."

He moves so that both of our backs are against the wall. He takes my hand.

"Tell me."

And so, I do. I tell him about the island, and what we found. About the Mad Scientist. I tell him about Ahmed and our conversation. How there is another way, perhaps, to survive if he comes through, but how the haven isn't going to last forever. In fact, it might be falling apart, considering all the glitches.

By the time I finish, he's no longer on his feet. Instead, he's sitting down, hands on his face and elbows on his knees.

"I'm sorry," I say. "I know that the Sheriff and Viola Hershall and your aunt and your cousin and Nadine, they all want this revolution more than anything. I know that in a way, you do, too. But it's too dangerous to think we can bring people here from the Wasteland to outlive the apocalypse."

"They're not going to listen to me if I ask them to stop," he mumbles from behind his hands.

"Perhaps you don't ask them to stop. Instead, we follow my new plan. We wait to hear from Ahmed. And we figure out how to create spigots and protective suits for those in San Francisco because doing something is better than nothing. And we never give anything else to the Oasis again. We let it fall."

Rico moves his hands away from his face. And I don't know why I'm nervous to ask him to follow my lead, but I am.

He stares at me as if he doesn't recognize me. As if people can change that much in less than two weeks.

I think he's going to tell me that I need to stop, but he responds, "What do we need to do?"

I let out a chuckle, slide down to join him on the floor, and kiss him once more, his lips tasting of freedom. "We wait for Ahmed to call us back. But before that, we need to get Sidra." And Sam, I can't forget about Sam. I made a promise to him as well.

"And how in the world do we do that?"

"Very carefully," I respond. "Or very irresponsibly. Viola is trying to send me alone, though."

"That's not happening. I'm with you, Jules. And we'll need backup," Rico says, then stands and takes my hand. He leads us back past the now-empty conference room, to another smaller office, which I take is Viola's, considering she's sitting behind a desk. Tía Linda is in the room, as well as Jesus and Nadine.

"We're going to go get the girl, and we'd like backup," Rico says.

He doesn't tell them anything else. But I see him exchange a look I can't fully read with his cousin, who exchanges one with Nadine, as if the three of them are speaking to each other without talking.

"It's too risky to spare anyone else right now," Viola says.

"What will happen when Sheriff Ramos comes and he doesn't find his granddaughter with us?" Rico asks.

"We can go," Jesus says.

"No, none of you should go anywhere." It's tía Linda who speaks now. "It's too dangerous for children."

"We're not children," Nadine says, cutting in, tone bitter.

"Nadine's right," Jesus adds. "We've grown up. Maybe not in your eyes, but it doesn't take away from the fact that living in the Wasteland has forced us to adapt."

Viola clasps her hands together. "The answer is still no. You two need to stay put and not cause any disruption. Your job is to remain hidden until we make a move, like everyone else. That is the role I want you to play. Juliana's already been to the mansion and can get in and out."

Rico nods. "Okay. It'll just be Jules and me," he relents. I want to argue more, but there's something in the way he squeezes my hand that makes me stop. And for once, I don't bicker, since it won't get me anywhere. I simply plan my own little rebellion.

"We'll leave you to it and get out of your way," Rico adds. Viola stares him down but finally gives a small nod in approval.

"Be safe," tía Linda says.

We walk side by side out of the office. I have no idea where Rico is going, but he presses something into my hand after a few minutes—when I take a look, it's some kind of weapon.

"A Taser, for safety when we're outside," he says as we reach what I now recognize as the bunker entryway.

I breathe deep, accept the weapon, and immediately know that despite what Viola Hershall said, Rico is mine, and he's once again proving that he's the one person I can trust.

We're breaking Sidra out.

CHAPTER 23

Jules

The train ride back to the North Shore is one filled with gratitude. I'm thankful that Viola's plan didn't get Rico killed. Still, I can't keep my leg from shaking, or my mind from running at a million miles an hour. That is, until Rico sets his hand on my knee before interlacing his fingers in mine. Suddenly, everything that's made me anxious withers.

I take in everyone around us. The people out on a late lunch or those typing away on tablets, finishing out their workdays or planning something in their lives. I'm sorry for anyone who doesn't know the truth—who genuinely thinks they're safe here.

Peace must be blissful.

Still, a part of me would rather be privy to what's going on than not, even if it complicates my life.

Once we're off the train, our plan is to find a motorcycle we can rent and head to Burberry's to get Sidra together.

I'm deep in thought at a crosswalk, Rico's hand still in mine, as we wait for the pedestrian sign to turn green, when

Sheriff Paul's face comes into view across the street. It's so odd to see him out of Burberry's mansion that for a moment, I'm not fully sure if it's him or a lookalike. But worst of all is the way he's not alone. At least ten deputies are with him, and when Sheriff Paul's eyes lock on us, like he's found exactly who he's searching for, panic rises in my stomach.

"Rico, run!" I turn us around and run down the street we've come from, even as Sheriff Paul calls out my name. The howling screech of pods stopping rings out behind us. Mechanical voices tell the sheriff to head back to the sidewalk for pedestrians. I pray they slow him down.

My legs burn furiously in a way I haven't felt since the last time Rico and I worked the Scar. My chest thumps so loud I hear it in my ears. Sweat runs down my face and neck, and my lungs struggle to keep pace as Rico takes the lead. Who knows what'll happen if Sheriff Paul catches us?

"This way," Rico says and guides us around another building, aiming to zigzag so we can lose Sheriff Paul in between the shops near the train depot.

"Juliana!" I hear behind me, just when I'm considering easing up.

I turn back around without really meaning to, tripping Rico.

Sheriff Paul stands a block away from us. My hand instinctively goes to the Taser Rico gave me, but there's no way I want to get close enough to Sheriff Paul to use it. Rico shields my body with his.

Some people in the area stop to gawk at us, then at the sheriff. I ignore them, and after a moment, they do the same.

None of them are willing to intervene on our behalf, to lose their spots in the haven, especially with Paul wearing his sheriff uniform today.

The rest of the deputies appear at his side. "There's no point in running. It's over, you two. Whatever game you've been playing at is through. Did you think we wouldn't ever realize you're not supposed to be here, kid?" he yells, eyes drawn to Rico as if he could smother him and enjoy it.

It takes a moment, but my brain reminds me that I'm not incapable, and I don't have to depend on Rico for everything. I can tell how tired he is. Can see how his body is sluggish, even as he stands upright. Even though he hasn't told me much of what happened over the last week, I know he's hurting.

Rico helped and taught me how to survive the Wasteland when I thought I couldn't without my parents. He always believed in me, not because he needed to or wanted a sidekick, but because he believed in my ability to stand on my own two feet.

I can get us out of this. I can be the one to hold our veil of hope together.

"Does my aunt know you're coming after me?" I call out, wondering exactly who is responsible for Sheriff Paul's mission today.

"No," he responds. "But it's for your aunt that I promise not to hurt you. All you need to do is let us take him. Your aunt never even has to know."

I grin, somewhat relieved that at least my tía isn't in on this. Perhaps if I can get to her, she might be able to help us. But do I really believe that? What is blood worth in the apocalypse anyway? Will she aid us after everything that's happened? All I've witnessed her do? No, I need a new plan. One that doesn't involve seeing if my tía would turn on me.

Paul takes one step forward and Rico readies himself into a fighting stance.

"Run, Jules," Rico whispers.

But how could I leave him? I had in San Francisco, and look at where it got us.

I ignore Rico and survey the area. There's a narrow passageway between two buildings. We can fit through it, but Paul will be too broad. "Well, I have one thing to say, Paul," I start, then flip him off from behind Rico's shoulder.

I pull Rico inside the passageway, moving as fast as I can toward the other side of the street. Behind us, there are orders being shouted, the chaotic shuffling of people pursuing. We need to get through before Sheriff Paul and his deputies catch us.

Sunlight blinds me as we exit the alleyway. Still, I don't stop as we cross the road, stalling a line of pods until one of them makes contact and thrusts me forward with enough force that I roll a good ten feet.

Everything and everyone in the vicinity freezes . . . and quiets. Rico is above me in a blink. He calls my name, but it's like I'm in a bunker and his voice is an echo.

The concrete road smells unnatural. Still, I inhale as deeply as I can, needing oxygen to get my muscles moving, the desire to get away from Sheriff Paul overwhelming. There's something about being on the brink of getting caught that makes me shake off the pain. I manage to get to my feet even as the ground tilts on its axis, and my gaze remains unfocused.

"Are you okay?" a man says as he comes out of the pod. He takes hold of my shoulders and steadies me.

"She's fine," Rico responds, searching around us, likely for an exit strategy.

Across the way, Sheriff Paul appears and shouts "Stop them!" to the man whose pod hit me.

The man searches my face, turns from me to the sheriff, from the sheriff back to me and to Rico.

"Please help us," I whisper, unable to get any other words out. Rico takes me by my elbows, holding me upright.

"Jules?" Rico asks, moving to cradle me.

I've never been too proud to beg, the way Mami and Papá never shied away from asking for support.

I don't know what the man sees in us. If he's another one of Viola's followers in disguise or simply someone in the Oasis who understands that giving us up to Sheriff Paul means our imprisonment or death. Instead of trying to stop us, he bites the side of his lips. Before Sheriff Paul gets to us, he murmurs, "Take my pod. Hurry now, you two."

I could kiss the man. Instead, Rico carries me into the two-seater pod. I hit the button to lock the door as soon as I've shuffled over to make room for Rico. I give the pod directions to Burberry's when Rico is in, too. The vehicle jolts forward, traffic continues, and Sheriff Paul is left to try to catch up to us on foot.

I turn to see out the back windshield. I'm left in horror as one of Sheriff Paul's deputies puts a black bag over the helpful man's head.

CHAPTER 24
Rico

"Are you all right?" I ask Jules once we're far enough away. "Who was that?"

"The Oasis's Sheriff," she replies. The same man who shot tía Linda years ago when we tried to break into the Oasis the first time. I should be angry, fuming at the man, but all I am is tired. When I don't say anything, Jules signals to her whole body and says, "I guess now we're both hurt."

I can't argue with that. Even though the medical pod fixed my arm, there are still times when it's all pins and needles, movements I make that cause it to ache. But I'm more worried about Jules.

I press gingerly on her ribs. "Does anything feel like it's broken or bleeding inside?"

She shakes her head, to my relief, and replies, "I don't think so."

"Maybe we should leave," I say. "Find a way out, even if we need to fight through."

"We can't leave Sidra," she responds, without giving it more thought.

I'm about to argue, but the sound of something hitting the pod windshield draws my attention.

"You two want backup?" a muffled voice says to our side.

"Is that Jesus?" Jules asks, voice alight in a way I thought it'd never be when it came to my cousin.

I press a button on the pod's central console and my window lowers and I joke, "I thought both tía Linda and Viola told you two to stay put?"

Jesus, holding on to Nadine as she drives their motorcycle, gives us a toothy grin in reply.

"Did you think we were going to let you have all the fun?" Nadine asks.

Behind us, a blast knocks one of the rearview mirrors off the motorcycle, which swerves for a moment, before Nadine straightens it once again and they go zooming forward.

I turn to see two cars and two bikes behind us.

"Faster," Jules urges the pod, which immediately picks up speed and trails behind the motorcycle.

I swallow the knot in my throat, ignore the pinch at my shoulder and the fact that my eyebrow's still far from completely healed and my eye is still swollen some.

"When the pod stops, you go into Burberry's and persuade Sidra to come with you," I say. "Jesus, Nadine, and I will handle the deputies."

"How?" she asks, voice masked in unease.

There's no time to think more on it, though, as the

bike comes to a stop at Burberry's gate, and our pod stops next.

Jesus and Nadine get off slowly. I recognize Nadine pulling something out from behind her. Where she got another Jian sword from, I have no clue, but I'm thrilled to see it.

I exhale and squeeze Jules's hand once. "We got this. I won't let you down."

"You never have, and we do. Got this," she responds, surer of herself than I've ever seen her. She kisses me before I press the button on the console of the pod that opens both doors.

Jules and I exit in tandem, heads held high, no hesitation.

"Hey, Cuz," I say. "Let's make a bet. Whoever knocks out more deputies gets to call dibs on Burberry's mansion when this is over."

"I'll take that bet," Nadine says.

The deputies stop their own vehicles and either slip off their bikes or get out of their pods. There're nine of them, dressed in protective riot gear. Against three of us. I don't like our odds.

I step in front of Jules. "Go," I whisper. I don't add in the *before it's too late* on the edge of my lips.

"Now, this is the showdown I've been waiting for," Jesus finally says, cracking his knuckles and shaking loose his arms, readying himself.

"This doesn't have to be a fight," the lead deputy says. "You can turn yourselves in."

Jesus, Nadine, and I snort.

"Why don't you all scurry back to wherever you came

from?" Nadine replies, moving her sword in fluid motions and stepping into position, sword at her shoulder, one leg forward.

I move into a fighting stance, my legs ready to pivot forward in attack mode. Tears fill my eyes at the pain in my shoulder, but I resist and press them back.

The deputies come at us all at once. To my luck, only two approach me. They take out batons like the deputies had at the warehouse.

"Rico," Nadine says, throwing me a smaller blade.

I grit my teeth and block a strike from the first deputy. The second runs at me and manages to hit me behind the knee, so I'm tripped up and fall on my back. I roll away, just in time, as the deputy's baton hits where my head was.

"Get up, Rico!" I hear my cousin yell.

I manage to get to my feet, but the deputy who knocked me down hits my leg and arm. Gashes appear, crimson and painful.

I block again, but this time, I also attack.

I see red, a flood of raw emotion overtaking me and making me charge in a way that's supernatural. I slice at his shoulder, and he drops his weapon. I don't stop, and before I know it, the deputy is on the ground as I'm about to deal him a final blow.

"Rico!" I stop at the sound of desperation in Nadine's voice. "Knock out, not kill," she says as she knocks one of the deputies out herself.

I nod, turn my blade to the blunt end, and hit the deputy on the side of his head. He passes out, and I'm left with only one foe.

As the other deputy presses my way, he's struck over the head by Jesus, who is actually laughing like he hasn't had this much fun in years. Maybe he hasn't. Either way, as much as I love my cousin, I never want to be like him.

He goes over to the deputy and kicks him. He's about to go at it again, when I grab him, pull him away. "This isn't how I want to win," I tell him. He laughs, but his face turns serious.

He wipes at his nose, the sweat from his brow, and shakes his head. "These people don't care about you. They would kill you if they could. Why stand up for them?"

"I'm not," I respond. "I'm standing up for my own humanity, and yours."

Before Jesus can reply, the world sways suddenly, and I become dizzy from the fight. Like I'm going to faint.

As Nadine's eyes grow wide, I realize it is something else.

The ground is shaking. I glance at Jesus. He freezes, along with the remaining deputies. The road suddenly splits, a canyon developing right underneath where Nadine and the last three deputies stand. She loses her footing. Jesus and I both leap after her, each of us taking a hold of one of her hands in time.

Jesus looks at me. I look at him.

We lift Nadine up as the deputies fall into an unending crevice.

The movement doesn't stop once we're all on our feet, away from the edge. For a moment, my stomach is in my throat as a brash crackling comes from above. If what Jules revealed about the dome is indeed true, it's weak, and an earthquake of this size, well, it might be what ultimately tears the crumbling shield down.

How long will the Masterdome last? And what happens if it stops working entirely? There's still at least an hour of daylight. The sun will be too strong, and we don't have enough protective suits for everyone. I don't even have mine with me at the moment, having left it behind at the train depot the day Nadine, Jesus, and I arrived. It's like the leaders of the Oasis thought they were gonna be invincible forever. But forever is never guaranteed.

"Jules," I say to Jesus and Nadine, who look ready to get back on their motorcycle and turn tail, but to where, who knows.

They don't fight me for once, though. Instead, they nod in unison. I also know another thing. I can't lose my cousin. I can't lose Nadine. They're my best friends. They're my family. "No more getting separated," I add. "We stick together, and we get through this. Then you can hate me all you want."

To my surprise, Jesus says, "Okay."

To my greater surprise, another bike appears. The boy from the train and a redheaded girl hop off in swift motions.

"Need more backup?" the boy asks.

"You're Rodrick, right?" Jesus asks as he exchanges a look of amusement with Nadine, as if they had a bet he'd show up or something. "One of Viola's right hands?"

Rodrick grins proudly. "Yep. We haven't formally met yet . . . Jesus and Nadine." He signals to his companion and adds, "This is Willa. We're Jules's friends. Here to help."

Willa gives us a salute. "Hey," she says. While Rodrick is overly sure of himself, Willa looks like she doesn't want to be here, her eyes scanning the Masterdome. I don't blame her. I don't either, not after the quake that just happened.

As if we have spare time, both turn to me, waiting for my official introduction. I step forward and smirk. "I'm Jules's fiancé."

"Oh, I've known who you are the entire time. I remember you from lottery day in Union Square. I also saw you and Jules together on the train. Thought I'd help prevent you two from getting caught too soon after your big shopping trip," Rodrick says, and I decide that I like him already.

CHAPTER 25

Jules

My heart is beating fast as the main gate scans my retina, and I'm let in. I approach the mansion with quick steps, walking up the stairs to the main door. I open the front door as quietly as I can, sneaking in.

My brow sweats; my hands won't quit shaking. I'm terrified that something will happen to Rico.

"You really thought you'd beat me here?" Sheriff Paul says as he comes out from behind the kitchen entryway.

He is intimidatingly huge, and no one is here to save me. By some miracle, my hand acts on its own. I take out the Taser from Rico and blast Sheriff Paul's neck with it, the device rattling in my hand as I struggle to contain its power.

When I let go, Sheriff Paul doesn't go down. In fact, he somehow manages to headbutt me, sending me reeling. I don't waste time wiping at the warm blood oozing from my nose.

"Stop, before you really get hurt." He smears away some foaming dribble that escapes his mouth as he comes at me.

I jolt him again, and this time, luckily, the volts of the Taser send him down. I follow and continue to shock him, kneeling on his body as it convulses on the tile floor. Eventually, he freezes.

Who knows how long he'll stay passed out for, though.

I move with a groan, rubbing my forehead, hoping the goose egg I get from the hit won't be too bad.

At this time of the day, Sidra likes to pretend to be doing homework in her room while she actually draws comics.

I take the left side of the imperial staircase up two steps at a time, rushing to get to her before I'm taken down. If nothing else, I can see her and finally tell her the truth about how her biological grandfather is trying to get her back. Doing that'll mean I've succeeded in being a decent person in some small way.

I crash into Sidra's room, my face sweaty and my nose burning something furious from where Paul hit me.

Sidra rests at her window seat, drawing with her headphones on. Judging by her calm demeanor, she hasn't heard a single thing that's happened downstairs.

Her face contorts with confusion, then alarm as she takes me in. She removes the headphones. "Are you okay? You're bleeding! What happened?"

"I don't have time to explain," I say, wheezing as I struggle to fully catch my breath. "I need you to trust me when I tell you that you're not safe here, and we gotta go."

"What?" Sidra takes a step back as if I'm speaking another language.

Checkers approaches us, licks at the bottom of my pants.

I pick up the cat, half knowing that wherever the cat goes, Sidra will surely follow. I spot his cat carrier in a corner and stuff him in, Checkers meowing furiously at my actions. I zip the backpack and hand it to Sidra.

"What are you doing?" she asks, an edge to her voice—something like disappointment and distrust.

I lower to one knee, so I'm looking up at her instead of the other way around. "I know this is going to sound wild, but please believe I'm telling you the truth. Burberry is not your mother."

She scoffs. "I mean, we both know that—"

"That's not what I mean," I start. "You were taken from your grandfather. He's alive! You look exactly like him; it's uncanny. And I want to take you back home where you belong. He sent me here to do that." It's a bit of a lie, but not too far off from the truth. I do want to take her away, just not to her grandfather. I want to take her to Oregon, to a new life.

"I'm not leaving, Jules," she says slowly. "This is my home."

Burberry comes into the room, trailed by tía Ines and Sam and Sheriff Paul. The latter looks at me like he'd happily cook me for dinner. I hadn't expected that the whole damn household would be here, but now it's too late to form a better plan.

Sam's eyes are terrified as they lock on mine.

"Sidra, come to me," Burberry says in a calm tone that makes me seem like the threat.

Sidra moves toward Burberry but pauses midway. I shake my head at her and can't help the tears that run down my cheeks. God, I am so tired of crying, and the moment I get to Oregon, I'm going to figure out a way to get away from everyone except for Rico and find peace.

"I came to get you because I can't leave you here. I care about you," I confess.

I can tell that the wheels in Sidra's mind are turning as she tries to figure out who to trust: the person she's known for weeks or the one she's known most of her life?

She turns to Burberry and asks, "Is my grandfather alive?"

Burberry scoffs and tries to play it cool.

"Why is Jules injured?" Sidra asks next. When Burberry doesn't answer, she pivots to face Paul. "Did you hurt my friend?"

"She's not your friend," Burberry yells, drawing the attention back to her. "She's a nobody. An orphan who was barely getting by on scraps."

"If she was a nobody, why would you trust her to watch over me?"

Tía Ines steps in between us all. "Maybe we need to take a breath, sit, and figure things out a little bit more calmly." My tía's expression is calculating, and there's something in her eyes that begs me to stand down.

I stand taller. I don't want to fight. I've always had Rico for that, but I also won't accept defeat when I need to persuade Sidra to run away and never return.

Burberry is done with being calm. In a fast move, she pulls out a gun like the ones we have in the Wasteland, ancient and deadly. "I can't let your niece take my daughter, Ines," she warns.

"She isn't your daughter," I say. "So let her go home with me. We won't cause you any more trouble. We'll leave."

You would think I asked Burberry to crawl on her knees to the Wasteland and live there for the rest of her unnatural life.

She stands straighter, holding her nose haughtily high, like everything has suddenly clicked into place, and she moves her gun, aims it, and shoots tía Ines in the stomach without a single moment of hesitation.

"No!" I scream, my throat immediately becoming raw. I rush to my tía, who falls to her knees, her hands holding tight to her belly.

Burberry grabs Sidra, even as the girl screams "Mom! Stop! Please, let me go!" and squirms to break free. Even as Checkers goes frantic in his carrier on her back.

Sam stands stock-still. His eyes dart from Sidra to me to the President and Sheriff Paul, who doesn't say anything either. He simply stares at tía Ines, as if this whole day hasn't gone according to plan. Then he says, "Sam, safety off."

"Sir?" Sam asks, still unmoving.

Sheriff Paul points his weapon in my direction. "You heard me, Deputy. We're in shoot-to-kill mode."

Sam takes out his blaster. He moves his pinky in an obvious way, as if to assure me that our pinky promise still stands.

Paul glances at my tía again, then his eyes lift from her body to me.

Still, he doesn't move to apprehend Burberry or even to save my aunt, someone I know he cares for. I recall the way he smelled her hair the day we met.

"She's your best friend," I say to Burberry. "Why would you do this?"

My tía might be a loose end for Burberry, one she doesn't actually mind getting rid of, like Dr. Urreal. Valuable members of the Oasis are expendable. And in this moment, I know for sure that President Burberry was the one who killed the people we found on the island.

I shut my eyes, waiting for Sheriff Paul or Burberry to finish what they've started.

This isn't the way I wanted to die, but I will gladly go doing something I think is right.

Only the noise that sounds is not a bullet, but the beginning of something worse.

The ground quakes and shakes, and the walls rattle violently. This isn't just any earthquake. This is a big one. A wild one. One that has very bad timing. You would have thought those who built the haven would have considered that fate would have a way of finding them up here. But I guess their hubris got the better of them. They built the haven somewhere they thought no one would ever get to without a representative. But Mother Nature has her way of slipping in anywhere.

The glass windows shudder before suddenly shattering.

"President?" Paul beckons, his voice coated in fear for the first time.

"Sam! Get Sidra!" I shout, seizing the moment. He takes Sidra's hand, pulling her to him.

Paul shifts the direction of his weapon toward Sam. But Sam is steadfast and doesn't even flinch, his hand unshaking. We've been through so much in the Wasteland, it's wild for them to actually think they can scare us with their weapons. We've faced threats a thousand times over out there. The thing that scares me is thinking that the people I love, like my tía, might die.

On the second floor of the mansion, things begin to sway back and forth and, for a moment, I think the house might collapse and take us with it.

Instead, the floor cracks between us, separating our part of the room from where Burberry stands by a few inches, a space that continues to expand.

"President, we need to go!" Sheriff Paul says, tone urgent. His eyes land on me like he's done us a favor.

Burberry doesn't even look back once, not even at Sidra, before she vanishes.

Even as the earth continues to shake, I exhale in relief that at least one immediate threat is gone.

"Leave me. There's no time," my tía murmurs. "I won't make it out of here." I shake my head. I didn't abandon any of my family. They all died one by one, in the arms of their people. If that is all we can give at the end, so be it.

Sam comes and assists me with tía Ines. Sidra tightens the straps of the carrier holding Checkers, helps me to my feet.

We jump the now-foot-wide crack the earthquake has caused without any problem, and we follow behind Burberry and Paul, knowing well that something is very wrong.

At the top of the stairway, Sidra stops and turns around, her eyes wide. "I have to get something," she says.

"Wait!" I shout after her.

"Go get her," Sam says, taking on my tía's full weight.

"Don't wait for me," I reply before following Sidra as she heads in the opposite direction, where I know President Burberry's office and sleeping quarters are located. Sidra goes into Burberry's room while I shout after her, "We have to go before the mansion is destroyed! There's no time."

"We can't leave without this," she replies, face flushed as she holds up a small and golden circular jewelry box with a sunburst embedded into the top.

"What is it?" Why is it worth risking her life?

"This device holds all my mom's secrets," she says, pockets the device, then takes my hand and leads us back toward the stairs. "If there's a way to get everyone to see that she's a fraud and isn't worthy of being the leader, it'll be in these files."

Sam is already down the stairs when we return. Sidra and I rush to catch up, only to watch as Sam loses his grip. He and tía Ines stumble to the ground.

I hurry to them, but Willa appears, getting there first and catching tía Ines before she hits the tiled floors. "Mom?" she croaks, a sob already caught in her throat.

Rodrick helps Sam back to his feet, and I take my place on the other side of my tía, who says, "Willa? You should all go, find shelter, a way down from the mountain before the Masterdome collapses on you."

"We can carry you," Willa argues.

My aunt's eyes roll, so I know she's close to her last breath. Despite all that's transpired, she is the last of my family. I can't lose her.

"You're coming with us." I grab her by her arm, bring her up to her feet, but she pushes me away.

"Mom!" Willa says, pulling her along, only for tía Ines to evade her grasp as well.

On her knees now, she glances at Willa and me, blood dribbling from her mouth.

"I'll slow you down," she says, falling back again.

"The medical pod!" Sidra says. "We have one upstairs."

My eyes dart up—we're so far.

"Jules," Sam says gently, touching my shoulder.

"Sam, you have to take Sidra and go," I say, my tone serious.

"We're not leaving without you," Sidra says.

Rodrick picks my aunt up, but she suddenly goes limp and doesn't move.

"Mom?" Willa asks, fear distorting her face as she checks for a pulse, then adds in broken speech, "There's nothing there."

My body shakes; the sobs come along with the burn of pain. I scream, so loud and shrill that my throat aches afterward. When I take one last look at tía Ines, I see the rest of my family in her, and recall how they all stilled in death as well. I relive the pain of losing each one of them. There's a feeling that has no name, a hurt deeper than anything you could ever imagine, that paralyzes me. I can't even blink.

"We have to go! Now!" Sam says, the walls around us breaking apart, dust and debris making it hard to see clearly. He hooks his pinky into mine. "I know you're hurting, but we need you."

Thanks to Sam, whose presence reminds me that I still have my friends, I finally manage to blink. Tears fall on my cheeks and snot drips out of my nose. I try to wipe it all away, but it makes it worse. Still, I move and hug my aunt's body with all my might. "I love you, tía," I tell her. After everything that's happened, everything she's done, I still mean the words.

Willa kisses tía Ines's forehead, her hand shaking as she lets go of her stepmother's hand, before Rodrick sets her back down.

We take off running as Burberry's mansion comes undone. This will be onc moment out of so many that'll haunt me for the rest of my life, however long that might be.

CHAPTER 26
Jules

The ground is violent and angry, as if the mountain wants to swallow the Oasis whole. Or as if the mountain will collapse upon itself.

I've lived through my fair share of earthquakes back in San Francisco, some worse than others, but this one is unlike any of those in its ferocity.

If we were in San Francisco, the earthquake might have been over. However, this high up in the mountains, there is a shift happening between tectonic plates that hasn't yet ended. With every aftershock, I glance up, expecting to see the metallic honeycomb sections of the Masterdome rain down on us. If it was weak already, what will something of this caliber do?

I take Sidra's hand, holding her tight and fighting to keep us both on our feet as the soil beneath us rolls.

When it doesn't seem like it wants to let up, I squeeze my eyes shut and count.

One. Oh Gods, please protect us.

Two. Mami, I might be joining you finally.

And maybe that's not so bad. I've thought about it so many times before—what it might be like to reunite with my family.

Three. Four. I can't breathe. Can your heart stop beating from fear?

Then his voice cuts through.

"It's okay, Jules," Rico whispers. I open my eyes, and he's somehow right in front of me. My muscles relax at the tenderness of his hand on my cheek. "It's stopped."

"We need to get down this mountain," Nadine says, breaking the silence.

"How?" Sam adds in at my side.

"I might know a way," Sidra replies, still holding my hand. "Sometimes my mom used to travel down the mountain via an unknown railroad track that she saved for herself. It's probably where she's heading now . . ." Of course she has a secret way down.

"Where?" I ask at the same time Rico does.

"Is this train safe?" Nadine questions, which might be more important to know.

"The station is hidden in the North Shore, in the shopping district. She used to tell me that it's the safest way down. The tunnels for this train are, like, reinforced or something," Sidra says. "In case of an emergency."

Rico and Jesus exchange a strange glance.

"That means we need to get everyone in the haven that we can onto that train and off this mountain," Rico responds.

There are ten thousand people in this city. I think of all the kids. The elderly people. No one deserves to be buried under rubble.

"If we're going to go, we should hurry," Sidra adds, pulling me fiercely toward the gate.

"Okay, so we have a two-seater pod and one bike," I say the moment we're on the other side of the metal fence that surrounds the mansion, trying to figure out realistically how many of us both can carry.

"Two bikes," Rodrick says.

"And those of the deputies?" I add.

"Those won't work," Willa retorts with a sniffle, her whole being deflated. I should be the same as her. Tía Ines's death should have me bawling, but what is losing one more person? It's a terrible way to think, but it's how I've survived until now. "They're unique. Made for the deputies and powered by their fingerprints."

I turn to Rico, already knowing what he's going to say before he says it, always the hero.

I shake my head, letting go of Sidra to pull him along to the pod we came in. If we squish together, I know he and I and Sidra can fit. But he takes a step back.

"You can't," I say, chest squeezing like it did the day of the lottery. I won't let him sacrifice himself for me again.

"I'll find my way. Just tell me where you're going," he says.

"I'll stay with him," Jesus says, moving to stand next to Rico.

I repeat, "You can't."

"She's right. Why stay, when you can catch a ride?" a voice behind us says.

We all turn toward what appears to be a caravan led by the women of the hour: Viola Hershall and Rico's tía Linda.

CHAPTER 27
Rico

The Masterdome creaks above us, a deafening sound of metal breaking apart even from inside one of the armored vehicles in our caravan. I almost want to laugh that same maniacal sound that Jesus sometimes makes. This is all too ridiculous, unlucky. I'd thought it was just the computer system of the Masterdome that was glitching, but it seems like the physical Masterdome was starting to break apart, accelerated now by the earthquake.

Or perhaps it's the opposite, fate. Can fate be tragic?

Or is the planet simply trying to tell us that the Oasis was never the answer? Jules was right to have a backup plan. Right about the spigots and the protective suits. About how for so long we've depended on a false paradise.

My dream for so many days was to get Jules into this haven. I thought if I did, she would be happy. She doesn't seem happy. I need to fix this somehow and give us the best fighting chance at survival like I've always aimed to do.

"The Masterdome is done for," I finally say, turning to

Viola Hershall and tía Linda, who sit in front of us. "The Oasis will fall. Will you please listen to us?"

Viola smirks. "I'm listening now that we have proof."

"Burberry is heading toward the train station in the city center," I say. She tilts her head at the news, then laughs.

"Why is that hilarious?" Jules asks, crossing her arms at her chest. She doesn't know that we've sent the train down to pick up Sheriff Ramos.

"Burberry is attempting to take a train down the mountain that won't be there," Viola replies, her amusement fading. "It's the same train that Rico and Jesus have sent to pick up Edgar and bring him into the Oasis."

Jules turns to me, her gaze questioning why I've told her so little. I swallow hard, guilt writhing on my tongue.

"I guess Burberry's secret way down wasn't as secret as Sidra thought," I say. "She has no way to escape."

"But if the train isn't there, doesn't that mean we're stuck until it comes back, too?" Jules asks, eyes growing wide with concern. I shift toward the window, eyeing the Masterdome.

"It's going to be a rough time if the quakes keep happening, but we'll figure out a way through it," tía Linda says, reaching for my hand.

I give her fragile hand a small squeeze. I can't believe she's back. She's here. Being with my tía now means so much after I spent so many years missing her. Years living with unimaginable guilt. There's no way we've made it this far just to be crushed by debris or taken out by Burberry's deputies.

"Either way, we need to take the train station from Burberry. If she still controls it by the time Edgar arrives, we'll be stuck on this mountain. So that's what we'll worry about first," Viola says.

I nod in agreement, but Jules slouches into her seat, her hand holding down the stack of protective suits she made that Viola brought with her. She exhales loudly. "How are we going to do that?" I notice the growing bruise on Jules's forehead and nose. On impulse, I touch my own eyebrow, which I didn't even realize the medical pod had healed. I ease my eye up, no longer needing to squint.

Viola tilts her head, studying Jules. "You don't always have to be the strongest to win," she says. "But you do have to be the smartest. Burberry has had everything handed to her since she was a little girl. Has never had to struggle a day in her life. Not really. Not like everyone else. We'll win. I guarantee it."

"Being smart only gets you to the door, force helps you break in," I say. And I should know. I definitely learned a few lessons from what happened the first time we tried to take the Oasis.

That time, neither my computer skills nor storming in by force worked.

If we fight, how many would we lose, though? I try not to think about it when we have no choice. If we fail, if we can't take the train, we might be dead by tomorrow.

"When I was being held captive," tía Linda says, squeezing my hand tighter, "I kept replaying what went wrong all those years ago at the hangar. Rico is right." She turns to Viola.

"Which is why," Viola starts, "we also have the force to make miracles happen. A lot of planning has gone into this moment. Whether we get to keep the Oasis or not doesn't matter. This is the beginning of a Third Epoch nonetheless."

As if to reinforce this, the ground shakes below the vehicle. The movement sends us side to side as the world sways. Jules squeezes her eyes shut until the rocking stops, then meets my gaze. It's a terrifying thing, to know that you can't protect the people you love from something like an earthquake. But I'll die before I let anything happen to Jules.

That is a promise I aim to keep.

PART V

THE TRUTH & THE THIRD EPOCH

CHAPTER 28
Jules

"I hate this plan," I say bluntly, staring at Willa and Sam. In order to regroup, we've stopped at the side of an underpass that might at least offer some kind of protection should the Masterdome fall.

"But splitting up was your plan," Willa retorts, then adds in quickly, "We need to alert everyone to what is happening, and we need to reveal whatever evidence is on the device Sidra took from President Burberry's office. We can only do that at the broadcast station."

"I think—" Rodrick starts.

"That is the plan," Willa says firmly, cutting in.

Rodrick swallows hard. It'll be a moment before Willa gets over what he hid from her. But I hope that they are able to one day move on.

Rodrick turns my way, eyes downturned, frown on full display. I reach out to take his hand. He saved me in San Francisco, and he's had my back ever since. It's time for me to do the same for him and show him that I understand why he joined Viola and Sheriff Ramos's revolutionaries.

So this becomes our final strategy: Sam and Willa will head to the broadcast station while the rest of us stop Burberry.

"I'm really happy you won the lottery," Willa says, as if it's the last time she'll ever see us as we prepare to depart.

Words clog in my throat. I pull her tight into a hug. "I'm sorry about your mom."

She holds me tighter, then walks past Rodrick and toward the two-seater pod we've brought with us.

"She'll come around," I tell Rodrick.

"You think I made a mistake?" he asks.

"Yeah, big-time," I say with a laugh. "You should have told her."

"I was scared."

I shake my head. "Well, what you were scared was going to happen, has. What are you going to do about it now?"

"I should go to her, right?"

I open my eyes wide, questioning how someone who literally made a revolution happen without anyone guessing it can be afraid of his girlfriend more than death.

Without waiting for my reply, he goes off toward Willa. For a moment, she doesn't react, but her face softens, she turns to him, and they hug, kiss. Say their possible goodbyes, and my heart cracks open for them.

Sam and I gravitate toward each other. Sidra joins us as she hands Sam the device she took from Burberry's.

"This'll have everything you'll need," Sidra says, and in that moment, she seems wise beyond her years.

Sam nods and hugs Sidra.

"Lottery twins forever?" he says to me, reaching out to interlock his pinky finger with mine.

"Thank you for being someone I could trust," I say, and he hugs me, too.

"Likewise," he whispers into my hair, messing it up afterward the way my older brothers used to. "Be careful."

"You too," I say as the ground begins to shake once more, the Masterdome crackling and buckling as the mountain shifts.

We don't waste any more time. We remount the bikes and vehicles, Rico helping me into the armored vehicle with Viola and tía Linda.

I try to focus as I take a seat, still holding Rico's hand. All we need to do is stop the President, get as many people off the mountain as possible, and wait for Ahmed to call.

Viola Hershall stares intently at me and Rico from the bench seat across the way. I grip the large hiking pack that Viola's given me, which contains the last three protective suits I've made but haven't handed out yet, along with my other belongings I'm grateful to still have with me.

"You two make a cute couple," she says, grinning. I don't know what she has to grin about, but I guess if I was getting exactly what I wanted—the fall of the closest thing to an empire that we have now—perhaps I'd feel the same.

We arrive at the city center around five as darkness

descends, the sun already setting behind the mountain range. The aftershocks have slowed. Still, every once in a while, there's a high-pitched creaking that echoes as if the Masterdome is hanging on by its hinges.

The streets are flooded with people, no one seemingly wanting to be in any of the buildings when they come down. With no way to get through the crowd, we park.

People are huddled together in groups whispering among each other instead of acting. If this was San Francisco, for all its faults, Sheriff Ramos would already have given orders and been fighting with his people instead of fleeing from them.

I think about my tía, who everyone might be waiting to hear from. Only they won't.

I ignore the burning in my throat.

High-pitched cries ring from a few blocks down.

The name *Burberry* calls my attention.

Everyone else turns, too; everyone stands. People push forward toward President Burberry. Pleas for help fly through the air. She won't help anyone but herself.

I can't breathe amid the crush of people, and I think this must be what Rico endures when he's claustrophobic, like all the air is vacating the universe.

I fight to catch my breath, tilt my chin up and try but struggle against the throng. Just like I had the day of the lottery.

Rico holds my hand until we're torn apart. I also can't find Sidra in the crowd anymore. The crowd reacts like a wave and sends us all forward, then back.

A hand takes my wrist. It's Nadine. In her other hand, Sidra hangs on for dear life. And thank God, Rodrick is behind them. I nod to her, mouthing a *Thank you*.

Suddenly, the lights flicker off, and the crowd stills. We all wait in silence.

A shot pops. When I look back, Viola is right behind us, holding a blaster in the air. Her dark brown skin glistens with sweat, and it almost feels like I truly know her.

I suppose I do.

I recognize the anger in her gaze.

The fear in her movements.

The overwhelming desire for things to be better. And how she's willing to fight for that world.

I realize that we need people like Viola and Sheriff Ramos. We need people like Rico's tía Linda. And we also need people like Rodrick. Jesus. Willa. Sam. Nadine.

Most especially, Rico.

And we need people like me.

All of us fighting in our own ways until one day, we figure out that we can be stronger together even if we often disagree with each other.

I might never like Viola Hershall, but I respect her and am aware I can learn from her.

I laugh, a strange sound while everyone around us remains silent in the darkness, eyes drawn to Viola, who is backlit by one of her people holding a powerful flashlight.

The others in our group gravitate to her. Rico takes my hand once more and kisses it. Rodrick is behind me. Nadine next to him. Jesus takes Rico's other side. Sidra stands in front of me, Checkers still in his cat carrier on her back. Two hundred people might not seem like a lot. Might not even be considered an army. But in this moment, the populace parts to make way for us, the revolutionaries.

CHAPTER 29

Jules

Rodrick leads our group, hand on the blaster at his hip, vigilant as he constantly glances around. Sometimes people who know him approach, shake his hand, ask him what's going on. But he gives few answers, so they quickly disappear to be with their own family and friends. Though he doesn't say it, I'm sure he's worried about Willa and searching for his pop among the crowd.

Someone must have handed a microphone to Viola, who follows behind Rodrick like a messiah come to claim her destiny. Her voice is loud as she says, "Citizens of the Oasis, my name is Viola Hershall. I was the very first representative this city had, but it's likely you don't know my name. At this moment, you might be wondering what is happening. Well, let me tell you . . . I have learned that the Masterdome is failing. A fact made worse by the earthquakes we are experiencing. The reality is, we might not have much time to get down this mountain. Not that President Burberry cares. She is seeking her own salvation—at the cost of all of our lives."

"Lies!" someone shouts from the crowd between us and Burberry.

Viola scoffs. "I assure you, what I'm saying is not a lie. But if you don't believe me, you will soon enough."

With that, our group continues forward.

Whatever regulated the temperature of the Oasis before isn't working, and as we walk, I strip off my golden shimmery button-up shirt and tie it around my waist, leaving my opalescent tank top underneath. Rico tries to take my pack from me, but I shake my head.

When we arrive at the storefront that groups have congregated around, there is a line of Burberry's deputies blocking anyone from getting inside.

"That's where the train is, camouflaged in plain sight," Rico says beside me.

The deputies stand with their blasters at the ready across their chests, their faces shielded by protective masks, their bodies covered in sleek bodysuits that can surely take a hit better than bare skin.

Viola raises her arms, hands outstretched, and everyone behind her stops, me included.

The deputies at the front shift, turn to one another, and stand more awkwardly.

Sheriff Paul comes out of the door and walks forward with measured steps. He's maskless and his eyebrows knit at the center of his forehead as he assesses the situation with concern. One of his deputies hands him their blaster, which he directs at Viola.

"I told her she should've kicked you out into No Man's Land," he shouts. "But I guess it's never too late."

Viola doesn't reply.

How does someone end up being the sidekick of someone so enormously terrible and live with themselves?

Those directly surrounding Viola meet the threat by taking out various weapons of their own.

"We need to hurry, Jules. It doesn't take very long to start the train," Sidra whispers at my side, pulling at the shirt tied around my waist, unaware that the train isn't actually there.

Without tearing my focus away from Viola and Paul, I tighten my shirt and say, "There's no easy way in." There's static in the air as the tension increases, making the hair on my arms rise, the skin on my neck prickle. I wipe at the sweat forming at my nape, unsure whether it's from the rising heat or nerves.

We're a half dozen rows behind the front of the line, so I hear clearly when Paul shouts, "Everyone needs to return to their homes immediately, or there will be consequences."

I've heard a similar line, with tía Ines at the northern border, when she killed all those people on Burberry's order.

Knots twist in my belly. The threat is real.

"What about the earthquakes?" someone yells at the same time someone else asks, "What about the Masterdome?"

Some residents are dressed in an array of metallic and opalescent clothing. Others are in jeans and bright colors like Viola. But it's clear that we're all up against the deputies and representatives in dark uniforms.

"There is nothing to worry about, and the President is

doing all that's in her power to ensure we are able to swiftly and securely fix the glitches happening," Sheriff Paul says.

I scoff. The lie is too much.

"Is that why she's here shopping?" someone else shouts out.

But this isn't a shop—it's a hidden way down the mountain, according to Rico and Sidra.

Before I can call Sheriff Paul out, we're plunged into another sudden darkness. It's enough to trigger someone on Sheriff Paul's side to fire a shot at the crowd, hitting somebody who screams out in pain.

There's a panic, feet shuffling. God, I wish this didn't have to be a fight.

It's always alarmed me, with so many problems in this world looming large over our shoulders, that humans resort to violence.

More shots are fired, this time from our side. The shots are reciprocated with a lightning storm that causes the crowd to scatter.

Sidra pulls me forward before I can react.

"How are we going to get through?" I yell when she gets us all the way to the front, where Paul and his officers stand firmly in place.

The lights flicker for a brief moment, then remain on once more.

There are people on both sides groaning and calling for help on the ground.

Sidra pulls me up to Sheriff Paul, who stands at the center and towers over her. His neck is scorched purple where I tased him. For a moment, I want to push Sidra behind me. But if there is anyone who can perform a miracle to save us, something in my gut is telling me, it's Sidra. So I give her the chance.

"Paul, you can't let her leave everyone behind," she says. "Don't you care about us at all? Don't you care about your own life?"

Sheriff Paul shifts his gaze from Sidra to me. There isn't hate in his eyes, though; there's finally a semblance of remorse. If I've come to love Sidra in such a short time, Sheriff Paul must have as well. Like I know he cared about my tía.

I shake my head, understanding his unspoken question—no, my tía is not coming.

His gaze goes blank before shifting to the people on our side who are injured, who need immediate medical help. He shakes his head. "I've had one job—protect President Burberry. That's what I'm paid to do. And I'll continue to do that."

He raises his hand in what must be a signal for his deputies to advance.

Rico's tía Linda moves forward then, stands in front of me and Sidra and Rico, shielding and protecting us.

"Hello, Paul," she says, familiarity in her tone.

"Linda," he replies. "Guess I shouldn't be surprised they broke you out."

"How long have we known each other?" she asks.

My mouth falls open as I wait for this revelation to unfold.

"Since we were five," he replies, expression cautious.

"The boy I knew who wouldn't hurt a fly is now willing to

kill anyone and everything for a woman who is running away instead of facing reality like a true leader?"

"What do I have to live for anyway?" he says. Which . . . what kind of reply is that? Because *he's* miserable, we all have to die?

It happens in a flurry. One moment, Sheriff Paul has his weapon pointed our way; the next, tía Linda moves and disarms him, giving us a new upper hand. The deputies who are with Viola move suddenly, pointing their weapons at those still in Burberry's pocket. Our side outnumbers them.

Sheriff Paul scans around him at those he thought were his deputies but were actually Viola's. He takes a step back and shakes his head.

Tía Linda smiles wildly, but there's also pain in her face, one I'm all too familiar with. "I know you think your life isn't worth anything. I know that you shot me and imprisoned me. Starved me. Left me for dead. Even though you knew me. I shouldn't worry about whether you live or die. But I do. I've always cared about everyone's right to live, and that isn't going to stop now. Move aside, Paul."

Several seconds pass before Sheriff Paul raises his hands, and the deputies lower their weapons.

The crowd moves forward, but only tía Linda and Viola and a few others enter with us.

"I'll go first," Rodrick whispers, blaster at the ready.

Nadine, who has appeared safely with us as well, pulls out her Jian sword.

"We shouldn't hurt her," I whisper-yell to them both. They

nod, but there's something in Nadine's eyes that doesn't seem so convinced.

The building may look like a storefront being remodeled, but we quickly come upon a stairway that drops down into a small train station.

I'm too far away from where Rico stands with Jesus and Viola, but we lock eyes for a moment, and it's the softness of his gaze that tells me we're forever on the same page.

We walk fast but quietly until we reach the platform.

Burberry doesn't see us as she throws trunks of items in front of one of the train's cargo bays in a hurry. Their crashing ricochets everywhere. To my surprise, the train is there. Could it be another? Or does this mean that Sheriff Ramos is already here?

"Mama, wait!" Sidra calls out. She runs to Burberry before any of us can stop her.

It's heartbreaking. Worse, as soon as she sees us, as soon as she takes Sidra in, Burberry grabs Sidra by the arm and turns her toward us, all while pointing a blaster at her daughter's torso.

The train hums to life. A screen on the side of the metal giant turns on to a broadcast. *The* broadcast, as Willa and Sam appear on-screen. No one else seems to notice them yet. But soon enough, all of the Oasis will believe us, understand, and turn against President Burberry, too.

"You were planning to leave your people?" Rodrick asks, voice hoarse. "Those who trusted you?"

"You trusted me? Why?" Burberry asks. "Because of my

father? And his father before him? None of you have any idea about the pressure I was under to uphold their legacy. And then one day, I realized that I didn't owe anyone anything. I could simply focus on myself, my own survival, and the weight on my chest disappeared."

"Did you kill Dr. Urreal to keep him quiet?" I ask.

On the screen, as if to answer my query, Willa and Sam vanish, and video footage of Burberry begins to play. It's some kind of video log she recorded of herself. She looks a mess—hair in a bun that's coming apart, mascara running, hand still on a blaster. "I killed them," she says in the video. "If my father knew what I've done, he would disown me. He should have. Dr. Urreal found out something that could end my presidency. I had no choice but to keep it a secret. The Oasis will fall. Someday. Soon. The Masterdome is failing, weak. My grandfather built this place with all the money in the world, but even then, it wasn't enough. And I can't do anything to fix it."

We wouldn't have this footage without Sidra, but there's something in the way she looks the sorriest of us all that rips open my heart. I don't know how Sidra knew about this, or how long she kept it a secret, but I hope that she can find peace someday in Oregon. That is, if Ahmed ever calls me back.

Burberry watches Willa and Sam, then screams at the screen. "That little brat, same as her mom."

I step forward. "We went to the island," I tell her, drawing her full attention to me now. "We've known about the Masterdome for a while. We have a way out of this, for everyone, a way to change our future. But you can't leave those in your charge to die on this mountain before we can make that happen."

"Things will never change." She sneers at me. "Not really. There are those who win at life, and those who lose. My parents taught me that. And their parents taught them before me."

"We *can* make things better," I say. "But we need to work together now to get people down the mountain safely. You need to stop. Otherwise, a lot of people are going to get hurt."

"You're a silly little girl. You think you can change the world, but you can't. I should have listened to my father, but your aunt convinced me not to. He told me to stop the lottery. To let all of you simply rot in San Francisco. Everyone there will die, and you'll—"

Before she can finish, the train door behind her opens.

Our whole group collectively gasps.

A man comes into sight. I look to Rico, who wears a smug half grin. He's proud of his role in this revolution. In a way, he should be. But why does this also feel like the end of us? Until we're safe, a Third Epoch isn't possible.

"Enough of this," Sheriff Ramos says. It shouldn't surprise me that he's here earlier than day ten of Rico's timeline. Nonetheless, Sheriff Ramos's expression is ready.

"Edgar?" Burberry asks, facing him now, disbelief coating her tone, eyes wide as if she's seeing a ghost. She steps back from where she stands in front of the train door. Sheriff Ramos jumps off and takes small steps toward the President. Burberry fires her blaster, but the Sheriff dodges it in time, and the shot hits a wall.

She turns her weapon on the rest of us. "You're all better off dead anyway."

Rodrick takes a stand next to me. Tía Linda takes a step forward, Viola following.

It happens in flashes. One moment, I see the future. Burberry killing Rico's tía the way she did mine. And doing who knows what to everyone else that I love, my beautiful found family, in her panic. I keep replaying how Burberry killed tía Ines, and anger bubbles in my chest. But more than that, I imagine how remorseful I'll be if I let Burberry keep hurting the people I care about. I look at my ring and think about how much I want the life it promises with Rico. I'm tired of horrible people destroying my future for their own power and benefit. Before I can even think straight, I'm taking Rodrick's blaster. And the next moment, I pull the trigger, hitting Burberry in the chest. She stops, her weapon falls, and she follows it to the ground face-first.

"Jules! No!" Sidra screams, falling to her knees over Burberry's body. I fight the tears that cloud my eyes, but I don't regret what I've done.

"It was the best way forward," Viola says, now beside me.

Something like admiration and relief shines in Sheriff Ramos's eyes.

Rico lowers my weapon and takes the blaster from my shaking hand, caressing my back as he does. His eyes search for mine, but I can't meet them. I've never killed anyone before. At least I know that I never intend to again.

Sheriff Paul appears and stares at Burberry's still body for far too long before he puts his hand on Sidra's shoulder.

She moves to hug his torso, which partially drowns out her wails. He signals to the five men he's brought with him to take Burberry away.

"I'm sorry," I say, but my voice comes out as a small whisper. I don't expect Sidra to forgive me, or to ever speak to me again. But I know that what I've done will mean she gets to grow up in a safer and better world. Burberry wasn't ever going to stop being a cruel person, doing the wrong things. People like her never do.

"We need to get people on this train. Now," Rico says to our group, but even his voice fades away as I'm left to deal with the choice I've made.

CHAPTER 30

Rico

On the third day since Jules spoke with Ahmed, we still have no word from him. I don't know if I was expecting him to contact us, or expecting disappointment. Either way, there's plenty of stress.

The Masterdome has continued to malfunction. One moment, it's morbidly hot, the next, it's freezing. That doesn't mean we've stopped working, though. Jules has met with friends and taken what she could from the fabric shop and clothing stores. I've been working with Arden at A Seat at the Table Books to ensure that all the books we can take with us are boxed up and set on the train. And the train, by some miracle, continues to run with the help of engineers from the Oasis.

The representatives who recently defected have been working with some longtime revolutionaries to help gather anything else deemed too important to leave under the rubble of the Masterdome. And to try to track down additional pieces for Jules's 3D printer, materials we know are nonexistent in the Wasteland.

I try not to think about the lack of a warm welcome everyone is likely to get from others back home once the dust has settled. But then again, with his granddaughter returned to him, perhaps Sheriff Ramos's harsh demeanor will soften and rub off on the people he governs.

The Masterdome overhead is still glowing a mesmerizing gold, but every now and then the color fades to a dark green, and a crackle echoes throughout the dome. And the heat has worsened. Even so, there is still so much water here that it's almost not so bad. If this were the Wasteland, everyone would have been dehydrated by now. But the deputies pass out water bottles, and we drink our fill.

I pass the time mostly by people-watching. It's strange to see people here with dazed gazes like those in San Francisco. It's hard not to feel sorry for them. After all, most probably thought life would be smooth sailing once they won the lottery. It's a harsh new reality. But it all means that everyone will need to figure out how to create a better and safer society. Together. And we'll really need to figure out how to fit everyone in the current underground bunkers, or a way to create more quickly, now that Ahmed coming through seems like a miracle we shouldn't count on.

I thought I would be relieved with the President gone, but I am still afraid that nothing good will come of her demise.

Jules sits alone, her back turned away from everyone. I take an extra water bottle and join her. "Are you all right?" I ask, handing her the water. She doesn't drink.

"I'll be better when we're off this mountain," she replies, leaning against me.

I kiss the top of her head, swaying us for a moment.

"You did the right thing," I say, knowing these are the words she needs to hear to move on.

She turns to me, examining my expression. "Did I?"

Her eyes drift to where Sidra sits with tía Linda, still crying. Close by, Sheriff Ramos looms, watching them. I haven't seen him say a word to Sidra, and part of me thinks he's terrified. If someone like him can be.

Regardless of how much everyone hated Burberry, she was Sidra's parent, and that's never easy to lose. It'll take time for her to heal. If she ever does.

Suddenly, someone calls Jules's name.

"Willa!" Jules shouts. She stands and runs toward Willa and Sam, who spent the last two days helping to gather food from the fields in the West Shore and portable technology from the East Shore. They're empty-handed now, so it's likely they've already stopped by the train.

Jules embraces them and they make their way to me.

I salute them, glad to see Jules's new friends safe.

"You two did good," I say.

Sam blushes; Willa simply nods, biting her lip as she looks around.

"There," Jules replies, pointing toward Rodrick. Willa runs to him, and he takes her, lifting her up and twirling her around. They lock lips.

A few minutes later, our group sits down and forms a circle outside the building that houses Burberry's secret train station, waiting for the train to return after refueling. Jules, me, Willa, Rodrick, Sam, Nadine, and Jesus—we make such an odd cohort, but somehow, it's also familiar. Like we were meant to find each other. Like Jules and I aren't so alone anymore.

Jules tries to call Ahmed again on the transceiver, but no one replies.

"How long ago was the train meant to be back?" she asks.

I glance at the time on my watch. "An hour ago. You think it got stuck? Or maybe we finally ran out of fuel."

"What if we go into the tunnel and follow the train tracks down?" Sam says as we try to brainstorm another way out of this mess should the train not return.

"That's a guaranteed death," Nadine replies. "You can't see anything. If there isn't a way out, we'd be stuck. And I, for one, want to get off this mountain alive."

"We might not have a choice," Jesus tells Nadine.

In turn, I look to Jules, who clings to the transceiver.

"Do you feel that?" Nadine asks, her hands stretched out on the ground, her eyes upturned toward the Masterdome.

"Another aftershock!" Viola's voice rings through the space, and we all stand.

We're used to aftershocks by now, having felt at least a hundred. So at first, I think it's going to stop. But it doesn't. Everything shakes more furiously, and this doesn't seem like an aftershock, but a new shifting of the mountain, another large quake. A whistle blows through the air in warning.

Jules's eyes find mine. I take her in my arms, even as those around us attempt to cram themselves into the train station. Being inside is dangerous enough. I want to tell them to stop, but when I open my mouth, nothing comes out. Sidra approaches us. I pull her in between Jules and me, her backpack with the cat at her feet. The girl doesn't fight it but takes hold of Jules as well. She can be angry at her later. Right now, she's surviving. A smart choice.

There's yelling all around us as Viola's people try to keep desperate people calm. I don't know what anyone else in our group is doing as I focus on Jules's face. If I die, I want her face to be the last thing I see.

The creaking of the metallic parts of the Masterdome coming apart at their hinges is deafening.

I move to shield Jules's head as much as I can with my arms, both our bodies shielding Sidra, while struggling to keep balance as the ground beneath us rolls.

There's something so familiar about this moment, as if we've lived a thousand times and died another thousand over. I guess living in the Wasteland you do. And this is nothing abnormal. Just another struggle, another day . . .

"I love you, Jules. I've loved you every single moment we've been together," I scream, reaching into my pocket where Viola's death pill still sits in its box. If one of us is painfully injured, we'll have a humane way out of life.

I can't understand what she says back.

Metal crashing nearby makes the back of my neck tingle with fear and melts with the guttural yells of scared people. The Masterdome is finally coming down. For those of us in the Wasteland, we never even thought we would see the Masterdome. It was a magical thing to think about, like outer space or something.

Jules doesn't scream. She nestles into my chest, her body tense.

I kiss Jules's forehead, holding her tighter as I let go of the pill box. I wish with all of my heart that I could save her and Sidra, but this place is literally falling on our heads.

The first pieces of the Masterdome to crumble don't land on Jules and me, but I watch in horror as they crush those a short distance from us. People scream for those they love as their bodies lie lifeless.

I keep repeating, "I love you, Jules. I love you."

Behind me, Nadine screams. I turn for a moment. She's okay, but she's trying to lift a large piece of the Masterdome off the ground as if someone's underneath it.

Another screech of metal breaking causes me to glance up.

My heart squeezes with fear as another piece of the Masterdome falls directly toward us.

It gets bigger and bigger, until all I see is black, and we're crushed.

Or so I think. As we're about to get flattened, Jesus pushes the three of us out of the way, the five-foot piece of the Masterdome falling so hard in the spot where we were, the concrete underneath crumbles and sinks two feet. Other pieces follow, landing on the building that was Burberry's secret train station. The entrance is sealed away, and now the train isn't an option.

"Are you loco, Cuz?" Jesus yells, voice shrill. "It's not over yet!"

There's a wild intensity to my cousin's eyes.

I nod once at Jesus, take Jules's hand in my left and Sidra's in my right, and pull them to run. We need to find some kind of shelter. But what shelter can withstand the weight of thousands of pounds of metal without crumbling?

Then the transceiver clicks on, and Ahmed's voice says something unintelligible through the chaos, followed by a clearer "Juliana, are you there?"

Jules pulls the radio transceiver's speaker from where she's stuffed it into her pack, simultaneously tinkering with it and continuing to run. "We're here! But we need help!"

There's static and then not, his voice muffled and cut short.

Juliana clicks the switch again. "We can't hear you, but if you hear us, we need your help!"

I add in, "The Masterdome is crashing down on us!"

I'm about to repeat my words when the sound of something approaching breaks through the darkness and the noise, and something that looks like a massive hovercraft enters where a large hole in the Masterdome has been made.

The door of the hovercraft opens, and a man appears. He waves his arms hectically at us, and at once, I know exactly who it is.

"Hello, my friends!"

Ahmed from Oregon, here to save us.

CHAPTER 31
Jules

I wave and laugh, calling to Ahmed on the transceiver. "It's me! I'm Juliana." Relief floods my chest and sets it alight.

Ahmed pulls out a microphone. "Citizens of the Oasis, we've come to rescue you! Hope you're ready for this!"

There're cheers from wherever people are trying to hide from the Masterdome.

The problem is that an aircraft this large, larger than anything I could even imagine flying, can't possibly stop in the city center.

Ahmed disappears inside the aircraft, the transceiver coming alive a moment later in my hands.

"Juliana, do you copy?"

I press the button. "I'm here! And I am so grateful you've come to help us!"

"We're going to land on the strip of grass by the lake," he says. "You need to get everyone who wants to make it there now!"

I turn behind me to Viola.

"I'll make it happen," she replies and takes out her loudspeaker to alert the last remaining people. "Listen up! Our way out of here will stop at Burberry Lawn. Anyone who wants to leave before the Masterdome collapses on us needs to make it there ASAP!"

She hands the loudspeaker to someone else, who keeps repeating the instructions.

Viola faces our group and says, "Come on!"

The way to Burberry Lawn is crowded and hectic. People run in one massive group. Several times Sidra falls, until Sheriff Ramos ends up swinging her over his shoulders and gives her a piggyback ride the way my brothers used to give me when I was little. I follow close behind them, ever so careful not to lose them in the crowd.

Without Burberry, everyone works together.

The aircraft whooshes overhead two miles away, then lowers.

The ground shakes underneath our feet.

Willa and Rodrick end up in front of Rico and me, holding hands as they run.

When I turn to my left, I see Jesus trip and topple, but no one else notices or stops.

I swerve until I get to Rico's cousin. I reach my hand down. He watches me with suspicion.

"I think I twisted my ankle," he says. "Leave me."

I roll my eyes at him and wrap his arm over my shoulder. We don't run so much as hobble fast, but we manage to keep up with the stragglers of the group.

There are people already getting into the aircraft, which is more than large enough to hold our remaining five hundred.

I swallow hard as Jesus and I arrive at the very back of the line. I don't know how far ahead our friends are, and nerves take over. My legs shake underneath Jesus's weight.

"We'll be okay," he assures me.

I nod, but I'm not at ease until I hear my name and see Rico fighting against everyone else to get to me.

"Well, there's a sight I never thought I'd see," he says, taking Jesus and me in with a crooked grin.

Rico hugs us tight.

The crowd pushes forward, screams, even as those who seem to be in Ahmed's group tell us to act calmly, to not panic.

"We'll be okay," I tell Rico, echoing Jesus, as his face shifts from comfort to worry in that too-familiar way.

There is a loud sound, and I know exactly what it is the moment we hear it.

The dam that holds the reservoir in place has broken. It's a flood of relief as well. The Oasis hoarded so much water for so long, and perhaps some of it now will make it to those who need it. Maybe some of it'll make it to San Francisco.

The ground beneath us cracks, forming a crevice between us three and the rest of the crowd that's moved forward now.

Rico and I act in unison, each grabbing one of Jesus's arms and putting them around our necks, then jumping together to the other side.

In seconds, we board the aircraft, tía Linda taking Jesus's

weight as soon as we get to her at the door. She kisses him on his forehead, and he hugs her tightly. It's a deep relief that at least one of us gets to grow up with our mami.

The belly of the aircraft is a huge gray space lined with rows and rows of seats: three seats to a row and a walkway down the middle, surrounded by an array of windows letting us see outside.

We're led to a few unoccupied seats near the front. I let Rico take the window seat, watching as Sidra and her grandfather take the row behind us. Viola sits on the other side of me.

"Everyone, hang on!" a voice orders overhead.

Outside, there is chaos as if the entire mountain is crumbling, the rest of the Masterdome splintering. A large chunk of it lands in the lake, and there is a giant wave that covers the aircraft, causing several people inside to yell.

My heart quickens in my chest.

"It'll be all right," Viola says, and there's a certainty to her voice that settles my stomach.

The door closes, and we begin to move, lifting off into the air right as the ground underneath us breaks open. The Masterdome comes apart, and we weave and turn to avoid the largest of the pieces.

Yet somehow, we make it out alive.

As the sun at dawn crests the horizon, we head toward a new beginning.

CHAPTER 32

Jules

For miles and miles, there is nothing. But as Oregon's dome comes into view, it stretches out farther than the human eye can see, twinkling like the diamond ring that I now take from my pocket and place back on my finger.

Where I was so awestruck by the Oasis's Masterdome, Oregon's is beyond what words can express.

The closest word I have is *magic.*

It is pure magic.

How has this place sustained itself? I guess Dr. Urreal played a part in that, and we'll learn about it all soon enough. We could be responsible for helping to maintain it, too.

I clutch Rico's arm so tight that my knuckles ache, and his cheek presses against mine as we look out the window. He doesn't complain about my grip, and I'm reminded of why I love him so much. Ever since I met Rico, he just lets me be me.

Mami would be so relieved by that. My papá, too. I don't know what to really believe about the afterlife, but I think if my family were watching me now, they would finally be able to breathe again knowing that I'm going somewhere that might be truly safe.

As I let the tears roll, I exhale and lean back, holding a book that Rico got for me in my lap.

I peek behind us where Sidra rests against her grandfather's shoulder, sleeping, Checkers passed out in her arms. I don't know how she can in this moment, not when my whole body is buzzing and literally shaking with excitement, but I'm relieved that even during dark times, she can find comfort in the aftermath of bleak moments. Sherriff Ramos mouths *Thank you* to me, and I'm surprised to find that some miracles do come true.

Tía Linda is next to them with her eyes closed, though I can tell she isn't sleeping. Her lips are drawn into a peaceful grin.

Sam and Jesus whisper to each other across the way. I don't know what they're saying, but every once in a while, I see a twitch of Sam's lips, a blush of his cheeks.

Nadine is in the window seat, looking out. As if she can tell I'm staring at her, she turns my way. We make eye contact and somehow both grin. She gives me a slight nod, then turns back to the mesmerizing view.

Willa and Rodrick don't say anything in the seats in front of us. What can anyone who has lost so much so suddenly even say?

A man approaches them, his soot-covered and slightly bloodied face crumpling as soon as he takes Rodrick in. "Son?" he says.

Rodrick stands, hugs the man, and cries, "Pop! You're okay! I've been looking for you. I was so worried."

I turn away as Rodrick's dad replies, another wave of relief washing over me.

Then there's the woman of the century: Viola Hershall. I study her the most as she stares out the large window near the exit, out of her seat even though we've been told to stay in ours, a smile spreading so large on her face you'd think the worst thing imaginable hadn't just happened to her home. I don't know this woman. But there's something about her. Perhaps it's the way she tilts her head and breathes so calmly that makes me happy she succeeded. To my surprise, Sheriff Paul joins her.

Once we land, we deboard close to a tunnel that leads into the Masterdome of Oregon.

We don't rush to get off. None of us fully eager to possibly face a new disappointment. But there's also Rico's veil of hope and the opportunity to try again.

We wait until Ahmed walks over. He has olive skin, a perfectly crafted beard, warm eyes that smile.

"You all ready?" he asks. And in his expression, I see something I never saw in Burberry's: sincerity.

And at once, I know that yes, I am so ready to live again.

CHAPTER 33

Rico

There is so much to see outside the Wasteland, outside the Oasis, outside California. Still, in this new society, I can only stare at Jules. Her face beams in a way it hasn't since I met her as we climb onto a rugged SUV. And all I want to do is keep that brightness alive. Her grip is looser now than during the flight.

She turns to me. I wink. I want to kiss her and never let go of her.

Ahmed promises to take us on a full city tour tomorrow, and I can't wait to explore more of a place that seems to be the real deal, led by someone who was elected by the people, who seems to not want anything but to protect those under his care.

I don't know what tomorrow will bring, or the next day, or the next year of our lives. I don't know if this dome will fail eventually as well, but we can survive here—all of us who want to.

"And this is a housing unit for you," Ahmed says to Jules and me.

I help Jules off the vehicle, and we walk toward our new home as Ahmed drives a little farther to drop off Nadine and Jesus and tía Linda at a place they'll share.

In front of us is a smaller dome. The housing units all look like miniature versions of the larger Masterdome, shimmering gold refracting back. The door is more organic than the one in the Oasis. It's a wooden door, reminding us that we're still on Earth.

I hold a key, an actual key, and use it to open the front door. We step inside. The layout is simple. A brown leather couch in a living room that has shelves filled with worn-out boxes of games and used books.

A small kitchen.

One bedroom.

One small bathroom with a shower, no tub.

It's perfect in every single way. A haven for us.

"We can cuddle for five minutes, then I need to take a look at your shoulder," Jules says as she sets her pack down by the entrance.

"Deal," I say and take off my shoes, then fall onto the bed. Jules joins me, burrowing her head into my neck and kissing me there.

We remain silent for some time, simply enjoying the lull of each other's breathing and the bliss of quiet.

"What are you thinking?" she finally whispers. I touch her stomach, noting that I can no longer trace her ribs, then pull her closer. The engagement ring on her finger sparkles.

"That we're finally safe, and I'd like to stay in this bed with you forever," I say, tears in my eyes as I take in the real meaning of the words.

We are safe.

And that is what true love in an oasis is.

EPILOGUE

Jules

Five Months Later

Underneath our new Masterdome in Oregon, Rico and I kiss, and then cheering erupts among our wedding guests.

"Congratulations, you two. I now pronounce you married!" Heath, who is officiating, squeals.

Rico's face is lit up as he takes my hand. He is the hottest when he's happy, and he's been so happy in our new lives, in this Third Epoch.

We walk down the illuminated forest path in a secluded part of Oregon's Masterdome. Me wearing a vintage white wedding dress Heath secured, and Rico in a tuxedo I handcrafted.

Ahmed gives us his brightest smile as we walk past him, and I'm so grateful to have him as our leader here. He's our hero. Not only because he saved us all when the Oasis was falling apart but because this wedding wouldn't have happened without his help and encouragement, especially not in a place so beautiful.

There are streamers and ornate lamps hung up everywhere this evening. Our family and friends throw rice at us as we walk past them.

We take a million pictures. We give a million hugs. We eat the most delicious dinner of chicken legs and vegetables. We cut our cake. Pass it around.

There is laughter and dancing.

Willa comes up on my side, eyes wide with joy, her hand rubbing her belly. God willing the baby will keep, and we'll have new life with us in a few months. "Sometimes I can't believe we're living in this new world," she says.

"But wc arc," I remind her. She sighs before giving me a big hug. The baby kicks between us, and it makes us both laugh.

Sam kisses Jesus when he hands him a glass of wine, Nadine's newest creation, and I fight back the biggest smirk. They are way too cute, but Jesus especially hates being told so.

"We need a toast from the newlyweds! Who wants to do the honors?" tía Linda says, hugging Rico. It's something special, having her in our lives. Tears burn hot in my eyes. My own mami isn't here, nor my papá or brothers. And as much as that hurts, at least we have tía Linda.

At first, all eyes turn toward Rico, but he only has his eyes on one person: me.

I search the faces of all those around us, the ones who have made our dream possible. I try not to cry as the feeling of being loved by all of these amazing people overwhelms me.

"It's taken all of us," I start, "working together to change the world for those outside this Masterdome. We have all been through more than any living person should have to suffer. We have all survived. But above all, we have all loved and been loved. So, cheers, my friends, and my love." I raise my glass in Rico's direction.

"Cheers!" they all say in unison.

"I love you," Rico tells me as our glasses clink together.

Nadine and Rodrick come carrying a large perfectly wrapped gift out of the woods.

They set it down in front of us.

I pull one end of the bow on the box, undoing it.

I cover my mouth with my hand as I take in our very first spigot prototype from our 3D printer. Rico holds my hand as Rodrick tinkers with it. It'll offer fresh water to a tenth of the population of Oregon's Masterdome. And if it works, we've been gathering enough plastic from scavenging nearby to send more to Sheriff Ramos and Viola Hershall and citizens in San Francisco, starting with the people Rico and I once shared a home with in Gustav's care and those in Mictlān.

It's been hard not seeing Sidra, but I hope that when I finally do again, she might be able to forgive me for what I did. Ahmed flew them home to San Francisco two months ago, to take the twelve hundred protective suits that I designed and helped create with seamstresses here. It feels incredible that I've played a small role in the start of a new future, one in which the people of the Wasteland don't owe any oasis anything.

"Just ease it on," Rodrick's pop says from beside them.

The adorable miniature spigot whirs and Rico carefully sets it in the large tank of water we're testing it with. It moves, sucking water into its belly, then expelling that water into another tank it's attached to.

Ahmed does the honors of filling a glass first. He takes out a machine that'll test the water's purity and dips it into the water. And we wait for the results with bated breath.

Nadine's next to him, peering over his shoulder, and it's the rare smirk on her lips that lets me know that we've done it.

"Victory!" Jesus shouts, approaching us, carrying several cups that he passes out before collecting our wine cups and setting them in a box. I take my cup of water with restrained eagerness, waiting.

When we all have a cup, we raise it to the air and drink, dance, and celebrate. It's something special, realizing that my plan, my wild, basically impossible plan, is actually working.

After a while, I find a corner of this open space in the forest to sit and watch my friends have fun.

"You okay?" Rico asks, coming up to me.

"Waiting for the moment," I tell him.

"What moment?"

It took days of Rodrick and Ahmed scouting to find this special place in the forest for us.

As we lose the rest of the daylight, the glow of butterflies begins.

"Are those . . . ?"

"Butterflies," I say. "Magic. Beauty. Hope."

Rico laughs. The best sound in the entire universe. "They're glowing."

“They’ve evolved, like we’re doing,” I reply.

He holds me close, kisses my temple, and whispers, “You know, every time I felt like there wasn’t any more hope, that it wasn’t worth fighting to live, I remembered you and found the strength to keep pushing. I love you. Not just for being my best friend. For trusting me. For being there when I need you. But most of all, for being my hope.”

I hug Rico tight, feeling his heartbeat against my own, and realize that for once, the anger and numbing sadness I’ve felt for years are gone. In their place, all that’s left is love.

ACKNOWLEDGMENTS

This story has been over a decade in the making, which means there are going to be people who I forget to mention, but I am so grateful to everyone who kept this story alive throughout the years. If you have read this story in any of its previous forms, I hope you love this version just as much.

At its heart, *The End of Us* is a story about how we need each other, and how only through love, friendship, and understanding can we do amazing things. Jules and Rico have evolved from the first time I wrote about them. They both have different names. They both go on very different adventures within the story. Both have different interests than in the original version. But they also haven't changed in many ways. Jules and Rico are two people who care so deeply about each other's well-being they end up realizing that in order for the two of them to be okay, everyone else around them needs to be, too. This is a notion I learned from them. And a powerful thread throughout the story.

We need each other.

This is also true in publishing. Nothing happens without each other. Every book has a plethora of amazing people coming together to make a project happen, and I am so grateful for getting to work with some of the most talented and passionate folks in the biz.

To Nicola and David Yoon, Joy Revolution was a dream imprint for me. I can't even express the gratitude I feel to both of you for inviting me to be a part of it. Thank you both for believing in Rico and Jules and their love story.

Thank you to my editor, the incredible Bria Ragin, for believing in what this story could be outside of its original form, and to editorial assistant Elizabeth Cervantes for helping the story evolve into its final product. You both offered me incredible feedback, and every time I got onto the page, I knew the story was getting better and better. Best of all, I was always genuinely so excited to jump back into your notes—that's something special, and I don't take it for granted. You gave me a dream editorial experience.

Thank you to my amazing literary agent, Kate Testerman, who is someone I know I can reach out to with even the silliest questions and always gives me the agency to reach my goals. I appreciate you so much. Thank you to Kelly Van Sant, Renee Nyen, and Katherine Welsh for all you do. And a big hug to Adria Goetz, who is my picture book agent at KT Literary.

Thank you to Mallory Loehr and Wendy Loggia for seeing potential in this Latiné story. I recently read the story of another Latiné author whose work, many years ago, had been rejected for the sole fact that it was Latiné. The team considering it for publication didn't believe the book was marketable. That things have changed in this industry is because of professionals like you who continue to push for greater diversity and who see the true market potential in stories with diverse heroes.

Thank you to my managing editor, Tamar Schwartz; production editor, Jamie Johnson; production manager, Shameiza Ally; cover and jacket designer, Tatiana Guel; cover artist, Leonardo Silva; my copy editors and proofreaders, Nicole Brugger-Dethmers, Kerianne Okie Steinberg, and Kerry Johnson; text designer, Megan Shortt; and anyone else I may have missed. I am enormously grateful. Thank you Ashlee Latimer, social media guru extraordinaire. I am forever grateful to you all for helping me bring this story to readers.

Thank you also to the amazing authors who spent time to blurb this book: Aiden Thomas, Angela Montoya, Pascale Lacelle, and T. A. Chan. Your support means the world to me!

Thank you to all of my family, especially Joe and Rio, for being my absolute best friends. I am beyond lucky to spend my life with you, and I love you both with all my heart. Joe, you are my Rico! Thank you to my mum and sister, who are always so excited for me to keep following my dreams. Big hugs to the rest of my family: my dad and little brother, my nieces and nephews, my sisters-in-law, brothers-in-law, and father-in-law. To those who have passed on, Linda and Natasha, who would have been so proud of me. I love you all.

Thank you to my critique partner, Shannon A. Thompson, for always believing in me. It was because of this story that we became friends and I'm forever grateful to it for that.

Thanks also to the incredible Tiffany Liu and Brian Park, who read this one way too long ago—I'm as grateful to you as ever.

A big hug to everyone at GZLA: Marietta, Nancy, Ellen, Linda, Beth, Erin, Saribel, Ashlee—thank you for always being excited when I have new books coming out. You're all the best. And a hug to everyone at Story Sunbirds and #LatinxPitch.

Another big hug to all of my amazing literary clients—you know who you are—who inspire me all the time. Getting the chance to love books and tell stories with you is an honor.

Most of all, thank you from the bottom of my heart to every reader who picks up this book. To every librarian and teacher who add it to thcir library. To every bookstore, indie or not, that stocks this book, thank you. A special shout-out to one of my favorite local indies, A Seat at the Table Books, that makes a special appearance in this book. To everyone who helps spread the word about it. I've dreamed of publishing dystopian, my favorite genre, from the very beginning of when I started pursuing publishing. This story is very special to me, and I had so much fun writing it. I hope *The End of Us* inspires you and helps you know that you can always make a difference in the lives of those around you, and you can always fight for how you want the world to be.

With endless gratitude,

Sandra Proudman

ABOUT THE AUTHOR

SANDRA PROUDMAN is a Mexican American author of unabashed Latinx stories, including the YA romantasy *Salvación*, which was a Kirkus and YALSA best of the year selection. When she's not writing or working as a literary agent, you can find her spending time with her amazing husband and adorable child, catching up on her shows, and working in her garden in California. *The End of Us* is her first dystopian novel.

WRITESANDRAWRITE.COM
@SANDRAPROUDMAN

THE END OF US
DISCUSSION QUESTIONS

1. *The End of Us* blends dystopian fiction with romance. In a world full of hardship and grief, do you believe love is enough to keep moving forward?

2. We are taught as young readers to look for the "moral" of a story. Do you think this story has a moral? If so, what do you think it is?

3. Jules and Rico struggle to trust each other inside the Oasis after they're pushed down different paths. What moments did you think would lead to the end of Jules and Rico's relationship? Were you rooting for their love to win?

4. How did Rico and Jules grow and mature throughout the story, individually and as a couple?

5. This story explores the importance of family, of both choice and origin. How does the idea of family shape Rico and Jules's vision of what the future can hold for them?

6. *The End of Us* explores social issues that are relevant in our world today (for example, class hierarchy and poverty, violence against immigrants, war, and climate change, among others). What message does the book have on one or more of these issues?

7. *The End of Us* is dual-perspective; do you think that the story would still work through only Jules's POV or only Rico's? What does seeing both of their perspectives add to the story?

8. Supporting character Rodrick shows that one person can change everything for everyone. Why do you think that Rodrick took Jules into the Oasis the day of the lottery instead of forcing Rico to go with him? In what ways did that small decision lead to a big impact?

9. Using examples from the novel, compare the characters' decisions to ones you might make if placed in similar situations.

10. Jules makes a decision toward the end of the story to stop President Burberry from harming others, even though it means destroying her friendship with Sidra. Do you think Jules made the right call? Why or why not?

11. *The End of Us* culminates in the idea of a Third Epoch, in which those with little don't have to put themselves at risk working for those with everything. Do you think that a Third Epoch would have been possible for the revolutionaries if they had been able to stay in the Oasis? Why or why not?